MAX BRAND

THE SACKING OF EL DORADO

LEISURE BOOKS   NEW YORK CITY

A LEISURE BOOK®

December 1997

Published by special arrangement with
Golden West Literary Agency.

Dorchester Publishing Co., Inc.
276 Fifth Avenue
New York, NY 10001

THE SACKING OF EL DORADO: Great Western Adventures by
Max Brand™ was first published by Chivers North America.
Copyright © 1995 by Jane Faust Easton and Adriana Faust-
Bianchi. "The Man Who Forgot," which now appears for the first
time in book form, has been added to the contents of this edition.

Further copyright information can be found at the end of this book.

ISBN 0-8439-4335-1

THE SACKING OF
EL DORADO

TABLE OF CONTENTS

A Note to the Reader

From the mid 1960s until 1988, when Dodd, Mead & Company ceased doing business, the Max Brand books it published, increasingly, were heavily and sometimes substantially rewritten by others. The three Max Brand story collections gathered by William F. Nolan were in most cases so completely rewritten as not to be recognizable if compared with the original stories. Many readers, who remembered the stories in those collections from when they had first appeared in magazines and loved them for what they are, were understandably dismayed, as have been critics who have increasingly focused essays and books on the extraordinary achievements of Frederick Faust, the man who wrote under the byline Max Brand. The stories gathered together in this collection have restored the original texts of the stories of Max Brand, based on the magazine versions and, wherever possible, on the original typescripts left by the author.

BAD EYE: HIS LIFE AND LETTERS

"Above the Law" was the first Western story Frederick Faust wrote. It was published in the issue of *All-Story Weekly* dated August 31, 1918 under the byline, Max Brand. Less than two months later "Bad-Eye: His Life and Letters" by Max Brand appeared in the same magazine in the issue dated October 19, 1918. It was Faust's second Western story. "Above the Law" has been reprinted by the University of Nebraska Press in *The Collected Stories of Max Brand* edited by Robert and Jane Easton. This marks the first book publication for "Bad-Eye: His Life and Letters."

Bad-Eye:
His Life and Letters

Everything about James Jerrold Melrose was educated except his imagination and one eye. His imagination spoiled his mind and a cast spoiled his eye. Otherwise, in the opinion of Mac, the bartender, "he was a good enough guy except that he was a tinhorn sport." Everyone called him Bad-Eye.

Melrose's residence varied all the way from Truckee to Warring, but his address was Masters's place. Here he gave out that he was interested in mining, and after the fourth drink he even made large off-hand statements which concerned dim millions he might invest in the right sort of mining property. Men took him seriously at first. Buck Walters even spent two days showing him his lead and enlarging upon its possibilities. Bad-Eye's offers dropped from tens of thousands to thousands, and from thousands down to hundreds. Buck waited till they got back to Masters's place. Then he told the crowd what he thought of Bad-Eye and his wrath held out longer than his vocabulary.

After that men revised their opinion of James Jerrold Melrose. They noted that toward the end of each month he rarely bought drinks and spent his time hugging the stove. Then came a letter addressed in a small, feminine hand and containing crinkling bills. The miners drew their conclusions rapidly: Bad-Eye must be living on his womenfolk.

Whatever they thought they kept to themselves, particularly after one of these letters arrived and Melrose was drinking heavily; for then his imagination ran riot, and he became what Mac called an imitation man-killer. When Bad-Eye shot the mirror full of holes, Mac protested to Masters. The owner was a big, good-natured man with a rather educated vocabulary, the repute of a fighter, and a gentle eye which belied his reputation. He shrugged his shoulders and reminded Mac that Mr. Melrose paid for the damage done.

When Bad-Eye decided one evening that the barroom was not large enough for his expanding spirit, and attempted to carry the stove out into the snow, Mac appealed to Masters again, but the boss smiled and refused to interfere.

"I'm speaking for the cross-eyed sucker's own good," said Mac, deeply irritated, "because one of these days I'm going to lose my temper and use him for a mop."

"Go as far as you like, Mac," agreed Masters amiably, "but don't spoil the floor."

It was very plain that Bad-Eye's imagination had run amuck. He thought he had penetrated to the inmost depths of the Western heart. His humor consisted of foul anecdotes. His idea of a Western party was a good deal of liquor, a shouting voice, and a bit of gun play to polish things off.

In fact, he was trying to recreate an atmosphere which ceased to exist thirty years before, and even then was more fiction than truth. The miners bore with him, partly because they looked on him as a harmless though rather disgusting curiosity, partly because they disliked a quarrel with a gun-fighter. They knew that such affairs usually wound up with a funeral. Even in Nevada, funerals are not popular.

Therefore, Bad-Eye continued to fill his days with noise and the smell of powder. The letters addressed in the fine feminine hand continued to arrive, and his prosperity flooded at the beginning of each month and ebbed sadly toward the end of it. Yet there is a period to all earthly prosperity. The day came which brought the letter that contained only a small sheet of note paper and not a sign of a greenback. Bad-Eye sat dumb for a moment, tearing the letter into small bits. Before he found his voice to curse, Mac exchanged glances with the half dozen men in the barroom and the grin of understanding went its rounds.

"Step up and liquor, boys," said Bad-Eye at last, rising from his chair and approaching the bar, "this is my day to treat."

He rapped authoritatively on the bar, but not a man stirred.

"What's the main idea?" asked old Pete Hanley. "You borrowed a buck off me this morning. Have you struck it rich since?"

Bad-Eye glared about the room. On all sides he met the same broad grin.

"I don't need money to drink at this bar," he announced. "My name is good for it."

"Not by a damn sight," said Mac coolly. "Let's

see the color of your money or you don't liquor here."

"Why you infernal old red-headed, lantern-jawed, squint-eyed, bow-legged baboon," began Bad-Eye, easing gradually into the vermilion parts of his vocabulary, "I've spent enough money here to build this one-horse joint!"

"Around these parts," said Mac calmly, though his eyes narrowed, "a man don't brag about the money a woman gives him."

At this Bad-Eye produced his inevitable gun and smote on the bar with it. "Step up," he commanded, turning on the miners; "step up and liquor. Mac, feed 'em what they want."

Not a man stirred. Mac leaned his elbows against the shelf behind him. It maddened Bad-Eye. He cursed every individual in the room and wound up with a special ration on Mac. The bartender's peculiar smile never varied.

"If you're about all through," he said, when Bad-Eye paused for breath, "you better go on up to your room and sleep it off. The air around here is getting a lot too hot for you, my friend."

"By God!" raved Bad-Eye, leveling his gun at Mac's head. "Come around from behind that bar. You're going to dance for the boys, and you'll need lots of room for it."

Old Hanley slipped from his chair and stole toward Bad-Eye.

"Go back to your place, Dad," said Mac. "There ain't no use of you getting mixed up in this."

Hanley stepped back. Mac walked quietly around the bar and stood before Bad-Eye.

"Now," he said, "what do you want of me?"

"Dance, damn you!" yelled Bad-Eye, and fired close to the bartender's feet.

Mac danced, but only one step, and that was forward. At the same time his fist shot out and struck Bad-Eye in the throat. He fell coughing and strangling against the wall, and Mac lunged after him. It was over in a minute. As they struggled on the floor Bad-Eye shot point-blank into the bartender's face. Mac struck the gun aside barely in time, but the bullet nipped his ear. An instant later he gripped the barrel of the revolver and the two rolled over and over on the floor in their struggle. The gun exploded again. Bad-Eye relaxed with one deep-drawn breath, and Mac rose, letting the weapon fall clatteringly to the floor.

The coroner reached Masters's place by night-fall, and his jury reached a decision in five minutes. Four men carried the body up the hill behind the roadhouse, and by midnight the last sod was heaped up on Bad-Eye's grave. When Masters came back from Truckee the next day, he turned the page on the incident by staring at the floor as he rolled a cigarette and remarking that Mac hadn't spoiled the floor after all.

Bad-Eye received his last letter in April. Time runs quickly in the mountains. In May he was an anecdote. In June he was a legend. Yet his spirit went marching on all that time, and on a white-hot summer day it entered Masters's hostelry again. When the owner rode back from a trip to his diggings, he found Mac collapsed in a chair in a corner of the room with his chin dropped upon a burly clenched fist. He regarded Masters with a blank eye.

"What's the matter, Mac?" he asked, "hot weather getting to you?"

Mac surveyed the big form of Masters from

head to heel and then turned away his eyes disconsolately.

"Loosen up," commanded Masters. "Something happened to your kid brother?"

The bartender rose and led him to the guest register. He pointed out a name inscribed latest on the list.

"Take a slant at that," he said heavily.

"Jane Melrose," read Masters. "Well, what of it? It isn't the first time a woman has stayed here, is it?"

Mac supported himself against the bar and gazed sadly into space.

"What does she look like?" asked Masters.

"Tall," said Mac, "clear eyes, square jaw. Looks like a fighter."

"Look here, Mac," said the owner seriously, "you're sick. You slide a saddle onto the roan and go over to Truckee for a few days. I'll take care of the bar while you're gone. You need a change of air."

"I reckon I do," said Mac, without enthusiasm, "and I reckon I'll get a change of residence, all right."

Masters regarded him with a frown. "Thinking of leaving me, Mac?"

"Yep."

"Where you going?"

"Behind the bars, I guess."

Masters caught him by both shoulders. "For God's sake, Mac, what've you done?"

"Bad-Eye."

"Bad-Eye?"

"She asked for him! His name was Melrose, too."

Masters mopped his forehead with his bandanna. "They can't get you for that. The coroner came all regular and. . . ."

Mac shook his head disconsolately. "She'll get lawyers after me. Lawyers can do anything. A man ain't got a chance against them. You know what happened to Barney!"

Masters lowered his voice. "What did she say?"

"She said: 'I believe that a gentleman named James Jerrold Melrose lives here?' She had a sort of frosty rise in her voice at the end of the question. I grabbed the bar and felt my throat go dry. 'Lady,' I said, 'I ain't remembering exactly. Maybe he did.' 'Ah,' she says, 'are you in authority here?' "

"Did she say it like that?" queried Masters.

"Worse'n that," answered Mac. "There must have been snow in her throat when she said it. 'I am not,' I said, 'but Mr. Masters is out.'

" 'Then I'll wait for him,' she said, 'if you will show me to my room.' I went upstairs with her. She went to the window of her room. Out there on the hillside I saw the grave of Bad-Eye. 'Ah,' she said, 'what a glorious view!' I turned and beat it down here."

Masters was pacing up and down the room with his head bent in study. "There's just one thing to do," he said, "and I have it, Mac."

Mac shook his head sadly. "It won't work," he said. "By her get-up she hasn't much money, but she isn't the kind you could buy off. She's got a educated voice."

"Then," said Masters with decision, "there's only one thing left. Mac, you've got to go to her and make a clean breast of it!"

"Me?" breathed Mac. "Me go and tell her that? You ain't seen her! She'd grab the next stage for Truckee and have a warrant out for me in a day."

"Look here," said Masters, "what's the matter with you? She's human, isn't she? She doesn't wear a gun."

Mac groaned. "I wish she did," he said, and added after a moment, "she must be his wife."

Masters started. "Bah!" he said, glancing again at the register to reassure himself. "She's got no 'Missus' in front of her name."

"No Missus?" queried Mac, in disgust at this ignorance. "Don't you know that they don't use no such titles in the East? Ah, she's his wife, all right. She's got the same name, hasn't she, and she come clear out to the dropping-off place to see him, didn't she?"

To these unanswerable arguments Masters listened with bowed head.

"Mac," he said at last, "I'm sorry, that's all. Think of you coming to trouble for a skunk like Bad-Eye. I should of give him the run before he got down to his gun play. Now, if she brings you up to the courts. . . ." He broke off sharply. "Run for it, Mac. Beat it while the going's good!"

"I suppose I'll have to," groaned Mac, "but it's hell, Bill. I been so long around here, it's getting like home to me."

"Mac," said Masters, "I'm going up to talk with her myself."

"Go to it, old man," Mac said. "I'll have a toddy ready for you when you come down. Maybe you can put her off the trail."

Masters shook his head. "No, Mac," he said. "The thing to do is to keep her here until she knows you well enough to feel sorry for you. Too bad you haven't got a wife and seven kids dependent on you. That always makes a hit with a woman."

"I got a kid brother," suggested Mac.

"H-m," pondered Masters, "that may help. Anyway, we aren't going to break it to her right off the jump. I'll try to amuse her for a few days and keep her away from the boys. When she knows us, she'll take it better. I know all about women, Mac. I got a sister. Where's my coat?"

"Coat?" queried Mac in dismay.

"Yes, coat, you blockhead. Got to make a neat showing when you talk to a woman like this one."

"You ain't had a coat on in three years."

"Don't lie!" said Masters. "I wore it not later'n last winter, when Jerry Douglas got married."

They found the coat in a corner closet. It was gray with cobwebs and a little stained in places, but vigorous brushing brought it back to a semblance of its original color. A more prolonged search discovered a necktie. Masters squinted at himself in the cracked remnant of the mirror which Bad-Eye had shattered several months before.

"How do I look, Mac?"

"Never better."

"Fit all right around the shoulders?"

"Pretty fine. How about those boots, though?"

Masters looked down to his heavy shoes. Clay of three colors streaked them.

"Boots?" he echoed. "I guess they will do! Gimme my hat. How's your gun, Mac? This six of mine is new, and I haven't got just the hang of it yet."

"What do you want a gun for? She doesn't carry one."

"She doesn't?" asked Masters. "Well, you never can tell, and I wouldn't feel natural talking to a dangerous party without a gun. All right. Now I'm ready. Look me over again, Mac."

The bartender walked slowly around him with a gradually brightening face.

All this time Jane Melrose sat in her room with her elbows resting on the windowsill, and her eyes roaming the wild outlines of the mountains. She smiled as she stared, for her heart wandered as freely as her eyes. A road girdled with a white line the mighty shoulders of the mountain. She guessed at a thousand trails through the wilderness.

A strong, sharp knock at the door startled her to her feet. She turned as the summons was repeated and saw the door quiver at the stroke.

"Come in!" she called.

The door opened on a figure which completely filled the aperture. He reminded her of a statue of Hercules draped in a grotesque modern costume. His chest seemed struggling to escape from the pressure of a coat several sizes too small and held by one button across his breast. The sleeves fell at least two inches short of the big brown wrists. The corded column of his throat was also confined by a narrow crimson necktie which was done in a small and hard knot and pulled so tight that the veins of the upper part of his neck were penciled in blue.

"Are you Jane Melrose?" said a booming voice.

"I am," she answered, "and are you the boss?"

She said this in a voice so caressing that Masters allowed his hand to fall against the butt of his revolver. The pressure was like the hand clasp of a friend, for looking at her he remembered that the bronco with the softest eyes was often the wickedest bucker.

"I'm Bill Masters," he said.

"Will you come in?" she asked amiably.

He stooped his head to enter and made one long stride into the room, slamming the door behind him. It seemed to her that such a man might have ridden but a moment before around that same white road which she had seen wandering from earth to the blue heaven.

She went to him and said: "I am very glad to know you, Mister Masters. Mister Mac told me that you could answer a few questions I have to ask. Will you sit down?"

With her hand in his, Masters felt that he gained power. Therefore, he relinquished it unwillingly. As he sat down, he remembered his hat and jerked it from his head, exposing a mop of fiery red hair, innocent of the comb. Jane lowered her eyes to the floor to cover her smile

"I won't keep you long, Mister Masters," she began. "I have come to make some inquiries concerning Mister James Melrose. Do you know anything of him?"

Her deep anxiety drew her brows together in a frown which made Masters shift in his chair.

"Melrose? Melrose?" he repeated vacantly. "Lady, I don't remember the name just at this time, but maybe it'll come back to me. We have a whole herd of folk stayin' here most of the time. I can ask around for you if you want me to."

"This was his address a few months ago," she said. "Were you the owner of this place then?"

"For six years," said Masters miserably. A great idea struck him. "Maybe he was working in one of the mines around here and just had his mail sent to my place?" he suggested.

"Working?" She shook her head decidedly. "No.

Whatever else Jimmy might have done, he wouldn't have worked."

"The cur!" muttered Masters to himself. "He must have made her life one long hell, but she still loves him."

She sighed, and her glance wandered out over the ranges again. Masters looked out also and his eye fell on the grave of Bad-Eye and stayed there. A peculiar hot sensation passed up and down his spine, as if someone were pouring steaming water down his back. In due time she was sure to find out. Pete Kilduff had promised to come down from the "Mamie Lode" that afternoon. If the girl spoke with him, she would learn the true history of the life and letters of Bad-Eye. Then woe to Mac! Something must be done to keep her away from the house while Pete was there.

"It will be a great disappointment if I don't find him," she said. "His letters stopped some time ago, and I've come a long way to get track of him."

"Oh, you'll find him all right," said Masters cheerily. "The boys will tell me if he's been around these parts. Say, if you'd like to kill some time to-day, we could take a ride out through the hills."

"Ride?" she repeated with shining eyes. "I had rather ride than do any other thing in the world."

Masters smiled back, but then his face fell. "There's two troubles," he said. "In the first place, the only spare horse I have is kind of high in the head from being in the stall so much, with no exercise. In the second place, I haven't any side-saddle."

She made a sweeping gesture which tossed these objections into the discard. "I have a divided riding-skirt that will do for a man's saddle," she answered, "and I'll chance your horse. I like them with a high head."

"Just like me," grinned Bill Masters. "Let's go down and take a whirl at the roan. I'll get him out while you're dressing."

On the way down he stopped in the barroom.

"Hang around, Mac," he said. "She's going to go out riding, and she's going to take the roan."

Mac regarded him with great eyes. "The roan, Bill? Why, the roan hasn't had a saddle on for six weeks."

"That's the joke!"

Mac turned grave. "Look here, Billy, I know you're my friend, but I don't want you to do any homiciding just to make things easy for me. Killing a skunk like Bad-Eye was different, but his widow looks like a human being to me."

"Take it easy, Mac," answered Masters. "I'll be on the spot, and I'll see that the roan doesn't do her any harm. She's got to learn that Western folk are different from Eastern, and she might just as well start in by finding out what a Western horse is, compared with the ones she used to ride around the park."

He went out the back door and soon reappeared from the stable with a stalwart roan, a full sixteen-and-a-half hands in height. They had scarcely cleared the door of the stable when the horse reared with a shrill whinny and struck out with his fore hoofs. Masters wrenched at the reins with his whole weight behind the pull and brought the horse down to all fours again. After that he tethered him to a hitching-rack at one side of the yard and went back to bring out his own bay. When he came out again, Mrs. Bad-Eye stood in the yard gazing at the roan. She was dressed in a short corduroy skirt and a small, round hat.

"What a splendid fellow!" she cried. "And see the spirit he has."

The roan was rearing back against the rope and shaking his head furiously.

"He and I will get along wonderfully together," she went on.

"He's a good horse, lady," said Bill Masters, frowning to conceal his smile. "Shall I help you into the saddle?"

He untethered the big roan and held his head tightly while she swung up into the saddle. Masters's eye fell upon her slender-toed riding boot.

"By thunder, lady," he cried, "are you going to use *spurs* on him?"

"Of course," she answered, settling herself in the saddle. "I'm lost on a horse when I haven't spurs. You can free his head now."

With his head released the big roan stood quivering a moment. She reined him sharply across the neck, and then the trouble began. Instead of swerving according to her guidance, the big fellow lunged out toward the open road. She threw herself back at a great angle, bracing her feet in the stirrups, and reined in with a mighty jerk that brought him up, rearing.

There was a frightened cry from the house and Masters caught a glimpse of the white face of Mac pressed against a window.

"Steady," shouted Masters. "Hold tight! I'm coming."

He ran for the roan's head.

"Keep away!" she shouted. "He's wonderful!"

The horse came down on stiff forelegs with a jolt that jarred her hat a little to one side, then to his utter astonishment Masters saw the rowel of her wheel spur touch the side of her mount.

"No spurs!" he yelled.

It was too late. The roan began to buck in the most approved style.

"Keep his head up!" thundered Masters.

Her shrill laughter, marvelously shaken by the bucking, answered him. She struck her mount on the flank with the open hand, and he responded with a furious burst of pitching. He did not cover more than fifty square feet of ground in all his antics, but in that narrow space he performed about all the tricks known to the equine mind. Her laughter was gone now, and Masters saw her teeth set; her hat fell to one side and then tumbled off. He picked it up mechanically. At the window the pale face of the bartender still gaped. In another moment the roan stood trembling and bright of eye, but quiet.

"Are you safe? Are you all right? Are you hurt?" asked Masters eagerly as he ran up to her. "Here. I'll help you down. I guess you've had about enough riding for one day."

"Stop now?" she laughed, rather breathlessly. "After I have got all introduced? If you say that, I'll begin to think you don't know horses, Mister Masters. The roan and I are going to be great friends. If you will give me my hat again . . . ?"

He handed it to her in silence, but his face was flushing with understanding and admiration.

"Aren't you going with us?" she asked.

"Watch me!" said Billy, and he vaulted into the saddle. "Lady, you've got my ballot."

A moment later they galloped off down the road and around the side of the mountain. They came back late in the evening and she was so tired that

29

she went up to her room at once and Masters sent the Chinaman with supper to her. In the meantime he held a whispered consultation with Mac.

"We got to play for time, Mac," he said seriously, "because she's a fighter and, if she gets started, she's going to raise hell. She's three times the man that Bad-Eye was."

"I told you so," groaned Mac. "I seen it in her eyes. I seen it in the way she stuck to the roan. She'd fight a man the same way."

"Steady," said Masters. "We'll give her time to get used to things . . . seeing guns on the hip and things like that. It takes time to get a woman gun-broke just the way it does a horse. Give me ten days and I'll have her thinking that death is the most common thing in the world in these parts. I mean sudden death. Take most Easterners and they think that 'sudden death' and 'murder' equal one and the same thing. They got to get practiced up in these Western ideas. I started work on her today."

"Bill," said Mac, "you're sure my best friend. Break it to her easy and maybe she won't sick the lawyers on me. What did you do with her today? I could of dropped when I saw you start off with her."

"I thought it all out before we got on the horses," said Masters with pride. "I took Tuvee Road. Pretty soon we came to the rock where Henderson fought the Stillwater gang. 'Over here, lady,' I said, 'a man called Henderson was waylaid by a gang made up of old Jimmy Stillwater and his brother and three sons. They potted Henderson. . . . '"

" 'They did what?' she said.

" 'They shot him through the calf of his leg.'

" 'Oh,' she said, 'the vile murderers!'

" 'He dragged himself behind that there rock and tied up his leg with a piece tore off his shirt. Then he opened up on the Stillwaters, who were stalking his rock. First crack out of the box he got old Jimmy through the lungs and he choked up with blood so he couldn't even cuss. . . . '

" 'Good heavens!' said Missus Bad-Eye. 'Why doesn't the government police this country with soldiers?'

" 'Then he shot one of the boys though the shoulder,' I went on, 'and the rest of the gang beat it, leaving Jimmy to die on the side of the mountain. Henderson dragged himself back to his horse and rode all the way to my place. He fainted on the floor of the barroom from the loss of blood.'

" 'And did they hang him?' asked Bad-Eye's wife, and she had fire in her eye."

"Did she ask that?" groaned Mac.

"She did," said Masters, "and she looked me straight in the face when she said it. I sort of sized her up with a side glance and figured that she wasn't dippy . . . just raised different from the way I was. You see, Mac, Easterners just naturally figure that, if one man shoots another one he gets hung for it."

"I knew she was that sort," sighed Mac.

"I made up my mind to put her straight about the way people figure in these parts," said Masters. "I said to her: 'No, they didn't hang him for his game fight. When his leg got well, he went out gunning for what was left of the Stillwaters. He got the other two boys down by Sandy Warren's, and then their uncle and the boy he'd potted, when he was fighting from behind this rock, they up and left the country.'

"She turned around in her saddle and looked me

square in the eye. 'And he wasn't hung then?' she said.

" 'He's alive to this day, lady,' I said, 'and he's one of my best friends.'

"She tickled the roan with her spur and we went lickety-split down the road. After a while she sort of eased up her horse and looked at me again.

" 'Mister Masters,' she said.

" 'Yes, lady,' I said.

" 'There's an old maxim!' she said. 'When in Rome, do as the Romans. I suppose I shall have a good deal to learn before I learn to do as the Romans of Nevada.'

"Why, Mac, when I heard her say that it sort of warmed my heart. 'Lady,' I said, 'if you were to stay around here, you wouldn't be a tenderfoot more'n six months!' And she laughed, Mac, like the singing of a bird. Honest, when I heard her laugh I begun to wish that it was *me* who did the shooting!"

"Bill!"

"Well? Don't look at me like a fish out of water. What's the matter?"

"Bill, I feel powerful sick."

"What's the matter?"

"Wait a minute." He sank down into a chair, still with wide eyes of horror fixed upon his boss. "What did you say about her laugh and a bird singing?"

Masters tilted back his head with a reminiscent smile. "It's something I can't describe, Mac. You should of heard her. The valley all below was drifting full of mist with the sun making streaks of light along it, but the air up on the road was clear as crystal, and her eyes. . . ."

"Bill, are you going to Truckee tomorrow?"

"Why?"

"To get some store clothes?"

"How'd you guess that, Mac?"

"I dunno. I just sort of knew it."

"You see, it's this way. A man can't go riding around with that sort of a woman in clothes like this. I seen her look at my coat once and sort of smile. That decided me."

"Who'll keep her away from the boys while you're gone?" asked Mac in despair. "Who'll keep her from asking about a thousand questions?"

Masters grinned significantly. "She won't go far from her room tomorrow. Like as not she'll have the Chink bring up her chow. The roan ain't any rocking-horse, Mac, and this was her first day on a horse for a long time."

He left for Truckee in the dawn and came back late the same night, his team half dead with fatigue. The next morning he and Mrs. Bad-Eye started out again with their horses and for a week their program scarcely varied. It developed that the widow did not press the topic of the missing James Melrose and Masters avoided the subject with enormous tact. He informed Mrs. Bad-Eye that he was having inquiries made through the neighborhood and would soon be able to let her know exactly how much they knew of the object of her search. When they arrived at this understanding, the matter was dropped between them. The week passed; the tenth day came; Mrs Bad-Eye informed Masters that she must leave for her home on the morrow.

That evening and until far into the night Masters paced up and down his room thinking of many things. It seemed to him that the widow was particularly kind to him. Sometimes he even felt that her remarks might be construed as leading toward things which he dared not discuss, for the moral code of Bill Masters was as straight as the edge of a sword.

He was hollow-eyed when he stood before his little round hand mirror the next morning and tied with painful care the purple and green necktie which he had bought in Truckee and had saved for the great occasion. With the arm of a flannel shirt he rubbed the tight shoes. With the cuff of his coat he polished his derby hat. He had to pass through the barroom before he went up to the widow's room. He went rapidly but not quickly enough to avoid the glance of Mac. The latter leaped over the bar and caught him by his flying coattail as he vanished through the door.

"Lemme go!" breathed Masters, crimson with shame and anger.

"Not a hop," said Mac. "Not till you tell me why you're wearing that cardboard dice box in a respectable house. Bill Masters, you're changed a damn' sight from the man you once was."

"Mac," said Masters solemnly, "this is the first and the last time I wear this outfit. That damned shoe on my off foot is squeezing a corn and I'm near choked by this infernal necktie."

"Bill," said Mac, "you look to me as if you was tied, roped, and branded. I'm going back to get a drink. I'm powerful sick, Bill, and it isn't because I'm thinking of myself."

Masters paid him no more heed but went hastily up to Mrs. Bad-Eye's room. At his knock a cheery voice bade him enter. When he strode through the door, she received him with a demure smile. Perhaps it was admiration, but Masters delayed only a moment to enjoy the effect of his outfit upon her.

Even from where he stood he could glance out of the window and see the tell-tale mound of earth which marked the burial place of Bad-Eye.

"Lady," said Masters, for he clung scrupulously to this title and never addressed her as Mrs., "have you really made up your mind to leave us today?"

"I suppose you've come to say good bye?" she asked, as she shook hands with him.

"Say good bye?" repeated Masters with difficulty, and his grasp retained her fingers a moment. "No, I've come to find out just why you want to go?"

"It isn't entirely a matter of wanting," she answered, "but I have to go home sometime."

"I suppose to a city?" he queried cautiously.

"Yes."

"Look here," said Bill Masters. "You don't seem cut out for a city life . . . not after I saw you handle the roan."

She frowned at him, puzzled.

"What I mean is this," explained Masters carefully, and he counted out the points of his argument upon his fingers. "The city is all right for men who're a good deal like women, and for women who aren't a good deal like men."

"Do you think I'm very masculine, Mister Masters?"

"That ain't it," denied Masters, "and yet you're a lot more of a man than a lot of people in pants. There ain't room in a city for a woman like you."

"Oh," she said, "I can get along without spaciousness."

"Yes," said Masters, "but you don't find the room for a fight down in the city."

"Fight?" she asked with wide eyes.

"H-m," growled Masters, who found the way

more difficult the farther he went. "I mean, you got to have room to sort of wrestle around with things . . . with life in general . . . you got to have room to breathe in. Look at that mountain top out there."

He pointed commandingly out the window.

"Well?"

"You couldn't find a better place than that for breathing . . . or for a fight . . . could you?"

She laughed, and her eyes lingered on him after the sound died away. He was deathly serious.

"It is wonderful," she said, "and I suppose it would be ideal for a . . . fight."

"From my way of looking at it," went on Masters, "you couldn't find a better place for a home than this country right around here. I've seen you look at the trees and the mountains away off in the purple distance. You're made to live where roads are wild and the people are wilder."

"Yes," she nodded, and her eyes were misted with a new seriousness, "I do love it. But I can't afford to build a home out here."

"Suppose you don't have to build."

"Rent a place?" she murmured with sublime blindness. "Yes, I might be able to do that. Some day I may come back and settle down here. I do love it. You'll never know just how I hate to leave it. Why, last night I lay awake and looked out at the big black outline of the mountains. The stars were behind them, and I thought of the times we rode down the trails."

Bill Masters glowered at the floor. "I'm a fool," he muttered to himself. "How can I expect her to understand what I mean? She still thinks she's a married woman and, when she finds out her husband is dead, she'll start fighting me just the way she fought the roan." He drew a great breath and found that he dared not look at her. "Lady," he said in a voice whose sepulchral depths surprised him, "I got something to say before you go."

Her eyes widened a significant trifle and a flush touched at her cheeks. Bill Masters ground his teeth. Certainly she could not love this dead husband of hers. Yet, when she came to know just how he had died. . . . However, his duty was plain to him. He must go straight on to the bitter end.

"I got to tell you a story. Sit down over there where you can look out the window."

She sat down without a word and her eyes roved ceaselessly across his face and up and down.

"Look out there on the hillside," said Masters.

Her head turned for a brief glance which immediately came back to him.

"There's a mound out there," he said, "and under the mound lies a man whom the boys around here called a skunk. Maybe you'd think he was something else." He paused, looked at her again, glanced from the ceiling to the floor. "I can't talk in this damned . . . I beg your pardon . . . coat."

He jerked it off with a force that snapped two buttons and sent them rattling across the floor. She looked at the floor with the demure smile which was becoming familiar to him.

"Why not take off the necktie, too, Mister Masters?"

He stared at her, fascinated. "Would you mind?"

She laughed. "I'd *love* to have you!"

He ripped it off and sat back in his chair, planting his hands on his knees. "For the first time in ten days," he said, "I'm taking a real breath of fresh air."

"That's what I thought," she said.

37

He regarded her with a new interest, but the duty before him called him back to his tale.

"Now I can talk," he said, "and I want to talk about the fellow that's under that mound. He was an Easterner, and he came out here with a lot of funny ideas about the West. We didn't live up to those ideas, so he started making a little wild West of his own. His favorite amusement was shooting up my place downstairs. He made the barroom a wreck and spoiled the best mirror between here and Truckee. Once a month he got a letter addressed in a woman's handwriting and in the letter there was money. Then for a while he was drunk all the time and, when he was drunk, he was crazy. When he wasn't drunk, he was just plain mean. That was his nature . . . like a mule's! We stood for him. We didn't care when he tried to carry the stove out into the snow because he didn't have room enough in the barroom, but my bartender cared when he started shooting into the floor to make him dance. Yes, ma'am, Mac got real mad! He hit that badman flush on the jaw and knocked him into the wall and, while he was still down on one knee, that Easterner took a shot at him with his gun."

"The cur!" she whispered.

The short remark was like wine to Masters. "Yes, sir, shot straight into his face. But Mac knocked the gun aside and started wrestling with him around the floor. In the middle of it he got the gun out of the fellow's hand and shot him through the body. Now, lady, stand up like a man and tell me what you think of Mac? Is he a murderer?"

She rose even before the command. "No!" she cried. "He's a hero, and the other man was a cur.

I'd like to go right down this minute and shake Mac's hand."

Masters felt a rosy flush of relief flood his very soul. "And out there is where he lies," anxious to follow up this first good impression with the truth of the disaster. "His name was . . . well, we called him 'Bad-Eye' because he had a cast in one eye."

She started and leaned forward to search his face more closely.

"A cast in one eye . . . an Easterner . . . ?" she repeated.

"Yes," said Masters, rising and gripping his hands, "and his name was James Jerrold Melrose!"

A trembling hand rose slowly to her throat and closed there tightly. Her face grew sickly white, even to the lips. From her eyes Billy Masters saw all the horror of hopeless grief. "My God," he groaned aloud, as though he were speaking to himself, "I wish the bullet had hit me instead."

She dropped into the chair and pressed her hands to her face. Masters felt as if someone had shot a bullet straight into his heart. He dropped to one knee beside her chair.

"For God's sake, look at me! Weep . . . scream . . . anything is better than this silence."

She answered nothing.

In his desperation he caught her hands and drew them down from her face. She was pale, but in the eyes which looked out at him there was not the sign of a tear. For a moment Masters stared in utter bewilderment.

"Did you hear what I said?" he asked.

"Yes, yes," she said. "Thank God. Thank God!"

It was a hysteria beyond a doubt. Masters looked about. There was no water in the room. In a moment she might scream. "Be calm," he pleaded. "It will be all right in the end."

"Right!" she cried. "I tell you it's the rightest thing in the world. Man. Man! Why didn't you tell me this ten days ago?"

The world reeled before the eyes of Masters. He supported himself against the wall with an outstretched arm.

"I thought that you . . . his wife . . . ," he stammered feebly.

"Wife!" she cried. "So that's the meaning of it all."

She broke into a long peal of laughter but checked herself suddenly at sight of the pitiful bewilderment of Masters. "Poor fellow!" she cried. "Were you trying to spare my feelings? You've made me happier than I've been for years."

Masters seized the back of his chair to support him and fixed upon her great, staring eyes. "Happy? Happy?" he repeated stupidly. "But Bad-Eye . . . I mean Melrose . . . your husband . . . ?"

"Husband?"—she could scarcely speak for laughter, and Masters felt a cold shudder of fear pass up his spine. It was the wild laughter of the mad.

"He is dead!" cried Masters. "Don't you understand? He lies there on that hillside under the mound. Look. You can see the spot with your own eyes."

She controlled herself with a mighty effort. "Jim Melrose and I were cousins, very, very distant cousins, thank heaven. He was the black sheep of his family . . . bad and worthless and a spendthrift from the beginning. But he managed to marry my dearest friend. He lived on her money. He wouldn't work. He gambled away half her fortune. Finally she separated from him, but she couldn't bear the disgrace of a divorce and so she sent him some money every month and I and all of her friends waited and hoped and prayed for the end of him. Some time ago she stopped hearing from him and, as I was making a trip West, she asked me to take the stage to this place and make some inquiries. And now . . . now I can go back and tell poor Mildred that this is the end of his letters . . . and even of his life."

The dawn of understanding was very red on Masters's face. "Lady," he said, "if there ain't any more cause for me to talk about Bad-Eye, there's still something back in my mind that I want you to hear. Will you listen to me?"

"Without that purple necktie," she answered, "you talk very well."

"It's more or less of a real estate agent's talk," he said apologetically.

"All right. What is it?"

"It's a boost for the country around here," he said, "as a place for a home."

She sighed. "I wish I could, with all my heart," she answered, "but it takes more money than I have. I told you that before."

"H-m," said Masters, "but there are ways it can be done without money."

"Without money?" she cried, astonished. "Do you mean to say that people around here will *give* away their homes to strangers?"

"It wouldn't be charity," said Masters gravely. "It'd be a sort of partnership."

Which is the reason that there are potted flowers, now, in the windows of the Masterses' place.

THE GHOST RIDES TONIGHT!

When Frederick Faust began contributing regularly to *All-Story Weekly*, having been encouraged to do so by its editor, Bob Davis, he used his own name for the first two stories published in the magazine but with the third, "Mr. Cinderella" in the issue dated 6/23/17, the *nom de plume* Max Brand was born. In time, it came to overshadow his own name and it is now his trademark. "The Ghost" by Max Brand first appeared in *All-Story Weekly* (5/3/19). It was reprinted in *Crack-Shot Western* (8/40), a new Western magazine launched that year by the Frank A. Munsey Company with the hope that the popularity associated with the name Max Brand would attract readers. Popular Publications, Inc., presently bought out the Munsey Company and in December, 1949, launched *Max Brand's Western Magazine*. Each issue of this monthly usually featured a Max Brand story. This story was reprinted under the title "The Ghost Rides Tonight!" in the issue dated 2/50. Because Frederick Faust subsequently published another short story in the revamped *Argosy/All-Story* (7/24/20) titled "The Ghost"—a story that is *not* a Western—the earlier story which appears now for the first time in book form retains the 1950 reprint title.

The Ghost Rides Tonight!

The gold strike which led the fortune hunters to Murrayville brought with it the usual proportion of bad men and outlaws. Three months after the rush started, a bandit appeared, so consummate in skill and so cool in daring that all other offenders against the law disappeared in the shade of his reputation. He was a public dread. His comings were unannounced; his goings left no track. Men lowered their voices when they spoke of him. His knowledge of affairs in the town was so uncanny that people called him the Ghost.

The stages which bore gold to the railroad one hundred and thirty miles to the south left at the most secret hours of the night, but the Ghost knew. Once he stuck up the stage not a mile from town while the guards were still occupied with their flasks of snake-bite. Again, when the stage rolled on at midday, eighty miles south of Murrayville, and the guards nodded in the white-hot sun, the Ghost rose from behind a bush, shot the near leader, and had the cargo at his mercy in thirty seconds.

He performed these feats with admirable finesse. Not a single death lay charged to his account, for he depended upon surprise rather than slaughter. Yet so heavy was the toll he exacted that the miners passed from fury to desperation.

They organized a vigilance committee. They put a price on his head. Posses scoured the region of his hiding place, Hunter's Canyon, into which he disappeared when hard pressed, leaving no more trace than the morning mist which the sun disperses.

While two score men rode almost within calling distance, the Ghost appeared in the moonlight before Pat McDonald and Peters and robbed them of eighteen pounds of gold dust which they carried in their belts. When the vigilance committee got word of this insolent outrage, they called a mass meeting.

Never, in the history of Murrayville, had there been so grave and dry-throated an affair. William Collins, the head of the vigilantes, addressed the assembly. He listed the Ghost's outrages, pointed out that what the community needed was an experienced man-hunter to direct their efforts, and ended by asking Silver Pete to stand up before them. After some urging, Pete rose and stood beside Collins, with his hat pushed back from his gray and tousled forelock and both hands tugging at his cartridge belt.

"Men," went on Collins, placing one hand on the shoulder of the man-killer, "we need a leader who is a born and trained fighter, a man who will attack the Ghost with system and never stop after he takes up the trail. And I say the man we need is Silver Pete!"

The audience stirred, caught each other with side-glances, and then stared back at Silver Pete. His reputation gave even Murrayville pause, for his reputed killings read like the casualty list of a battle.

"I repeat," said Collins, after a pause in which he allowed his first statement to shudder its way home, "that Silver Pete is the man for us. I've talked it over with him before this, and he'll take the job, but he needs an inducement. I propose that we give him any loot which may be on the Ghost's person. If the Ghost is disposed of in the place where he has cached his plunder, the finder gets it all. It's a high price to pay, but this thing has to be stopped. My own opinion is that the Ghost is a man who does his robbing on the side and lives right here among us. If that's the case, we'll leave it to Silver Pete to find him out, and we'll obey Pete's orders. He's the man for us. He has a straight eye, and he's fast with his six-gun. If you want to know Pete's reputation as a fighting man. . . ."

"He'll tell you himself," said a voice, and a laugh followed.

Silver Pete scowled in the direction of the laugh, and his right hand caressed the butt of his gun, but two miners rose from the crowd holding a slender fellow between them.

"It's only Geraldine," said one of them. "There ain't no call to flash your gun, Pete."

"Take the drunken fool away," ordered Collins angrily. "Who let him in here?"

"Misher Collins," said Geraldine, doffing his broad-brimmed hat and speaking with a thick,

Max Brand

tell-tale accent, "Misher Collins, I ask your pardon, shir." He bowed unsteadily, and his hat brushed the floor. "I plumb forgot I was in church with Shilver Pete for a preacher!" he went on.

"Take him out, will you?" thundered Collins.

The two men at Geraldine's side turned him about and led him toward the door. Here he struggled away from his guides. "Misher Collins!" he cried in a voice half whining and half anger, "if I capture the Ghost, do I get the loot?"

A yell of laughter drowned the reply, and Geraldine staggered from the room. "What do you say, men?" roared Collins, enraged by these repeated interruptions. "Is Silver Pete the man for us?"

There was a deep muttering of consent.

"I'd hire the devil himself," murmured one man, "if he'd get rid of the Ghost."

"All right," said Collins, and he turned to Pete. "You're in charge here, and it's up to you to tell us what to do. You're the foreman, and we're all in your gang."

"Speech!" yelled a miner. "Give us a speech, Pete."

Silver Pete favored the speaker with a venomous scowl. "Speech nothin'," he answered. "I ain't here to talk. I ain't no gossipin' bit of calico. I got a hunch my six-gun'll do my chatterin' for me."

"But what do you want us to do, Pete?" asked Collins. "How are we going to help you?"

"Sit tight and chaw your own tobacco," he said amiably. "I don't want no advice. There's been too many posses around these diggin's. Maybe I'll start and hunt the Ghost by myself. Maybe I won't. If I want help, I'll come askin' it."

As a sign that the meeting had terminated he pulled his hat farther down over his eyes, hitched his belt, and stalked through the crowd without looking to either side.

Thereafter, Murrayville saw nothing of him for a month, during which the Ghost appeared five times and escaped unscathed. The community pondered and sent out to find Pete, but the search was in vain. There were those who held that he must have been shot down in his tracks by the Ghost, but the majority felt that, having undertaken his quest alone, Pete was ashamed to appear in the town without his victim.

On the subject of the quest Geraldine composed a ballad which he sang to much applause in the saloons of the town. It purported to be the narrative of Silver Pete's wanderings in search of the Ghost. In singing it Geraldine borrowed a revolver and belt from one of the bystanders, pushed back his hat and imitated the scowling face of Pete so exactly that his audiences applauded wildly. The ballad concluded with a wailing stanza:

> I don't expect no bloomin' tears;
> The only thing I ask
> Is something for a monument
> In the way of a whiskey flask.

Geraldine sang himself into popularity and many drinks with his song, and for the first time the miners began to take him almost seriously. He had appeared in town shortly after old John Murray struck gold six months before. He was a slender man of thirty-five, with a sadly drooping mouth and humorous eyes. He had introduced himself as Gerald LeRoy Witherstone and was immediately christened Geraldine.

Thereafter, he wandered about the town, with

no apparent occupation except to sing for his drinks in the saloons. Hitherto he had been accepted as harmless and amusing, but his ballad gave him an Homeric repute, particularly when men remembered that the song was bound to come sooner or later to the ears of Silver Pete.

For the time being Pete was well out of earshot. After the meeting, at which he was installed as chief man-hunter of the community, he spent most of the evening equipping himself for the chase. Strangely enough, he did not hang a second revolver to his belt nor strap a rifle behind his saddle; neither did he mount a fleet horse. To pursue the elusive Ghost he bought a dull-eyed mule with a pendulous lower lip. On the mule he strapped a heavy pack which consisted chiefly of edibles, and in the middle of the night he led the mule out of Murrayville in such a way as to evade observation. Once clear of the town he headed straight for Hunter's Canyon.

Once inside the mouth of the canyon he began his search. While he worked, he might have been taken for a prospector, for there was not a big rock in the whole course of the canyon which he did not examine from all sides. He climbed up and down the cliffs on either side as if he suspected that the Ghost might take to wings and fly up the sheer rock to a cave.

The first day he progressed barely a half mile. The second day he covered even less ground. His search went on with the vision of the outlaw's lot before him. Soon his food supply was exhausted. Even his coffee gave out. For ten days he lived on flour, salt, and water, and then, as if this saintly fast were necessary before the vision, Pete saw the Ghost.

The Ghost Rides Tonight!

It was after sunset, but the moon was clear when he saw the phantom rider race along the far side of the valley. The turf deadened the sound of the horse's hoofs and, like an apparition, the Ghost galloped close to the wall of the valley and disappeared.

Pete rubbed his eyes and looked again. The horse, with its rider, had vanished into thin air between him and the sheer rock of the valley wall. A little shudder passed through his body, but the dream of plunder restored his courage. He carefully observed the marks which should guide him to the point on the rock at which the rider disappeared. He hobbled the mule, examined his revolver, spun the cylinder, and then started down across the canyon.

He had camped upon high ground, and his course led him on a sharp descent to the stream which cut the heart of the valley. Here, for two hundred yards, trees and the declivity of the ground cut off his view, but when he came to higher ground again he found that he had wandered only a few paces to the left of his original course.

The wall of the valley was now barely fifty yards away and, as nearly as he could reckon the landmarks, the point at which the rider vanished was at or near a shrub which grew close against the rock. For an instant Pete thought that the tree might be a screen placed before the entrance of a cave. Yet the rider had made no pause to set aside the screen. He walked up to it and peered beneath the branches. He even fumbled at the base of the trunk to make sure that the roots actually entered the earth. After this faint hope disappeared, Pete stepped back and sighed. His reason vowed that it

51

was at this point that the horse turned to air, and Pete's was not a nature which admitted the supernatural.

He turned to the left and walked along the face of the cliff for fifty paces. It was solid rock. A chill like a moving piece of ice went up Pete's back. He returned to the shrub and passed around it to the right.

At first he thought it was merely the black shadow of the shrub. He stepped closer and then crouched with his revolver raised, for before him opened a crevice directly behind the shrub. It was a trifle over six feet high and less than half that in width. A man could walk through that aperture and lead a horse. Pete entered the passage with cautious steps.

Between each step he paused and listened. His progress was so painfully slow that he could not even estimate distances in the pitch dark. The passage grew higher and wider—it turned sharply to the right—a faint light shone.

Pete crouched lower and the grin of expectancy twisted at his lips. He scarcely dared to breathe, for fear of the bullet which might find him out. Before him was the light which must outline, however faintly, the figure of anyone who lurked in wait. With these things in mind he went on more rapidly. The passage widened again and turned to the left. He peered cautiously around the edge of rock and looked into as comfortable a living room as he had ever seen.

The rock hung raggedly from the top of the cave, but the sides were smooth from the action of running water through many long years. The floor was of level-packed gravel. Silver Pete remained crouched at the sharp angle of the passage until he heard the stamp and snort of a horse. It gave him heart and courage to continue his stealthy progress, inch by inch, foot by foot, pace by pace toward the light.

A tall sinewy horse was tethered at one end, and at the opposite side sat a man with his back to Pete who leveled his revolver and drew a bead on a spot between the shoulder blades. Yet he did not fire, for the thought came to him that if it were an honor to track the Ghost to his abode and kill him, it would be an immortal glory to bring the bandit back alive.

Once more that cat-like progress began until he could see that the Ghost sat on his saddle in front of a level-topped boulder. The air was filled with the sweet savor of fried bacon and coffee. Pete had crawled to the very edge of the cave when the horse threw up his head and snorted loudly. The Ghost straightened and tilted back his head to listen.

"Up with your hands!" snarled Silver Pete.

The Ghost did not even turn. His hands raised slowly above his shoulders to the level of his head and remained there.

"Stand up!" said Pete, and rose from the ground, against which he had flattened himself. For if the Ghost had decided to try a quick play with his gun, the shot in nine cases out of ten would travel breast high. "Turn around!" ordered Pete, feeling more and more sure of himself as he studied the slight proportions of the outlaw.

The Ghost turned and showed a face with a sad mouth and humorous eyes.

"By God!" cried Silver Pete, and took a pace back which brought his shoulders against the wall of rock, "Geraldine!"

If the Ghost had had his gun on his hip, he could have shot Pete ten times during that moment of astonishment, but his belt and revolver hung on a jutting rock five paces away. He dropped his hands to his hips and smiled at his visitor.

"When they put you on the job, Pete," he said, "I had a hunch I should beat it."

"Damn me, Geraldine," he growled. "I can't believe my eyes!"

"Oh, it's me, all right," Geraldine nodded. "You got me dead to rights, Pete. What do you think the boys will do with me?"

"And you're . . . the Ghost?" sighed Silver Pete, pushing back his hat as though to give his thoughts freer play. "What'll they do with you?" he repeated. "I dunno. You ain't plugged nobody, Geraldine. I reckon they'll ship you south and let the sheriff handle you. Git away from that gun!"

Geraldine had stepped back with apparent unconcern until he stood within a yard of his revolver.

"Gun?" grinned Geraldine. "Say, Pete, do you think I'd try any gun play while *you* have the drop on me?" He laughed. "Nope," he went on. "If you was one of those tinhorn gunmen from the town over yonder, I'd lay you ten to one I could drill you and make a getaway, but you ain't one of them, Pete, and seeing it's you, I ain't going to try no funny stuff. I don't hanker after no early grave, Pete."

This tribute set a placid glow of satisfaction in Pete's eyes. "Take it from me, Geraldine," he said, "you're wise. But there ain't no need for you to get scared of me so long as you play the game square and don't try no fancy moves. Now show me where you got the loot stowed and show it quick. If you don't. . . ."

The threat was unfinished, for Geraldine nodded. "Sure, I'll show it to you, Pete," he said. "I know when I got a hand that's worth playing, and I ain't a gent to bet a measly pair of treys against a full house. Take a slant over there behind the rocks and you'll find it all."

He indicated a pile of stones of all sizes which lay heaped in a corner. Pete backed toward it with his eye still upon the Ghost. A few kicks scattered the rocks and exposed several small bags. When he stirred these with his foot, their weight was eloquent, and the gunfighter's smile broadened.

"Think of them tinhorns," he said, "that offered all your pickings to the man that got you dead or alive, Geraldine."

The Ghost sighed. "Easy pickings," he agreed. "No more strong-arm work for you, Pete."

The jaw of Silver Pete set sternly again. "Lead your hoss over here," he said, "and help me stow this stuff in the saddlebags. And if you make a move to get the hoss between me and you. . . ."

The Ghost grinned in assent, saddled his mount, and led him to Pete.

"Now git your hands up over your head ag'in, Geraldine," he said, "and go out down the tunnel about three paces ahead of me."

Geraldine stopped at the boulder to finish off his coffee. He turned to Pete with the cup poised at his lips. "Say, Pete," he said genially. "Anything wrong with a cup of coffee and a slice of bacon before we start back?"

"By gosh, Geraldine," grinned the gunfighter, "you're a cool bird, but your game is too old." Nevertheless his very soul yearned toward the savor of bacon and coffee.

"Game?" repeated the Ghost, who caught the gleam of Pete's eye. "What game? I say let's start up the coffee pot and the frying pan. I can turn out flapjacks browner than the ones your mother used to make, Pete."

Pete drew a great breath, for the taste of his flour and water diet of the past few days was sour in his mouth. "Geraldine," he said at last, "it's a go! But if you try any funny passes, I ain't going to wait for explanations. Slide out the chow."

He rolled a large stone close to the boulder which served as dining table to the bandit and sat down to watch the preparations. The Ghost paid little attention to him but hummed as he worked. Soon a fire snapped and crackled. While the bacon fried, he mixed pancake flour in a tin plate. The Ghost piled the crisp slices of bacon on a second tin plate and used the fried-out fat to cook the flapjacks.

"What I can't make out," said Geraldine, without turning to his guest, "is why you'd do this job for those yellow livers over in the town."

"Why, you poor nut," he answered compassionately, "I ain't working for them. I'm working for the stuff that's up there behind the saddle."

The Ghost stared at him. "Say," he grinned, "do you think they'll really let you walk off with all that loot?"

The face of the gunman darkened. "I know they'll let me," he said with a sinister emphasis. "That was the way they talked."

Geraldine turned back to his work without further comment. In a few moments he finished. He put the food on the boulder before Silver Pete and then sat on the other side of the big stone. The gunfighter laid his revolver beside his tin cup and attacked the food with the will of ten. Yet, even while he ate, he noted that the Ghost stared at him with a curious and almost pitying interest.

"Look here," Pete said, "just what were you aiming at a while ago?"

Geraldine shrugged his shoulders and let his eyes wander away as though the subject embarrassed him.

"Damn it!" said Pete with some show of anger. "Don't go staring at me like that. What's biting you?"

"It ain't my business," the Ghost said. "As long as I'm done for, I don't care what they do to you."

"Wha'd'ya mean?" Pete blurted. "D'ya mean to say them quitters are going to double-cross me?"

The Ghost answered nothing, but the shrug of his shoulders was eloquent.

"Geraldine," Pete said, "you ain't playin' fair with me. Look what I done for you. Any other man would of plugged you the minute they seen you, but here I am lettin' you walk back safe and sound . . . treating you as if you was my own brother, almost."

Geraldine met his stare with a steady eye. "I'm going to do it," he said in a low voice, as if talking to himself. "Just because you come out here and caught me like a man, there ain't no reason I should stand by and see you made a joke of. Pete, I'm going to tell you."

Pete settled back on his stone with his fingers playing nervously about the handle of his gun. "Make it short, Geraldine," he said with an ominous softness. "Tell me what them wall-eyed cayuses figure on doin'."

right between the eyes, was a little round hole, powerful-like a hole made by a .45. They say. . . ."

"They lie!" yelled Silver Pete, rising.

"Huh?" said Geraldine. "Of course they lie. Nobody could look at you and think you'd plug a pal . . . not for nothing."

Pete dropped back to his stone. "Go on," he said. "What else do they say?"

"I don't remember it all," said the Ghost, puckering his brows with the effort of recollection, "but they got it all planned out when you come back with the loot, they'll take it and split it up between them . . . one third to Collins, because he made the plan first. They even made up a song about you," went on Geraldine, "and the song makes a joke out of you all the way through, and it winds up like this:

> **I don't expect no bloomin' tears;**
> **The only thing I ask**
> **Is something for a monument**
> **In the way of a whiskey flask.**

"Who made up the song, Geraldine?" asked Pete.

"I dunno," answered the Ghost. "I reckon Collins had a hand in it."

"Collins," repeated the gunfighter. "It sounds like him. I'll get him first!"

"It was Collins who got them to send out three men to watch you. They was to trail you and see that you didn't make off with the loot. Ever see anybody trailing you, Pete?"

"I never thought of it," he whispered. "I didn't know they was such skunks. But, I swear, they won't ever see the money. I'll take it and line out for new hunting grounds."

"But what'll you do if they're following you up?" suggested the Ghost. "What'll you do if they've tracked you here and the sheriff with them? What if they get you for Red Horry?"

The horse had wandered a few paces away. Now its hoof struck a loose pebble, which turned with a crunching sound like a footfall.

"Watch out!" yelled the Ghost, springing up and pointing toward the entrance. "They've got you, Pete!"

The gunfighter whirled to his feet, his weapon poised and his back to the Ghost. Geraldine drew back his arm and lunged forward across the boulder. His fist thudded behind Silver Pete's ear. The revolver exploded and the bullet clicked against a rock. Pete collapsed on his face, with his arms spread out cross-wise. The Ghost tied his wrists behind his back with a small piece of rope. Silver Pete lay trussed and unconscious. The Ghost turned him on one side and then, strangely enough, set about clearing up the tinware from the boulder. This he piled back in its niche. A string of oaths announced the awakening of Silver Pete. Geraldine went to him and leaned over his body.

Pete writhed and cursed, but Geraldine kneeled down and brushed the sand out of the gunfighter's hair and face. Then he wiped the blood from a small cut on Pete's chin where his face struck a rock when he fell.

"I have to leave you now, Pete," he said, rising from this work of mercy. "You've been good company, Pete, but a little of you goes a long way."

"For sweet sake!" groaned Silver Pete, and Geraldine turned. "Don't leave me here to die by inches. I done some black things, Geraldine, but never nothing as black as this. Take my own gun and pull a bead on me, and we'll call everything even."

The Ghost smiled at him. "Think it over, Pete," he said. "I reckon you got enough to keep your mind busy. So long!"

He led his horse slowly down the passage, and the shouts and pleadings of Silver Pete died out behind him. At the mouth of the passage his greatest shout rang no louder than the hum of a bee.

Grimly silent was the conclave in Billy Hillier's saloon. That evening the Ghost had stopped the stage scarcely a mile from Murrayville, shot the sawed-off shotgun out of the very hands of the only guard who dared to raise a weapon, and had taken a valuable packet of dust. They sent out a posse at once, which rode straight for Hunter's Canyon and arrived there just in time to see the phantom horseman disappear into the mouth of the ravine. They had matched speed with that rider before, and they gave up the vain pursuit.

It was small wonder, therefore, if not a man smiled when a singing voice reached them from a horseman who cantered down the street:

> **I don't expect no bloomin' tears;**
> **The only thing I ask**
> **Is something for a monument**
> **In the way of a whiskey flask.**

The sound of the gallop died out before the saloon, the door opened, and Geraldine staggered

61

into the room, carrying a small but apparently ponderous burden in his arms. He lifted it to the bar which creaked under the weight.

"Step up and liquor!" cried Geraldine in a ringing voice. "I got the Ghost!"

A growl answered him. It was a topic over which they were not prepared to laugh.

"Get out and tell that to your hoss, son," said one miner. "We got other things to think about than your damn foolery."

"Damn foolery?" echoed Geraldine. "Step up and look at the loot! Dust, boys, real dust!"

He untied the mouth of a small buckskin bag and shoved it under the nose of the man who had spoken to him. The latter jumped back with a yell and regarded Geraldine with fascinated eyes.

"By gosh, boys," he said, "it *is* dust!"

Geraldine fought off the crowd with both hands. "All mine," he cried. "Mine, boys! You voted the loot to the man who caught the Ghost."

"And where's the Ghost?" asked several men together.

"Geraldine," said Collins, pushing through the crowd, "if this is another joke, we'll hang you for it."

Geraldine said, "I'll give him to you on one ground."

"Out with it," said Collins.

"I don't want him strung up. Is it a bargain?"

"It's a bargain," said Collins quickly. "We'll turn him over to the sheriff. Are you with me, boys?"

They yelled their agreement, and in thirty seconds every man who had a horse was galloping after Collins and Geraldine.

At the shrub beside the wall of the valley, Geraldine drew rein, and they followed him in an awed and breathless body into the passage.

"I went out scouting on my own hook," explained Geraldine as he went before them, "and I saw the Ghost ride down the canyon and disappear in here. I followed him."

"And what did you do to him?"

"You'll see in a minute. There was only one shot fired, and it came from his gun."

They turned the sharp angle and entered the lighted end of the passage. In another moment they crowded into the cave and stood staring at the tightly bound figure of Silver Pete.

"Untie his feet, boys," said Collins, "and we'll take him back. Silver Pete, you can thank your lucky stars that Geraldine made us promise to turn you over to the law." "How did you do it?" he continued, turning to Geraldine.

"I'm not very handy with a gun," said the Ghost, "so I tackled him with my fists. Look at that cut on his jaw. That's where I hit him."

A little murmur of wonder passed around the group. One of them cut the rope which bound Pete's ankles together, and two more dragged him quickly to his feet.

"Stand up like a man, Pete," said Collins, "and thank Geraldine for not cutting out your rotten heart."

But Silver Pete, never moving his eyes from the face of the Ghost, broke into a long and full-throated laugh and never said a word.

"Watch him, boys!" called Collins sharply. "He's going loony! Here, Jim, grab on that side and I'll take him here. Now start down the tunnel."

Yet, as they went forward, the rumbling laugh of the gunfighter broke out again and again.

"I got to leave you here," said the Ghost when

they came out from the mouth of the passage. "My way runs east, and I got a date at Tuxee for tonight. I'll just trouble you for that there slicker with the ghost rider's dust in it, Collins."

Without a word the vigilance man unstrapped the heavy packet, which he had tied behind his saddle. He fastened it behind Geraldine's saddle, and then caught him by the hand.

"Geraldine, " he said, "you're a queer cuss. We haven't made you out yet, but we're going to take a long look at you when you come back to Murrayville tomorrow."

"When I come back," said Geraldine, "you can look at me as long as you wish." His eyes changed, and he laid a hand on Collins's shoulder. "Take it from me," he said softly, "you've given me your word that the boys won't do Pete dirt. Remember, he never plugged any of you. He's got his hands tied now, Collins, and if any of the boys try fancy stunts with him . . . maybe I'll be making a quick trip back from Tuxee. Savvy?"

His eyes held Collins for the briefest moment, and then he swung into his saddle and rode east with the farewell yells of the posse ringing after him. By the time they were in their saddles, Geraldine had topped a hill several hundred yards away and his figure was black against the moon.

The wind from the east blew back his song to them faintly:

I don't expect no bloomin' tears;
The only thing I ask
Is something for a monument
In the way of a whiskey flask.

The Ghost Rides Tonight!

"Look at him, boys," said Collins, turning in his saddle. "If it wasn't for what's happened tonight, I'd lay ten to one that that was the Ghost on the wing for his hiding place!"

A SAGEBRUSH CINDERELLA

"A Sagebrush Cinderella" by Max Brand was first published in *All-Story Weekly* (7/10/20). There was about Faust's Western fiction, almost from the beginning, something of the archetypal, and often his short stories as well as his serials have about them qualities commonly associated with legendry, myths, parables; they draw their vividness from the same primal sources as folk tales. Jacqueline During in this story is reminiscent of another of Faust's most enduring characters, Jacqueline Boone, one of the two heroines in "Luck," a six-part serial which had run the previous year in *The Argosy* under the byline John Frederick. The first book version of "Luck" As Faust wrote it was published as a Circle Ⓥ Western in 1996. "A Sagebrush Cinderella" appears here in book form for the first time.

A Sagebrush Cinderella

I
"WHISKERS"

She lay prone upon the floor, kicking her heels together, frowningly intent upon her book. Outside, the sky was crimson with the sunset. Inside the room, every corner was filled with the gay phantoms of the age of chivalry. Jac would not raise her head, for if she kept her eyes upon the printed page it seemed to her that the armored knights were trooping about her room. A board creaked. That was from the running of some striped page with pointed toes. The wind made a soft rustling. That was the stir of the nodding plumes of the warriors. The pageantry of forgotten kings flowed brightly about her.

"Jac!"

Jacqueline frowned and shrugged her shoulders.

"Jac!"

She raised her head. The dreary board walls of her room looked back at her, empty, barren, a thousand miles and a thousand years from all romance. She closed her book as the door of her room opened and her father stood in the entrance.

"Readin' again!" said Jim During in infinite disgust. "Go down an' wait on the table. The cook's gone an' got drunk. I've give him the run. Hurry up."

She shied the book into a corner and rose. "How many here for chow?" she asked.

"Maurice Gordon an' a lot of others," said her father. "Start movin'!"

She started. Handsome Maurice Gordon. She had only to close her eyes and there he stood in armor—Sir Maurice de Gordon.

You might have combed the cattle ranges for five hundred miles north, east, south, and west, and never found so fine a figure of a man as Maurice Gordon. Good looks are rather a handicap than a blessing in the mountain desert, but Maurie Gordon was notably ready at all times for anything from a dance to a fight, and his reputation was accordingly as high among men as women.

He made a stir wherever he went, and now as he sat in the dining room of Jim During's crossroads hotel, all eyes were upon him. He withstood their critical admiration with the nonchalant good nature of one who knew that, from his silk bandanna to his fine riding boots, his outfit represented the beau ideal of the cowpuncher.

"Where you bound for?" asked the proprietor of the hotel as the supper drew toward its close.

"The dance over to Bridewell," said Maurie. "Damnation!"

For as he mentioned the dance, Jac who was bringing him his second cup of coffee started so violently that a drop of the hot liquid splashed on the back of Maurie's neck.

"Oh!" she cried, and seized her apron to wipe away the coffee.

" 'Scuse me," growled Maurie, seeing that he had sworn at a woman. "But you took me by surprise."

With that he stopped the hand which was bearing the soiled apron toward his neck, and produced from his pocket—marvelous to behold!—a handkerchief of stainless white with which he rubbed away the coffee.

"Jacqueline!" rumbled her father, and his accent made the name far more emphatic than Maurie's "Damnation."

That was her given title, but to every cowpuncher on the ranges she was known as Jac During who rode, shot, and sometimes swore as well as any man of them all. She was Jacqueline to her father alone, and to him only at such a time as this.

"Well?" she said belligerently, and her eyes fixed on her father as steadily and as angrily as those of a man.

"Your hands was made for feet. Go back to the kitchen. We don't need you till the boys is through with their coffee. Too bad, Maurie."

"Nothin' at all," said the latter heartily and waved the matter out of existence.

He might banish Jac from his thoughts with a gesture, but he could not drive away her thoughts of him so easily, it seemed; for she stopped in the shadow of the doorway which led to the kitchen and stared back with big eyes at the cowpuncher.

"Who you takin' to the dance?" said her father.

"Dolly Maxwell," said Maurie, naming the prettiest girl in many, many miles.

"That pale-faced . . . thing!" muttered Jac, relapsing into a feminine vocabulary at this crisis. But she sighed as she turned back into the kitchen.

She threw open the door of the stove so that the light flamed on her red hair, which was tied in a hard knot on top of her head—the quickest, easiest, and unquestionably the most ugly manner of dressing hair. A vast and unreasoning rage made her blood hot.

The anger was partly for her own blunder in spilling the hot coffee. It was even more because of Maurie's ejaculation. With that one word he had banished the vision of Sir Maurice de Gordon. The plumed helmet had fallen from his head; his bright armor had blown away on a gust of reality. In the fury of her chagrin Jac caught up the poker and raked the grate of the stove loudly. The rattling helped to relieve her as swearing, perhaps, relieves a man. In the midst of the racket she heard a chuckle from the dining room, and her blood went cold at the thought that someone might understand the deeps of her shame and wrath.

She ran to the door. There she sighed again, but it was relief this time. At least it was not Maurie who laughed. He was deep in conversation with his neighbor. She swept the other faces with a quick glance that halted at a pair of bright, quizzical eyes. Only one man had apparently understood the meaning of her racket at the stove.

"That bum!" said Jac, and turned on her heel.

But something made her stop and look back. Perhaps it was the brightness of those eyes; certainly nothing else could have made her look twice at this fellow. Even among these rough citizens of the mountain desert he was wild and ragged. His shirt was soiled and frayed from elbow to wrist. A bush of black hair was so long that it almost entirely hid his ears, and his face, apparently untouched by a razor for months, was covered by a tremendous growth of whiskers. She could only faintly guess at the features behind that mask.

It was very puzzling, but Jac would not waste time thinking of such a caricature of a man as he of the many whiskers. She turned back into the kitchen and broke off her meditations by kicking a box across the floor.

It smashed against the wall. Jac sat down to think and stared gloomily straight before her. Her throat swelled, and in her heart was that feeling of infinite age which comes upon women at all periods of their life, but most of all during the interim when a girl knows that she is mature and the rest of the world has not yet found it out.

"Why was I made like this?" said Jac miserably.

And from within a still, small voice that was *not* conscience answered her.

"Aw," said the voice, "quit kiddin' yourself!"

"Why," repeated Jac dolorously, "was I tied to such a face?"

"You might as well be askin'," said the voice, "how the colors are painted on a pinto."

"Them colors never rub out."

"Neither will your face."

"It's awful!"

"It is."

She stood in front of the speckled mirror. "There's something wrong with the way I fix my hair," she muttered.

It was tied so tightly that it pulled up the skin of her forehead and raised her eyebrows to a look of continual plaintiveness.

"There's *certainly* something wrong with the way I do my hair!"

"Is that all that's wrong with your face?" whispered the voice.

"My hair is red," said Jac.

"Like paint," said the voice.

"There's no help?"

"None!"

To escape from this merciless dialogue, Jac went back to her post of vantage. The square shoulders of Maurie Gordon were just disappearing through the outer door. All the others were gone, with the exception of her father, her brother Harry, and the man of many whiskers. The last was hardly to be considered as a human being. She felt practically alone with her family, so she entered the dining room and sat on the edge of the table, swinging her feet.

"Harry," she said, "d'you see anything the matter with the way I fix my hair?"

Her brother glanced at her with unseeing eyes. The man of many whiskers stopped stirring his coffee and glanced up with the keen twinkle which Jac had seen before.

She turned her shoulder upon him

"Throw me your tobacco, Pa," said Harry.

"Did you hear me ask you a question?" said Jac fiercely.

Harry rolled his cigarette before he answered. "Don't get so sore you rope an' tie yourself. What did you say?"

"I asked you if you was goin' to the dance at Bridewell."

The stranger chuckled softly.

"Say, what's eatin' you, Whiskers?" snapped Jac, but without turning.

"Sure I'm going," said Harry. "It's going to be a big bust."

"What girl are you takin'?"

"Nobody. I'll find plenty to dance with when I get there."

Jac blinked her eyes once, twice, and again. "Why not take me?"

The cigarette fell from Harry's lips. "What the. . . ." he began. "Say, Jac, are you sick?"

The ache came in Jac's throat again. Her face changed color and the freckles across the bridge of her nose stood out with a startling distinctness. "Don't I dance good enough, Harry?"

He had evidently been bracing himself for a straight-from-the-shoulder retort. At this gentle question he gasped and rose with a look of brotherly concern.

"Jac, if you was a man, I'd say you'd been hittin' the red-eye too much."

"Oh," said Jac.

Harry touched her under the chin and tilted back her head. The deep blue eyes stared miserably up to him.

"What's the matter with her, Pa?" he asked.

"Plain foolishness!" said the latter.

Jac struck the hand from her chin and leaped from the table to her feet. "Harry," she said, "if I was a man, I'd hang a bunch of fives on your chin!"

The chuckle of the stranger made her whirl.

"Get out, Whiskers," she commanded, "or I'll pull a gun and give you a free shave."

The man rose obediently and went from the room to the porch. Harry followed him out and swung into the saddle of his horse. His father delayed an instant.

"Now cut out this talk of goin' to the dance," said

Jim During. "You stay right here, an' if any of the boys come in late, fix them up some chow. I got to slide over to see old Jones on . . . some . . . some business."

"Sure you do," said Jac scornfully. "I know *that* kind of business. It comes five in a hand, and you draw to it."

The hair of her father seemed to take on a deeper tinge of red. "Well?" he said.

"Well?" she replied no less angrily. "If I couldn't play no better hand of poker than you do, I'd go no farther than solitaire, believe me."

"Jacqueline!"

"Don't swear at me!" said Jac. "If you think I ain't right, just sit down and play a hand with me."

Her father was so swelled with wrath that he could make no rejoinder. At length he whirled on his heel and strode toward the door, pulling his sombrero down over his eyes. At the door he turned back and pointed a long, angry arm.

"An' if I catch you leavin' this place tonight . . . ," he began.

"Well?"

His face altered and the anger faded from his eyes. "Jac," he said gently, "why in hell wasn't you born a boy?"

He went on out and a moment later his horse clattered down the road.

"Why?" repeated Jac.

II
"LAND"

She went out to the porch and stared after the disappearing horseman. When he had quite vanished in the rapidly fading light of the evening, she turned back. She stopped. The stranger sat on the edge of the porch, whittling a stick.

His black hair bushed out under the brim of his sombrero, and for some reason it stirred the latent wrath in Jac. She went to him and stood with arms akimbo, staring down.

"Too bad," he said, but did not look up.

"What's too bad?"

"The red hair."

It was a long moment before she spoke. "Huh?" she said. "If I was to talk about *your* hair, you'd think I was discussin' a record crop of hay. If I was to. . . ." She stopped, for the twinkling eyes were smiling up to her.

"I look like the land of much rain, all right," said the stranger.

Jac dropped to a cross-legged position with the agility of an Indian and, supporting her chin on both hands, she stared impudently into the face of the stranger. "What does the land look like when the forest is gone?"

"It ain't been surveyed for so long, I've forgotten."

He shifted a little to smile more directly into her eyes, and the movement caused her glance to drop to his holster. It was open. With a slow gesture— for no one, not even a woman, makes free with the weapon of another in the mountain desert—she drew the revolver out, looked it over with the keen eye of a connoisseur, glanced down the sights, spun the cylinder, and tried the balance with a deft hand.

"Clean as a whistle," she said as she restored the revolver. "*Some* six-gun!" With a new respect she looked the man over from head to foot. "Maybe under the mask," she said, "you look almost human."

"I dunno. Maybe."

Her eyes wandered far away, came back to him, frowned, wandered off again. "Can you dance?" she asked conversationally.

He broke into a deep laughter. Jac gathered as if for a spring.

"Go slow, partner," she drawled. "Maybe I ain't big but, believe me, I ain't a house pet."

"I'd as soon think of fondlin' a wildcat," nodded the man.

She hesitated between anger and curiosity and then glanced around with needless anxiety lest they should not be alone. "Give it to me straight, pal," she said. "How bad do I look?"

Her companion looked her over with a critical eye and a judicious frown. "I dunno," he said at last. "It's pretty hard for me to tell. If those freckles was covered up, maybe I could see your face."

As he spoke, he edged away, as if ready to spring from the porch when she attacked him. Instead she sighed. The other started and looked at her with a new interest.

"How old are you?" he asked sharply.

"Three years more than you think."

"Sixteen?"

"And three makes nineteen. You're right the first time. How'd you do it?"

He took off his hat and extended his hand. "My name is Bill Carrigan," he said.

Even in the dim light he could guess at the curiosity in her eyes.

"Mine is Jac . . . Jacqueline During. I'm awfully glad to shake hands with you."

There was a little pause.

"I suppose Maurie Gordon is nearly at the dance by this time?" he said tentatively.

She nodded. The lump in her throat kept her silent.

"How tall are you?" he asked suddenly.

"Five-feet-five and a half."

"What's your weight?"

"One hundred and twenty. Say, Carrigan, what you drivin' at?"

He looked away as if making a mental note. "What size shoes?"

She looked at him with a dark frown, but the twinkle of his eyes was irresistible. She broke into a laugh.

"Look at 'em!" She extended to his gaze a foot clad in the heavy shoe of a man, cut square across the toe. "Well, Columbus, what have you discovered?"

"Land," said Carrigan, and rose.

"You goin' so soon?" she queried plaintively.

"But I'm coming back," said Carrigan.

"Coming back?" repeated Jac.

"With bells."

She watched him swing gracefully into the saddle of a clean-limbed horse and gallop swiftly into the gloom.

"Well, I'll be . . . ," began Jac. She checked herself. An instinct which was born with Eve made her raise a hand to pat her hair. She began again: "I must look like. . . ." Once more she stopped, this time with a sigh. "What words are left?" murmured Jacqueline.

Carrigan pulled his horse up before the barbershop in the little village a mile away. He banged thunderously against the wall of the shanty with his gun butt.

"What the hell!" roared a voice above.

"Business," said Carrigan. "Come on down and open your shop."

A few moments later he sat down in the chair while the barber lighted his lamp. The latter groaned when he saw the face of his customer.

"How much?"

"The price of your best razor," said Carrigan instantly. "Now start . . . chop off the heavy timber, saw down the undergrowth, anything to clear the land. And do it on the jump."

Hair flew . . . literally. At last the barber stepped back, perspiring, and looked at the lean face before him. "I feel," he said, "more as if I'd made a man than shaved him."

"Maybe you're right," said Carrigan, and started on the run for the general merchandise store across the street, the only clothiers within a hundred miles, a place that carried everything from horseshoes to hairpins.

The proprietor was locking up the front door. "What's your rush, partner?" he asked. "Wait till tomorrow. I got some business to. . . ."

"Tomorrow is next year," said Carrigan. "Start goin'."

The door opened.

He began shedding orders and old clothes at the same time. The storekeeper, on the run, brought the articles Carrigan demanded.

"More light!" Carrigan said at last.

The proprietor brought a lamp and placed it close to a large mirror, the pride of his place.

Carrigan stalked up to it and, turning slowly around, viewed his outfit with one long glance.

A Sagebrush Cinderella

"All right," he said. "Now I'm ready to begin buying!"

The proprietor gasped and then rubbed his hands. "What next?" he asked.

"A beautiful girl."

The proprietor smiled in sympathy with the somewhat obscure jest.

"A beautiful girl," repeated Carrigan, "with red hair, weighing a trifle over one hundred and twenty pounds, standing five-feet-five and a half, and with feet . . . well, of the right size."

The proprietor moistened his lips and stepped back. His eyes were very large.

"Start for the ladies' department."

The proprietor was baffled, but he led the way.

"Dresses first," said Carrigan. "Something fancy. Best you've got. Here! Red . . . green! Green . . . red!"

He picked out a gown and held it out at arm's length, a soft, green fabric.

"What size do you want?" asked the proprietor.

"What's the perfect size for five-foot-five, eh?"

"Thirty-six."

"What's this gown?"

"Thirty-six."

"How much?"

The proprietor doubled the price.

"Taken," said Carrigan.

"But maybe the lady ain't thirty-six, and. . . ."

"You're right, old-timer. The lady ain't, but she will be. What's next? Petticoat?"

"Those are over here."

"I leave it to you, partner. Something that makes a rustle and a swishing like a light rain on leaves. You know the kind?"

"Taffeta will do that."

"Then taffeta it is. Now for the kicks. Something light. Slippers, eh?"

"Follow me." He set out an array of dancing shoes. "What size?" he asked.

"The right size."

The proprietor made a gesture of despair. "There ain't no woman in the world whose feet are the *right* size."

"Then we'll set a record tonight. How big ought they to be for a hundred and twenty pounds?"

"That all depends. If the lady is. . . ."

"The lady ain't," repeated Carrigan wearily. "I'm tellin' you, we're making her here."

The proprietor wiped his forehead. "Number four?" he suggested vaguely.

"Let's have a look. Make it something like this."

He indicated a pair of bronze slippers but, when the storekeeper produced the pair of number fours, Carrigan took one of them in the palm of his brawny hand and stared at it with something between awe and dismay.

"Are these meant for real feet?"

"Yep."

Carrigan thought of the mighty brogans he had seen on Jac's feet. "Do or die," he said, "she'll have to wear 'em! What's next? Stockings?"

"Here they are."

"These green ones will do the work. And now. . . ."

"Corsets?" He indicated a model bust clad in a formidable corset.

Carrigan sighed. "Friend," he said, "did you ever hear about the days when men wore armor?"

"Yes."

"When I'm dancin' with a girl that wears one of

them things, I feel as if I had my arms around a man in armor. Anything else?"

A malicious light gleamed in the eyes of the proprietor. "There's nothing else except these girdles that a drummer palmed off on me. They're just elastic, that's all. They don't give a girl no figger."

"H-m! But they're a long way from armor plate. I'll take one."

"What size?"

"How do they run? Large, small, and medium?"

"By inches."

"Make it something extra medium in inches."

Most of them *wish* they could wear twenty-one."

"Twenty-one, it is."

The proprietor grinned. "But if that's too small. . . ."

"Friend, what do you do when your cinch is too small for your hoss?"

"Pull."

"Well?"

The proprietor added the girdle to the heap in mute surrender. "And now that we've got down to the girdle," he said, "the next thing is. . . ."

"Look here, friend," said Carrigan, "don't go too far!"

"Well?"

"Well, fix up the underlining any way you want, but make it the best you've got. One thing more. There ain't enough color in this outfit. Something for her shoulders?"

"A scarf? Right here."

Carrigan picked out a filmy, orchid-colored tissue. "Now we've reached her face."

The proprietor groaned. "Paint?"

"Nope. I don't want to add anything. I want to make something disappear. Freckles."

The storekeeper grinned. "Vanishing cream and then rice powder. That's the latest hitch."

III
"CINDERELLA"

The bundle which resulted was bulky, but Carrigan sang as he raced back. He drew his horse to a walk as he approached the During hotel, for a light showed dimly from the dining room. There might be some new arrival in the place.

It was only Jac, however. She sat by the table with her face buried in her arms. He saw one hand lying palm up beside her head. It was small and the fingers tapered.

"I never noticed she was so small," said Carrigan to himself in a hushed voice. He stepped closer, softly. "Jest a kid," he added.

There was the sound of a controlled sob. Her body quivered, and Carrigan knew that she was struggling with some great grief.

"Cinderella!" he called gently and touched her shoulder.

Her head turned. Two marvelously deep blue eyes shone up to him. Her lower lip was trembling but, when she saw him, she stiffened with astonishment.

"What do you want?" she asked.

"A beautiful girl, five-feet-five and a half, one hundred and twenty pounds."

"Carrigan!" she stammered. "Is it really you?"

He dropped the bundle to the floor and turned slowly. "Look me over."

"Wonderful!" She had dropped into a chair and sat pigeon-toed, her hands clasped tightly in her lap and her mouth slightly agape. "Carrigan, how did you do it?"

"Look in that bundle, and you'll see."

He left the room hastily but, before he had gone far, he heard a thin, short cry. Happiness and pain are closely akin.

"If she only . . . " began Carrigan. He choked. "If this was only a masked ball," he said at last, "she might get by. But even then that hair. . . ." He swore softly again. "If Maurie turns her down after this, I'll bust his face wide open!"

He thought of Gordon's wide shoulders and sighed. After a time a voice called from the house.

"Carrigan!"

It was a marvelous voice. It was changed, as the tone of a violin changes when it passes from the hands of an amateur to those of an artist.

"Is that my name?" said Carrigan, and he walked slowly toward the house.

She stood in the center of the room, with a piece of the wrapping paper in which the bundle had been done up held before her face. Carrigan started back until his shoulders touched the wall.

"My God!" he murmured with indescribable awe. "They fit!"

"But . . . " she said behind the paper.

"Well?"

She lowered the paper. The freckles looked out at him, and the eyes with plaintive brows raised by the hard knot of the hair. At the base of her throat was a line of sharp division. All above was a healthy brown. All below was a dazzling white. He could not meet the despair of her eyes.

"Well?" she said.

"Well?" said Carrigan.

"I didn't choose this face," she explained sadly. "It was wished on me!"

Carrigan sank into a chair and looked upon her as a general looks over a field of battle and calculates the chances of his outnumbered army. His eyes fell to the slender feet in the shining bronze slippers with the small, round ankles encased in pleasant green. His heart leaped. His eyes raised and met the freckles. He clenched his hand.

"If it wasn't for them freckles. . . ."

"Yes?"

"I could see your face."

Crimson went up her throat with delicate tints, blending the clear white of the breast with the brown of the round neck. He jumped to his feet. He pointed a commanding arm.

"That hair!"

"I know, it's. . . ."

"I don't care what you know. Untie that knot!"

She obeyed. A red-gold flood rippled suddenly almost to her knees. Carrigan blinked.

"Sit down!"

She dropped to a chair, and Carrigan commenced to work. When a man has to do anything from roping a steer to jerking out a six-gun with the speed of light, he acquires a marvelous dexterity with his hands. Carrigan could almost think with his fingers. They seemed, in fact, to have a separate intelligence.

He gathered up the silken mass. The soft touch thrilled him as if everyone of the delicate threads carried a tiny charge of electricity. It was marvelous that such a shining torrent could have been reduced the moment before to that compacted, bright red knot. Carrigan closed his eyes and summoned up a vision of hair as he had seen it dressed, not on the heads of any of the mountain-desert belles, but in magazine pictures.

With that vision before him, he commenced to work, rapidly, surely. It seemed as if the hair, glad to escape from the bondage of that hard knot, fell of its own accord into graceful, waving lines. It curved low across the broad forehead. It gathered at the nape of the neck in a soft knot in the Grecian mode.

"Now!" said Carrigan.

She rose and faced him. "What's happened?" she cried, for his lower jaw had fallen.

He swallowed twice before he could answer. "I'm beginning to see your face!"

For the face, after all, is like any picture. The hair is the frame, and an ugly frame will spoil the most lovely painting. The eye does not stop at a boundary. It includes it.

"Once more!" said Carrigan, and seized the vanishing cream.

As he worked now, he felt like the artist who draws the human face from the block of marble. He felt as Michelangelo when the grim old Florentine said: "I do not create. I take off the outer layers of the stone and free the form which is hidden within." Or perhaps he was more like Pygmalion and the inevitable statue when the artist saw the first hues of life faintly flushing in the cold marble.

When he stepped back and looked at her, she seemed strangely aloof. She had drawn away a thousand miles and a thousand years. He discovered the most ancient of truths, that a beautiful woman is a world in herself upon which all men must look from the outside. She escapes from experience. It cannot stain her. She escapes from herself. Her beauty is greater than her soul.

"It's done," said Carrigan sadly.

"Isn't it any use?" she queried.

He thought of Maurie and hated the handsome face which rose in his memory.

"You look sick," said Jac. "What's the matter? Is it all in my face? Let me take a slant at the landscape after the snow has fallen."

She ran to the cracked glass. She was a tomboy when she whirled to a stop in front of it. He watched her eyes widen, saw her straighten slightly, wonderfully. She was inches taller when she turned; she was years older.

"Are you ready, Mister Carrigan?"

She moved to him with a subtle rustling like the fall of a misting rain on orchard blossoms. He could not answer for a moment. He had seen a miracle.

"Yes, Miss During," he said at last.

The light which came somewhere from the depths to shine in her eyes altered swiftly to a sparkle which he could understand. She ran to him and caught both his hands.

"Carrigan," said Jac, "you're a trump!"

"And you," said he, "are the ace of the suit. Let's go!"

"One thing first," she said, and ran into another room.

She came back almost at once with a chain of amber beads about her throat—a loop of golden fire, trembling and changing with every breath she drew. She slipped the orchid-colored scarf over her shoulders. It was like a mist tinged by the dainty light of dawn. Three times the rich color was repeated, first in the red-gold glory of her hair, then in the flash of fire that looped her throat, and last it splashed across the bronze slippers. But with the orchid-colored scarf the charm was complete; the spell was cast.

"How are we to go?" she asked as they stood beside his horse.

He looked on her with some doubt. The dim light caught at the amber beads. "Perhaps we'll have to ride double," he ventured.

Her laughter reassured him. She caught the pommel of the saddle as if to vault up, man-fashion. Then she remembered, with a murmur of dismay. "How . . . ?" she began.

He caught her beneath the arms and lifted her lightly to the saddle, then sprang up behind. The horse started at a slow trot.

"Carrigan?"

"Well?"

"Harry is at the dance. If he should recognize me?"

"He won't."

She chuckled. There was a brooding mischief in the tone that set him tingling. "Are you sure?"

"Did the people recognize Cinderella at the ball?"

"And if there should be trouble because I'm recognized?"

"This fairy godmother wears a six-gun."

They were silent a moment.

"How far is it to Bridewell?" he asked at last.

"Eight miles . . . by the road."

"We're late already. Is there any short cut?"

"Across the river, it's between two and three."

"The river?"

"It ain't very deep . . . sometimes. I've done it but never in duds like these."

"Are you game to try the short cut across the river?"

Her head tilted back as she laughed. That was her answer. It was not laughter. It was music. It was the singing of one whose dreams are coming true, and where it left off on her lips the sound was continued like a silent echo in Carrigan.

As she swung the horse to the left toward the ford of the river, a puff of warm wind floated the scarf against Carrigan's face. He could scarcely feel its gossamer web, but a faint fragrance came from it, and his heart beat fast. The moon rolled like a yellow wheel over the tops of the black hills, and its light touched the throat and the turned face of Jacqueline, so that Carrigan could barely guess at her smile. When he spoke to her, she did not turn. She stared straight before her, crooning a hushed, joyous melody deep in her throat.

She would not turn her head, for then the vision with which she rode would have vanished. While she looked straight before her, past the tossing head of the horse, it was not Carrigan who sat at her shoulder. It was not his voice which spoke to her. It was not his breath which touched her throat now and again. No! For though the horse had not journeyed far, Jacqueline had ridden a fabulous distance into the regions of romance. The amber beads were now a chain of gold and, where they touched cold against her breast, that was where the jeweled cross lay, the priceless relic before which she said her prayers at dawn and evening. The hair was no longer red. It was yellower, richer than that golden moon. The slight clinking of the bridle rein, where the little chain chimed against the bit, that was the rattle of the armor of her knight. He had ridden far for her that evening. He had stolen into the castle of her father. He had reached her chamber, where the tapestries made a hushing along the wall like warning whispers. He had lowered her from the casement on a rope made of twisted clothes. He had helped her across the moat. Then, with a rusted key, they turned the harsh lock of a secret portal and were free—free—free!

Jacqueline tossed up her arms. The air was like a cool caress upon them. Yes, she was free. They topped a hill. Below it ran the river, glimmering silver through the night, and jeweled by the shining of the stars. Suddenly she shook the reins and urged the horse to a frantic gallop down the slope.

"What's the matter?" cried Carrigan.

Yes, how could he know that even at that moment her father, with a band of hard-riding liegemen, had thundered into view behind them and that death raced closely on their heels? She drew rein, panting, on the edge of the river.

Then Carrigan proved himself a knight indeed. They dared not imperil that gown of green, so he sat in the saddle with his legs crossed in front of the horn and lifted her in his arms. Then he gave the horse its way, and the cunning old cattle pony picked a safe way along a sand bank. The water rose higher. They slipped, floundering into little hollows, and clambered back into shallower places. Once the water rose so high that Carrigan could have put down his hand and touched it.

"Steady!" he said encouragingly to the girl.

The voice was deep and vibrant. It blended with her dream of romance. Her tyrant father with his villain knights sat their horses on the bank of the river, not daring to attempt the passage, and now that her hero was about to bear her safely to the other shore. . . . She drew a long breath and relaxed in his arms, her strong young body now soft and yielding. The horse pawed for a footing and then lurched up the bank with a snort. Her arms tightened around Carrigan's neck; her lips pressed eagerly to his.

"Jac!"

How could he know that that word carried her dream away like dead leaves on a wind? She covered her face from him.

"We are late already," she said.

IV
"THE SONG OF SONGS"

The dance hall was the upstairs floor of Bridewell's general merchandise store. From the center of the ceiling was suspended a monstrous gasoline lamp that flooded the larger part of the dancing floor with dazzling light, but the flicker of the flame sent occasional seas of shadow washing into the corners of the room. A thick line of stools and chairs and empty grocery boxes made the seats for the throng around the wall. The floor glimmered and shone in mute testimony to the polishing which it had received earlier in the evening when a dozen strong men pulled about the room a heavy bale of hay with two men sitting upon it. Waxed hardwood could not have been more brilliant.

The music was supplied by a banjo, a slide trombone, a violin, and a snare drum, and the musicians operated their instruments with undying vigor. Lest they should falter in their efforts from weariness, glasses of liquor stood beside them at all times, supplied by generous cowpunchers who appreciated the soulful music. This stimulus was not applied in vain for, as the evening wore on, each piece of music was increased slightly but perceptibly in cadence beyond all which had gone before.

This applied to the two-step, which sent the dancers whirling over the floor with such violence that at the end of each dance there was a general stampede for the bar which stretched across the farther end of the room. Here four men worked with frantic haste to quench the thirst of the multitude and labored in vain. The exercise made the throat of every man as dry as that of Tantalus, and the glasses were snatched up and tossed off as rapidly as they were spun down the length of the bar.

Jac and Carrigan paused at the door to make a survey of the scene. The festivities were already well under way. Some of the men had removed their bandannas and stuffed the latter into back trouser pockets, from which they streamed like brilliant pennons during the dance. There were other tokens that the dance had passed the stiff formality of the opening moments. The musicians played with the fierce resolution of long-distance runners entering the homestretch. The violinist leaned back with eyes closed and jaw set in do-or-die determination, while his bow darted back and forth across the strings. The banjo man leaned far over and thrummed away with an expression partly of pain and partly of far-away yearning as he stared above the heads of the dancers. The expression was caused not by sorrow of soul but by a cramp in his right hand. The trombone player, however, was a far worse case than either of his two companions. He was very fat, very short, and his red, bald head shone furiously. Yet he would not diminish the vigor of his efforts. His long slurs were more brazenly ringing than ever. His upward runs raised the heart and the hair at the same time. His downward slides sent out a chill tingle along the spine. He jerked out his arm with such violence that it made his flabby body quiver like jelly, and the vigor of his blowing set a white spot in the middle of his puffed cheeks.

Orpheus stirred the trees as this orchestra stirred the citizens of the mountain desert. It sent them whirling frantically about the dance hall. It moved them to sit now and then in the shadow-swept corners, closely tête-à-tête.

A wild and ludicrous scene? Perhaps. But also there was beauty and youth as much as ever graced a ballroom. And there was rhythm. Rhythm of the dance, rhythm of the screeching, thrumming music. To the young, rhythm is poetry. It set a glamour upon the faces of the dancers; of the shadowy corners it made moonlit gardens.

"What is my name?" queried Jac. "We forgot that!"

He was dumfounded.

"Perhaps I'm your sister?"

He grinned. "Jac, you look as much like me as a yearling shorthorn looks like a longhorn maverick. Something fancy. Jacqueline Silvestre. How does that hit, eh? Miss Silvestre! You've come from the East. You're visiting at a ranch twenty miles away."

"What ranch?"

"Fake a name."

"Everyone knows everybody else for miles around."

"It's up to you. Can you do the Eastern lingo?"

She tilted her head to one side and gazed upon him with naive astonishment. " 'Lingo,' Mister Carrigan?"

"Good Lord!" breathed Carrigan.

Her laughter was low and filled with hints of many things. It made him distinctly uncomfortable.

"I've read books," she said. "I'll do my part. But you?"

"I'm simply a cowpuncher you've pressed into service to bring you here. Right? Now, who do you want to dance with? Watch their eyes!"

They walked slowly into the room and were met by a new sound over the clangor of music and voices. It was that buzz which to the heart of the débutante is the elixir of life, and to the city matron is the nectar which promises immortal beauty. In the dance hall at Bridewell it was less covert. Jacqueline stood in the spotlight like a queen.

She knew that her color had heightened. She knew that the flare of the gasoline lamp made her hair a glorious dull-red fire, touched with golden points of light which fell again on the necklace at her throat, the only heirloom she had received from her mother, and still further down on the bronze slippers. The admiration of the men filled her heart; the trouble in the more covert stares of the girls overflowed it. A sense of power flooded in her like electricity. She knew that, when she turned and dropped her hand on the arm of Carrigan, it sent a tingle through him.

Her smile was casual and her eyes calm. Her whisper was surcharged with a vital anxiety.

"Do you dance . . . well?"

"Regular fairy," grinned Carrigan, and she

95

wished his mouth was not so broad. "How about you?"

"Not so bad."

"Let's start."

Dancers are not made even by infinite pains and lessons. They are born, and Jac was a born dancer. With the smooth floor underfoot, the light slippers, the pulse and urge of the music, however crude, the new-born sense of dignity and womanly power, she became an artist. She danced not to the music, but to what the music might have been.

Through the film of pleasure she vaguely knew that people were giving way a little before her. She knew the eyes of the girls were upon her feet. She knew the eyes of the men were on her face and the sway of the graceful body, and among those eyes she found one pair brighter and more devouring than all the rest. It was Maurie Gordon.

He was dancing with a little golden-haired beauty, Dolly Maxwell. She let her eyes rest carelessly upon him. She smiled. Handsome Maurie started as though someone had stepped on his foot. He stumbled—he lost his step—his little partner frowned up at him and then flashed a look of utter hate toward Jac. A girl may guess at the heart of a man, but she can absolutely read the soul of another woman. It is a subtle system of wireless which tells a thousand words in a single smile; a glance is a spark driven by ten thousand volts. The heart of Jacqueline swelled with the Song of Songs.

"Do something!" she murmured in the ear of Carrigan.

He met her eyes with a cold understanding. "You've just seen Maurie Gordon?" he asked.

"You're dancing wonderfully," she pleaded, "but do something new."

"Do you know the Carrigan cut?"

"I'll try it."

"It's a cross between a glide, a dip, and a roll. Take three short steps, then take a long, draggy slide to the left . . . and let yourself go."

The trombone started an upward flourish. They followed it, running forward. She began the draggy step to the left and then let herself go. How it was done, she could not tell, but somehow he took her weight in the middle of the step, and they completed a little dipping whirl as graceful as the lilt of a seagull against a flurry of wind.

A gasp of applause broke out around them. The dancers veered further off to allow room for these beautiful new maneuvers. Jacqueline, dizzy with the joy of conquest, saw the set, white face of Dolly Maxwell. It was the golden drop of honey in the wine of victory. The music stopped, but the rhythm still ran in her blood.

Carrigan's rather coldly curious stare sobered her.

"What's the matter?" she asked.

"I see a freckle comin' out to look the landscape over. Sorry you ain't got that powder-puff with you."

"I have it, all right."

"I didn't know you had pockets in that dress."

"It's in my corsage."

"Your which?"

"Look at that funny trombone player."

He turned to stare at the shiny bald head and, when he looked back, she had just slipped something into the bosom of her dress. All traces of the freckle were gone. She flushed a little under his eye of inquiry.

Then, very anxiously: "Is it gone?"

"It's behind a cloud, anyway," said Carrigan. "Here's Maurie Gordon."

The big cowpuncher came up, earnest-eyed. "If you're not hooked up for this next waltz . . . " he began.

He stopped with a widening stare. She had glanced carelessly over him from head to foot, and now turned her back on him to take the arm of Carrigan. The movement was slow, deliberate, casual. It left big Maurie Gordon crimson and breathing hard, the butt of open laughter from all.

V
"THE SILVESTRE SLIDE"

Carrigan found Jac trembling with excitement, though her face was still calm. "What the devil," he began. "I thought Gordon was the man you wanted. . . ."

"Don't you get me?" she broke in eagerly. "None of those swell Eastern ladies would bat an eye at a bum who came up to them without bein' introduced."

"Oh!" said Carrigan. "And who . . . ?"

"You will," she answered without hesitation. "Take me over to a chair and talk with me a minute. Then you can side-step up to the bar and get a drink. When all the boys flock around and ask about me. . . ."

He growled: "How do you know they'll flock around and ask about you?"

There was something akin to pity in her smile.

The statue was walking away from Pygmalion. "Take it from me. They will. Your money ain't any good at that bar . . . take me to that chair standing away from the rest of them . . . because every man will be wanting to make your acquaintance an' buy you liquor. Drink beer, Carrie. I hate a breath. Then they'll ask about me, an' you tell 'em that I'm straight from the East an' don't understand Western ways. Tell 'em they'll have to be introduced. An' don't bring over anyone I don't point out."

"Beginnin' with Gordon?"

"Sure. Bring him first."

"Who's next? Are you goin' to corral 'em all"

"If I want to."

They sat down, Carrigan rather gingerly, and edging away from her.

"You see that skinny feller with the black hair?"

"Yep."

"That's Dave Carey. He's engaged to that girl with the smile an' the fluffy pink dress. She called me a 'horrible tomboy' once. You can bring Dave Carey next."

"Goin' to bust up the happy homes, Jac?"

"Miss Silvestre," she corrected. "Watch Jenny Hendrix stare at me! She's whispering, too. I hate her! Then there's Ben Craig, the tall man with the thin, sad-lookin' face. Once when he was at the hotel, he said my head was more like a turkey egg than a face. You c'n bring him third. I'll think of some more after a while."

"How're you goin' to keep up the bluff with all those fellers? They'll spot your lingo in a minute."

Jacqueline waved the suggestion airily away. "I read a book once," she said, and her smile was very close to the grin of Jac During, now no more. "It told about an Eastern girl who came West an' she was terrible thrilled about the Western men. She had a great lingo. I'll stick by what she said."

"What was it?"

"Mister Carrigan, have you lived all your life in the West?"

"Sure."

He started and stared at her. "Is that part of the lingo?"

"I knew you had been all your life out here in these big open spaces. It makes you so much more real than the Eastern men."

"Huh!" grunted Carrigan, and blinked rapidly.

"Do you know that I feel that you . . . but you would think me foolish if I said it."

"You bet your life I wouldn't!" gasped Carrigan.

She leaned closer and dropped a hand on his arm. Her gaze dwelt tenderly on his startled eyes. "I feel that you are the first *real* man I have ever known, Mister Carrigan."

"The devil you do!"

"Yes. All the men I have met have been so superficial. But you are like your own great West, Mister Carrigan, with a heart as wide as the desert and as open as the sky. I feel it. Am I foolish to tell you this?"

Carrigan loosened his bandanna. "Jac, are you goin' to pull this sort of a line on all the boys?" he asked hoarsely.

"Sure I am. Why not? Don't it get by?"

"There'll be gun play before the night is over, you c'n lay that ten to one."

"Why?"

"Don't look at me like that! You make me nervous. It ain't what you say so much as the way you say it. Where'd you learn that way of talkin'?"

"I been to the movies, an' I used my eyes. I've

seen Maude Merriam an' come home an' practiced at the mirror. Has she got anything on me?"

"She generally ain't got half so much on," groaned Carrigan, and rose.

"Wait a minute, Carrie!"

"Say, Cinderella, maybe I'm the fairy godmother, but don't go callin' me by a woman's name. The brand don't no ways look well on my hide."

"All right, Mister Carrigan. But just remember this: that ain't the Carrigan cut that we done in the last dance."

He rubbed a hand across his forehead.

"It's the Silvestre slide."

"What?"

"Sure. I introduced it in New York, an' everybody in the Five Hundred copied it an' named it after me. It made an awful hit!"

Carrigan fled. He went straight for the bar by instinct, for he began to need a drink. Jacqueline proved a prophet. As he dropped his coin on the bar, a broad hand swept it back to him. He looked up into the handsome, serious face of Maurie Gordon.

"Partner," said Maurie, "this drink's on me. My name's Gordon."

"Wait a minute, Maurie," broke in another voice. "You're lickerin' with me, friend. I'm Dave Carey. Glad to meet you. Two comin' up, bartender!"

"I'm drinkin' beer," said Carrigan, remembering orders.

An odd look, which he understood perfectly, came in the eyes of the other men.

"Look here," went on Maurie, "that girl you brung to the dance is a hell bender. If you ain't

Max Brand

dancin' all evenin' with her, maybe I could break in, eh?"

He reinforced his suggestion with a broad wink and a tremendous slap on the shoulder.

"Maybe you could," said Carrigan. "I'll have to introduce you. Miss Silvestre is straight from the East, an' she don't quite get the hang of our Western ways."

"Straight from the East?"

"Yep. New York an' all that. Blood as blue as hell."

"The devil!"

"It is, all right, till you get to know her."

"How'd you pick her up?"

"She's been visitin' at the ranch where I work. We sort of ran off together tonight. She was strong for some sort of a lark. Kind of nifty?"

"*Is* she?"

"But you got to talk careful to her, get me?"

"I'll hang onto my tongue like it was a buckin' bronco."

"Then foller me."

"Hold on," said Carey desperately. "Carrigan, don't I get no look in here?"

"What do you want to go hangin' around with every girl in the country for?" queried Gordon, and his frown was dangerous. "Ain't you engaged already?"

"Am I?" replied Carey, with an ominous lowering of the voice. "An' ain't Dolly Maxwell got you roped and throwed?"

"Suppose," broke in Carrigan anxiously, "that you get introduced at the same time, an' then Gordon c'n have the first dance an' you get the next."

They compromised on this basis and trooped obediently behind Carrigan.

102

"Wait a minute," said Gordon. "Maybe you'd like to meet Dolly Maxwell?"

"Sure," said Carrigan.

They stopped before the girl of the golden hair. There was soul-deep understanding in the cold eye she fixed upon Maurie Gordon. Carrigan received gushing recognition, not for him he knew, but for the partner of the sensation in green.

"The next dance? Sure you can have it. Good bye, Maurie."

But her parting shot was wasted on thin air. Maurie was headed for other and more pleasant regions, and the light of the discoverer was in his eye. He was a new Balboa looking out upon another Pacific. They ranged before Jac.

"Miss Silvestre, this is Mister Gordon, an' Mister Carey."

Maurie searched his memory, steeled his nerves, and spoke: "I sure feel it's a privilege to know you."

"Me, too," said Carey, and then bit his lips.

The scorn of a superior intelligence was haughty in the face of big Maurie.

"Thank you," Jac was saying. "Will you sit down?"

"Sure," said Maurie, and plumped into the chair beside her. "Maybe you ain't got the next dance taken. Can I have it? Thanks."

He glared his triumph at Carey, who turned away, dark-eyed with envy.

The cold glance of Jac cut short Carrigan's incipient grin. "So long," he said, and turned on his heel. He joined Dave Carey.

"Fourteen degrees of frost in her smile," said that worthy, "but I'm bettin' on a river runnin' under the ice."

"Are you goin' to dance?"

"Nope. I need a drink. Have one on me?"

"I got work ahead," said Carrigan, and made for Dolly Maxwell.

VI
"THE GIRL FROM FIFTH AVENUE"

" 'So long,' " quoted Jac. "Is that the Western way of saying good bye, Mister Gordon?"

There was a serious question in her eyes. Maurie leaned back and drew a deep breath.

"Maybe your friend Carrigan talks that way, an' I've heard some others say the same thing, but it ain't considered partic'lar choice. Most of us says '*adios*,' or something like that."

"Oh, I thought it was rather queer, but then Mister Carrigan is"—she paused—"rather queer in lots of ways!"

It was plain that she considered him different. The music began. They danced. The rather diffident arm of big Maurie gathered strength and confidence.

"You sure c'n throw your feet!" he burst out at length.

"You ain't travelin' very far behind," said Jac, amiably. She felt Maurie start. She knew—with a growing coldness of heart—that he was staring down at her face with question. With a great effort she made her eyes rise and rest artlessly upon his. She was hunting her book-vocabulary desperately. "I've picked that up from the Western vernacular, Mister Gordon. Does it sound natural?"

"It sure does."

The doubt was gone from his face. The triumph

reinforced her smile. Dolly Maxwell sailed by in the arms of Carrigan. They were dancing beautifully.

"Say," said Gordon with sudden anxiety, "what was that funny step you done with Carrigan?"

"That was the Silvestre Slide, as they call it in New York."

"Oh!"

"I invented it, and it was picked up all along Fifth Avenue. You've no idea how quickly things spread in New York. They named it after me."

In his awe he almost lost step. She enjoyed his consternation for a moment and then in pity spoke: "Shall we try it?"

"D'you really think I could get away with it?"

" 'Get away with it,' Mister Gordon?"

"I mean, d'you think I could be taught?"

"Oh, yes. It's this way. It's a cinch . . . as you say out here in the West."

They started the maneuver, but Gordon was afflicted with stage fright. He blundered miserably. A snicker sounded about them, and desire for murder flooded the heart of Jacqueline, for Carrigan and Dolly Maxwell had just executed the step perfectly. She set her teeth and drove ahead.

"Mister Gordon, have you lived all your life in the West?"

"Yep. Every day of it!"

She sighed. Then: "That is why you are so different. In the East the boys are so . . . well, so artificial!"

"Huh?" said Maurie vaguely. "That so?"

"But you are like your own wild West! With a heart as big as your mountain desert and as open as your skies."

The arm of Maurie tightened. She felt his breath

coming quickly against her hair, and she thought of the spilled coffee and the "damnation!" of earlier in that same evening. Life was sweet indeed.

"What makes you so unusual, Mister Gordon?"

Once, twice his lips stirred before the words came. "It's a hard life on the range. It takes a strong man to get by."

"You look strong, Mister Gordon."

Laughter makes the voice purr, and there was a caress in the tone of Jacqueline. He stiffened, throwing his shoulders back.

"In a pinch I've done a man's work," he said modestly.

"I've heard about men who can take a steer by the horns and wrestle until they throw the big animal . . . but I suppose that is just Western joking?"

"Nope. I don't think nothin' at all of throwin' a steer."

"Oh! And aren't you afraid of . . . of their nasty horns?" she stammered with admiration and wonder.

"I was brung up to take chances. Throwin' a steer ain't much . . . for a man like me. You see, I got the size for it. A feller needs weight on the range."

"But some of these cowpunchers seem quite slender."

"Yep. They don't count much for a real man's work. Take Carrigan over there. I guess he's a pretty fair sort when it comes to gettin' around, but he ain't got the weight. I guess he weighs about twenty pounds less'n I do."

"Do you know that I feel . . . but you would think me foolish if I said it!"

"Lady . . . Miss . . . Miss Silvestre, you c'n lay

ten to one I won't think anything you say is foolish."

"Well, then, I feel as if you are the only *real* man I have ever known."

"Honest?" said the deep, quivering voice.

"Yes. The rest I cannot understand. I'd stifle among them."

"You ain't stringin' me along?"

"What other men say are merely words. But such a man as you are speaks from the heart. I know! I could believe you."

"Miss Silvestre. . . ."

"Isn't it usual in the West to be called by first names?"

There was a sound of choking. Her wide, wondering eyes raised to his.

"Or is it wrong, Mister Gordon? To be called by one's given name seems to me . . . freedom."

"My name's Maurie."

The hoarseness of his voice was the music of the spheres.

"And mine is Jacqueline."

"It's a wonderful name!"

"Say it."

"Jacqueline!"

She looked up with childish curiosity. "I have never heard it spoken that way before. It seems . . . it seems to me free . . . like your own wild West!"

"Ain't you been free?"

Her head fell. Her left hand pressed his in her effort to keep back the bubbling laughter. He returned the grip with a mighty interest.

"I have lived all my life in a convent!"

He started. "I thought you was hangin' out along Fifth Avenue?"

It was a close squeeze. She blessed a sudden thundering on the slide trombone. All fat men have kind hearts, she decided.

"Yes, but only for a little while. Only for a few months. Then they brought me West." The last paragraph of a third installment rose word by word before her eyes. "They thought to bury me in the West. Even out here they guard me like a criminal. Tonight I had to run away to be with you . . . you all. But they cannot bury me in this country. I look upon the stars at night and do not feel alone. The desert is my friend. I feel its mystery. And I feel the truth and strength of the men of the desert. Somewhere among them I shall find *one* friend."

She bowed her head again. "Some memory, Jac," she was saying to herself.

The deep rumble of his voice, broken and passionate, broke in upon her. "By God, you *have* found that friend. I'm him!"

"Mister Gordon . . . Maurie!"

He could not speak. The music stopped and, as it died away, they caught a clear laugh from across the hall.

"The feller that come with you seems to be havin' a pretty fair sort of time," said Maurie.

Jac looked up. There was Carrigan laughing heartily with Dolly Maxwell. She seemed extremely beautiful when she laughed, and her voice was musical; it rose over the babble of the dance hall like the chime of a bell. Jac set her teeth. She remembered the Carrigan Cut—as Maurie had failed to do it. Dave Carey was approaching.

"Here comes my next partner," she said, "but. . . ."

Her pause said a thousand things. It made Maurie stand very straight. He was taking the burden of a woman's happiness upon his shoulders . . . and such a woman! "I will never forget." The tensity of his emotion made him grammatical. "Come with me and we'll sit out the dance. Send Carey away."

"But if he don't want to go?"

"I'll bust his jaw for him if he don't."

"Please . . . Maurie!"

"All right," he said, relenting slowly. "I'll see you later."

As he retreated, Jac turned to Dave Carey. He was standing stiffly, like a soldier awaiting orders.

" 'I'll see you later!' " she quoted. "I wonder if I should consider that a promise or a threat, Mister Carey? Or is it just a Westernism?"

Dave Carey expanded. He knew that the girl in the fluffy pink dress was watching him with a white face.

"Poor ol' Maurie," he said gently. "He ain't much on manners. He was never given much of a bringin' up. Maybe you noticed it sort of in his way of talkin'. You're lookin' sort of sad."

She was gazing pensively on the happy faces of Dolly Maxwell and Carrigan. Now she lowered a gloomy eye to the floor.

"I try to seem gay, Mister Carey."

"But there's somethin' eatin' on your mind?"

She looked up with childish admiration. "How could you tell? But you Westerners see everything!" The clear music of Dolly Maxwell's laughter floated to her. Her brow clouded. "I cannot help being unhappy, Mister Carey."

Carey's hand slipped down on his hip, and then he sighed. No one had been allowed to wear a six-gun into the dance hall.

"Somebody botherin' you? P'int him out!"

"If there were, you would protect me, Mister Carey, I know."

"*Would* I!"

"You've no idea how secure it makes me feel just to hear you speak that way."

"Honest?"

"Yes, for I know that you could keep danger and trouble far away from me."

He cleared his throat. His chest arched. "Which I'd say I throw a six-gun about as fast as anybody in these parts."

" 'Throw a six-gun,' Mister Carey?"

"Sure," he explained. "Flash a six . . . pull a cannon . . . draw my revolver."

"Oh, Mister Carey! Do you mean that you have ever drawn your revolver upon a man?"

"On a man? Me? I guess maybe you ain't heard any of the boys tell about me."

"Oh, yes. Of course, I've heard a great deal about Dave Carey. You're the first man Mister Carrigan pointed out to me when I came into the dance hall."

"Is that straight? Well, Carrigan ain't a bad hand himself, I guess, but you can see by the way he handles himself that he ain't much in a fight."

"Can you tell simply by looking at a man?"

"Easiest thing in the world. Watch their hands. Look at big Maurie Gordon over there. Too big. All beef. No nerve. If him an' me was to mix, I'd fill him full of lead before he ever got his gun clear."

"*Mr. Carey!* You wouldn't shoot at poor Mister Gordon?"

"He knows enough not to pick no trouble with me."

"Mister Carey, somehow I feel that I can talk frankly to you."

He swelled visibly. His face was red.

"Tag dance!" bellowed the announcer.

Carrigan was rising to dance again with Dolly Maxwell. The solemn face of Ben Craig drew near. His stare was a promise as she started off with Dave Carey.

With the rehearsal on Maurie Gordon to help, she talked very smoothly now. She reached her great point: "But they cannot bury me in this country. I look upon the stars at night and do not feel alone. And I feel the strength and truth of the men of the desert. Somewhere among them I shall find. . . ."

Here she noted Carrigan standing unemployed at the edge of the hall. He had been tagged quickly, of course, because of pretty Dolly Maxwell. She signaled him with a great appeal in her eyes, and before they had taken half a dozen more steps his hand fell on the arm of Carey. As she slipped into the arms of Carrigan, her smile of farewell to Carey was sad and wistful. He stood stock still in the middle of the floor, jolted freely by the passing couples. In his eyes was the melancholy light of the sea-bound traveler who sees the last towers of his home port drop below the horizon.

VII
"THE ROPING OF CARRIGAN"

"Carey and Gordon, roped, tied, and branded," said Carrigan. "But don't forget that powder puff."

"Carrigan, let me talk. I've been passing such a line of fancy lingo that my throat is dusty. I've been rememberin' everything that I ever read in love stories an' if I can't be myself for a minute I'll choke for want of fresh air."

"Thought you were having a pretty fair sort of time," said Carrigan absently.

His eyes were traveling over her head. She caught a glimpse of bright-haired Dolly Maxwell as they whirled. He was drifting away from her—that was plain.

"I've just been stringin' 'em along," said Jac. "But you're different, Carrigan."

Here her eyes rose slowly to his. Far away she sensed the somber face of Ben Craig. She had not much time. Carrigan was looking down at her now.

"Look here," he said bluntly, "you can't tie every steer in the corral to one rope, Miss Silvestre. Keep the brandin' iron away from me. The fire ain't hot enough to hurt me yet. The iron won't make no mark."

Jac thought of Maude Merriam at the great moment when her husband tells her that he loves another woman. She caught her breath. She made her eyes grow wide. "Do you really think that I would . . . ?"

"Damn it, Jac, ain't Maurie and Carey enough for you? And there's Ben Craig lookin' at you like a wolf at a calf."

"Carrigan!"

The timbre of her voice made him start. She knew that he would not forget her to look after Dolly Maxwell for some time.

"Well?"

"Do you think I'm a flirt?"

"Jac, I'm warnin' you now. Don't feed me the

112

A Sagebrush Cinderella

spur no more. I'm the fairy godmother. I ain't the prince in the story."

"Is it all a story?"

He groaned.

"I thought I would find one man who wasn't just part of the fairy tale."

"There you go with your book English. Jac, you can't rope me. I see the shadow of the noose flyin' over my head an' I'm goin' to duck out from under."

She turned away with a far-off sorrow in her face.

"There's tears in your eyes!"

A pathetic smile quivered an instant at the corners of her lips.

"Honest, ain't you jest throwin' a rope, Jac?"

"I thought *you* would understand me, Carrigan."

He was breathing hard. She remembered a caption which had been flashed on a Maude Merriam screen.

"I thought you were *big* enough to understand!"

"My God!" whispered Carrigan.

"What?"

"The rope's on me!"

"Carrigan, why do you play with me like this?"

"*Me* play with *you?*"

"Yes. Is it fair?"

The keen eyes searched her intently. She felt as the duelist felt when the rapier of a foe slithered up and down his steel. The violin started a run.

"The Carrigan Cut!" she cried.

He went through with it automatically.

"No one can dance like you," she whispered as the hand of Ben Craig fell on Carrigan's arm and, as she moved away with the solemn-faced cowpuncher, she saw Carrigan standing as Dave Carey

113

had done, with the far-away look, like a man who says farewell to everything that matters in his life.

Maurie Gordon and Dave Carey, their eyes fixed upon one object on the dance floor, came together at a corner of the hall. She drew closer. They started forward at the same time, then stopped and glared at each other with bitter understanding.

"Maurie," said Carey gently, "take my tip. Don't bother Miss Silvestre no more tonight. It won't bring you nothin'."

Maurie smiled from the depth of his pity. "Jacqueline," he said, with marked emphasis, "has found one man who understands her."

Carey shook his head slowly. He spoke carefully, as one would explain a difficult problem to a child. Jac was making the second circuit of the hall with Craig. She had reached the point: "But don't Westerners as a rule call each other by the given name, Mister Craig?"

"She's had a sad life, Maurie," said Carey, his eyes following the graceful vision in green. "You, with your bringin' up, you couldn't understand how to take to a swell girl like. . . ." He stopped, stiffening, and changed of face. "I guess that'll hold you, Maurie. Did you see her smile at me?"

"Smile at you?" said Maurie with unutterable scorn. "Why, you poor sawed-off runt, that was all for me! She smiled at me like that before. They've tried to . . . to bury her in the West, but she's found. . . ."

"One real man!"

"Me!" said Maurie

The music stopped.

"Maurie, aside from bein' a little thick in the head, you're a pretty straight feller in most ways.

A Sagebrush Cinderella

I don't want to see you make no fool out of yourself."

The smile of big Gordon came from an infinite distance, from a height of almost sacred compassion. "Jacqueline and me," he said softly, "we understand. She's led a sad . . . what the hell!"

As the dancers returned to their chairs, Harry During, lurching across the floor, stopped in front of Jacqueline. He had found it difficult to get dancing partners that evening and for consolation and excitement he had retreated to the bar and attended seriously and conscientiously to the matter of quenching his thirst. That thirst was deepseated and it had taken him a long time to reach the seat of the dryness. Now, however, he had become convinced that he had done his duty by his parched insides, and he started toward the door to take horse and ride home. On the way a vision crossed his path—a vision in green, with a floating mist of dainty coloring over her shoulders. He paused to admire. He remained to stare.

If he had been sober, he would have resumed his course with a shrug of the shoulders. But he was not sober. There was a film across his eyes and a mighty music swelling within him. Reason was gone and only instinct remained. But the eyes of instinct are far surer than the eyes of reason. He moved closer with a shambling step. He leaned over his sister.

"It's Jac!"

He burst into Homeric laughter. Ben Craig rose slowly, a dangerous man and a known man in the mountain desert. Even through the mists of redeye, Harry During sobered a little under the crushing pressure of the hand which fell on his shoulder. He pointed, grinning for sympathy.

"Look," he said. "Ain't it funny? That's my shister! That's Jac!"

Craig turned for an instant's glance at Jac. She had not changed color. There was a grave but impersonal sympathy in her steady eyes. She said: "Please don't hurt the poor fellow . . . Ben."

Craig turned back to Harry. "It's a disgrace," he said, "to let a drunk like you wander around insultin' helpless girls. By God, it's got to stop."

"My own shister . . . " protested Harry weakly.

"On your way!" thundered Craig, for he was conscious that many eyes were upon him.

Two formidable figures appeared on either side of him. They were Maurie Gordon, black of face with wrath, and Dave Carey, his lip lifted from his teeth like a wolf about to snarl. They were three formidable animals, facing the swaying figure of Harry. When men act under the eyes of a woman, the careful veil of civilization is lifted. The lovely Miss Silvestre was nearby. The three became ravening beasts.

"Out with him!" said Dave Carey.

"Move!" said Maurie.

"Start!" said Ben Craig.

But the same thing that made the hair of Jacqueline red made the blood of Harry hot. "I'll see you damned first," he said thickly.

Instantly six iron hands gripped him. He was whirled and, struggling vainly, borne across the floor toward the door. A universal clapping of hands came from the edges of the hall. It was understood that Harry had insulted the lovely stranger and in the West a woman, whether beautiful or ugly, *may* be treated with familiar words but *must* be treated with reverent thought.

At the very threshold of the door that led from

the main hall into the little anteroom where guns and hats were piled, Harry managed to wriggle loose. The fury of his anger was sobering him a little and restoring the nerves to his muscular control. He broke loose with a curse and swung feebly, uncertainly at the nearest of his prosecutors. Carey and Craig ducked to rush and grapple with Harry; but big Maurie with the thought of Miss Silvestre and 'real men' floating in his brain drew back his sledge-hammer right fist and smashed it into the face of young During.

Harry pitched back through the door as if a dozen hands had thrown him. The three turned and made straight for Jac like three little boys returning to their mother for praise due to a virtuous act after a day of naughtiness and spankings. The women around the hall were silent. They had heard the dull thud as that fist drove home. The men applauded the murmurs. It was the custom to applaud Maurie Gordon. But when the three reached Jac, she sat white of face and still of eye.

"This don't happen often," began Carey.

"I never see anything like it before," added Craig.

"Anyway," said Maurie complacently, "I've taught him a lesson."

A hard voice sounded at his shoulder. He turned to stare into the furious eyes of Carrigan. There was nothing bulky about the latter but now, with his lean, almost ugly face white with anger and his gleaming eye, he seemed strangely dangerous.

VIII
"THE THREE MUSKETEERS"

"Gordon," he said, "you need a lesson, yourself."

Maurie stepped back. "What's eatin' you?" he frowned.

"You hit him when he couldn't hardly raise a hand," snapped Carrigan.

There was no mistaking it. He meant fight. It shone in his eyes like hunger. It tensed his muscles till he seemed crouching to spring like some beast of prey.

"Please!" cried Jac, and stepped in between them.

"Shut up and sit down!" said Carrigan.

He pointed with a stern arm. She shrank back to the wall.

"By God," snarled Dave Carey, "you can't talk to girls like that, stranger!"

"Then come outside with me an' I'll talk to a man. You too, Gordon, you. . . ."

A thrilling cry from many women made them all turn. In the door stood Harry During with the light gleaming on his long six-gun.

"Gordon!" he called. "Git down and crawl like the dirty dog you are."

There was another flash of light on steel. It was the proprietor who had drawn, but he did not attempt to draw a bead on Harry During. His gun cracked. There was a clang of iron and a crash of glass as the big gasoline lamp went out. The hall was flooded with semi-darkness. And with the coming of the darkness fear rushed on the crowd. A stampede started for the door, but who could find the door in that chaos of struggling bodies and swinging shadows? Through the windows came the faint light of the early dawn.

"Jac!" cried Carrigan.

But tall Ben Craig was already beside her. "Leave it to me," he said reassuringly. "You didn't make no mistake when you picked me out. I'll show you that the mountain desert's got one real man to make up for a lot of coyotes."

"Wait," she pleaded.

"Jac!" called Carrigan again.

"Here!"

"Don't trust to no one but me," said Craig.

"Then get me out of this mob!"

"Follow me."

"I will if I can."

"Then. . . ."

He picked her up and lunged forward through the crowd.

"Drop her!" commanded the voice of Carrigan.

"Not for ten like you!"

He released Jac to turn and fight. A fist cracked home against his face, and he swung furiously. They grappled, and Craig felt as if he were fighting a steel automaton. The muscles his hands fell upon were rigid. The fist on his head and ribs beat a tattoo. Dave Carey had found Jac.

"Thank God!" he cried. "I thought you were lost. Trust to me. I'll see you through." Like Craig, he picked her up. "I'll take you home, if you'll go with me."

"Anywhere out of this crowd."

"Jac!"

"Here!"

A hand caught Carey by the shoulder and jerked him around. In the dim light he saw the convulsed face of Carrigan and dropped Jac to strike out with all his might. His blow landed on thin air and a hard fist smashed against his ribs. He went to the floor with a crash. Though his breath was half gone, he clung to his foe and struggled like a wildcat. Wild tales were told of Dave Carey in a fight. He lived up to all those stories now. Finally a clubbed fist drove against the point of his chin. He relaxed.

The burly shoulders of Maurie Gordon loomed through the semi-darkness above Jac.

"Jacqueline!"

"Maurie!"

"Thank God I've found you!"

"Yes, thank God!"

"This way after me. There's the door!"

"Jac!"

"Here!"

A demoniac shape sprang at Maurie through the dark.

Accustomed by this time to the dim light, the crowd was swirling rapidly through the door, and in the outgoing tide went Jac. The same confusion which made a hell of the dance hall reigned in the open air. But there was more space to maneuver, and Jac gathered her gown up high and slipped through the crowd to the place at which Carrigan had tethered his horse.

She caught the pommel and swung up to the saddle like a man. There was a sickening sound of ripping and tearing. The green gown was hopelessly done for. She gave no thought to it and landing astride the saddle—a position which completed the ruin of the dress—she gave the horse his head and drove forward with a shout like that of a drunken cowpuncher.

She was truly intoxicated with triumph. The men of her choice fought for her in the dance hall. They were her knights battling for the smile of their lady. To one of them would go the victory, but hers was all the glory. She shouted at the coming dawn and urged the horse into a faster run. The wind caught at her face and whistled sharply past her ears—the song of victory.

No delay for the fording of the river. She took it on the run, splashed from head to foot with mud and water. She did not care. The gown was a wreck. Her hair tumbled down on her shoulders. She reached the further bank and drove on at a gallop, shouting like one of the Valkyries.

A battle of giants waged in the dance hall, where Maurie Gordon and Carrigan raged back and forth, sometimes standing at arm's length and slugging with both hands, sometimes rolling over and over on the floor and fighting every inch of the way. If the great arms of Maurie gave him an advantage in the open fighting, the venomous agility of Carrigan evened matters when they came to close quarters.

Dave Carey drew himself up to a sitting posture with both hands pressed over his mid ribs while he watched the conflict. Ben Craig leaned against the wall, sick and white of face. Through his swollen eyes he could barely make out the twisting figures. And still they slugged and smashed with a noble will until, missing a swing at the same time, they were thrown to the floor by the wasted force of their own blows and sat staring stupidly at one another.

The growing daylight made them quite visible now. It showed two battered countenances. It showed equally torn clothes.

"Where's Jacqueline?" cried Maurie.

"Gone!" cried Carrigan, and started to his feet.

Gordon followed suit but slowly. He was badly hurt in both body and mind. The two heroes stared at each other.

"Done for!" groaned Dave Carey from the distance.

"Stung," sighed feeble Ben Craig.

"Beat!" growled Maurie.

"Roped!" said Carrigan.

"Fellers," said Carey, struggling to his feet and still caressing his injured ribs, "I got an idea we better see that Fifth Avenue swell before we do more fightin'."

"I got to find her," said Gordon stoutly. "She depends on me. I'm the one real man she's ever known."

"You be damned before you find her," said Carrigan, and the light of battle flared in his eyes again.

"Hold on," interposed Carey. "You ain't the real man she's found. *I'm* it!"

"You are?" sneered Craig. "They tried to bury her in the West, but she's goin' to be set free by a man who. . . ."

"Who tried to bury her in the Western desert?" asked Carrigan.

The other three spoke with one voice.

"Her uncle," said Carey.

"Her cruel father," said Craig.

"Her older brother," said Maurie.

They turned and stared at each other, stunned. Once more they spoke in one voice. "Stung!"

"I believe her," defended Maurie. "She's led a sad life in a convent all these years."

"In a boarding school, you mean," said Carey.

A Sagebrush Cinderella

"Wrong, a girls' school," said Craig.

They stopped again. Light from the dim distance was coming in their eyes. And Jac, after leaving the down-headed horse in front of her father's hotel, stole swiftly up the stairs to her room.

"Who's there?" roared the familiar voice from Jim During's room.

"Me."

"Where've you been all night?"

"None of yer business."

"Jac, I'm goin' to raise the devil if you try many more of these funny tricks."

"I been out walkin'."

"All night?"

"Ain't I got a right to walk?"

"Jac, why wasn't you born a boy?" groaned Jim, reverting to his old complaint.

"Because it's a lot more fun bein' a girl," said Jac, "when you've got the golden touch."

She went into her room. It was hard to look at herself in the faint light and with the little round pocket mirror which had been ample for all her needs before. The glory of Cinderella was gone— quite gone! The green gown was a wretched travesty; her hair was a tumbled mass; only in her smile and her eyes there was a difference, a new light of power which, having once come to a woman, dies only with her death. Truly the victory was hers. She started to remove her clothes.

It was a long task, but finally they were rolled into a small bundle and tucked into a little corner. She put on her old clothes and carefully retied the hard knot in her hair. The fairy godmother was gone. She washed the powder from her face. Cinderella once more sat in the ashes.

She was rattling away at the stove, preparing to

make the fire for breakfast, when a sound of singing down the road brought her to the window. There came another Three Musketeers. They were mounted—Porthos, Athos, and Aramis. And before them walked the new D'Artgnan—Carrigan. With one voice they sang.

It should have been a sad song for, as they came closer, she saw that they were battered of face and torn of clothes. Yet their song was glad. Experience, whether good or bad, makes strong men rejoice. They trooped into the dining room.

"Chow!" they thundered in unison, and Jac stepped to the door.

As one man they gaped.

Big Maurie Gordon walked to her with a scowl, took her face between his hands, and stared into her eyes. His own were so swollen that he was looking out of the narrowest of slits. "Where have I seen you?" he said.

"Maybe you been dreamin' about me, you big stiff!" said Jac amiably.

Maurie dropped his hands and turned away. "Yep. A nightmare," he said.

"I got a start, too," growled Carey. "An' when I seen Jac I thought about. . . ."

"Don't say it," broke in Craig. "It makes me see red."

"Hit the kitchen, Bricktop," said Maurie, "an' rustle some ham an' eggs. Lots of 'em!"

She smiled, and the expression changed her whole face. The Three Musketeers jumped and stared at her with a return of their first interest. The fairy godmother was waving the wand.

"This," said Jacqueline, "is worse than the convent."

"The devil!" groaned Maurie. "This ain't possible!"

"When I came West," went on Jac with the same smile, "I thought that I should find one real man."

They listened with mouths agape. It was like watching base lead being transmuted before their eyes to gold.

Carrigan winked his one good eye. The other was black and puffed.

"And I have found one," said Jac. She winked at Carrigan.

"I can leave it to you," said Carrigan, "to lead me a real man's life."

THE CONSUMING FIRE

"The Consuming Fire" by Max Brand first appeared in *Argosy/All-Story* (11/27/20). The previous month this magazine had serialized the second book in the Whistlin' Dan Barry series, *The Night Horseman*. Like *The Untamed* (that began this saga in 1918), this novel, too, would be filmed by Fox Film Corporation with Western star Tom Mix in the lead role. "The Consuming Fire" was subsequently reprinted as "Vengeance Trail" by Max Brand in *Greater Western Magazine* (5/35). It appears here for the first time in book form.

The Consuming Fire

Since the days of Bluebeard, the best way to make a man do a thing is to tell him to avoid it. The most jaded appetite tastes the forbidden with a relish. The boy climbs the fence not because he wants to get on the other side, but because the fence is there, telling him to keep out; and the heart of the débutante yearns toward the "dangerous" man whom her mother has "ruled out."

Consequently, though the world lay at the feet of young Ed Raleigh, and he could have traveled to Paris or Pékin with a full pocketbook and the consent of his father, the one region to which his heart turned was the forbidden Bald Eagle Mountains. It was his father who forbade it.

"In them mountains," he was wont to say, "they's jest enough gold to break a man's heart and turn him into a waster." Yet Pete Raleigh had made his stake and found his wife in those same mountains, and the very ground he cursed was the scene of the tales he loved to spin.

The Raleigh ranch had spread through the length and breadth of the valley but, while this

might be called the common-sense kingdom of
Pete Raleigh, the kingdom of his fancy to which
his memory inevitably turned was the Bald Eagle
Mountains—the burned, brown peaks along the
valley and the far-away crests of the upper range,
blue with distance and tipped with snow.

To young Ed Raleigh that land was a fairy realm
peopled with the men and women of his father's
stories. What the ancestral sword, rust-eaten, and
the battle-hewn shields were to the young squire
of the dark ages, the old mucking spoon and drill
set of Pete Raleigh were to his son. Until finally,
having one day ridden a pitching outlaw in a fashion to have swelled the heart of the most hardy
bronc peeler with pride, Ed Raleigh awoke to the
knowledge that he was a man. He reasoned not
without justification that, if he could stick to a
wild horse without a bucking-roll, he could fight
his own way and follow his nose through the
world.

When he arrived at this decision, the first place
his eyes turned was toward the Left-Hand Cut,
that deep defile like a knife cut through the Bald
Eagle range where the railroad slid over the
heights and down into the valley. The Left-Hand
Cut was the gate of fairy land, and in the center of
the cut stood the town of Sierra Padre, in whose
streets the men of his father's yarns had fought
and drunk and gambled and died.

Ed Raleigh was too wise to tell his father where
he was going. He merely kissed the white head of
his mother, whispered in her ear, and then fled
from her tears. An hour later he was plodding
down the valley behind a pack burro and seeing
the world through the long, flapping ears in the
most approved prospector fashion. In his hand he

carried his hammer and started chipping rocks within five miles of the ranch house.

To be sure he knew nothing, or next to nothing, about ore, but six feet two of arrow-straight manhood, twenty-five care-free years on the range, and nearly two hundred pounds of stringy muscles, hard as sinews, are an equipment complete in themselves. Ed Raleigh did not know the color of hematite from the color of wild violets, but he intended to learn. He was eager enough to dig for the center of the earth and about strong enough to get there.

Twenty-four hours brought him to the foothills, and two days more carried him into the cut. In the middle of the afternoon he drove his burro into Sierra Padre and paused at the head of the single street. He could have shouted with joy, for everything was in place, everything was exactly as it had been when his father was there. He closed his eyes and winked hard: it was almost as if he were himself Peter Raleigh, not Peter's son, Ed.

That shingle on the right announced the Wung Li laundry. The general merchandise sign was just as unreadable as it had always been since Garry the Kid shot up the town. The horses in front of the saloon were the very horses that had ridden through all his father's yarns since Ed's fifth year.

Straight to the saloon went Ed Raleigh and strode through the swinging doors. Then he stopped, as a man stops in mid ring when a straight left whacks against the point of his chin. For behind the bar stood a big man with grizzled hair and a prodigious paunch. Ed Raleigh winked again and then stepped to the bar.

"Are you Olaf Bjornsen?" he asked.

"Yep, that's me."

Ed Raleigh closed his eyes and clung to the edge of the bar. He felt breathless. Olaf Bjornsen! the same man, the same name. No, there was one discrepancy: the Olaf of his father's stories would have answered, "Ya, Ay bane that Olaf!" It was the son, then. But the rest of the room was the same. The stove in the center had three iron legs, as it ought to have had, and the fourth one was of wood, black as iron from age and much sooty droppings. The familiar cobwebs trailed across the ceiling of unfinished boards. Over to the side was a picture of the mighty Salvator spread-eagling his field, and doing a spread-eagle himself to accomplish the feat, behind the bar the resolute face of John L. Sullivan with an American flag draped around his waist—the Boston strong boy in his youth. It was all the same, down to the smooth, unvarnished surface of the bar—the same bar on which his father had rested his glass of red-eye in the glorious days of old.

"What'll you have?" Olaf Bjornsen was asking.

Ed Raleigh turned his eyes to right and left. There were half a dozen other men in the room. That fellow with the scar on his cheek and the sidewise trick with his eyes—surely that was Whitey, the gambler, and the old man with the solemn beard must be philosophic Dan Morgan who could deliver with equal impromptu ease an election speech or a funeral service. They were all there—all!

"Well?" Olaf was urging with a touch of irritation in his voice. "Come to life, kid. Sleepin'?"

"Come to life!" This fellow's vocabulary was the one jarring note in the entire picture.

"Red-eye," muttered Ed Raleigh, and mopped his forehead.

The Consuming Fire

The bartender stepped back along the bar and picked up bottle and glass. Ed waited, suspended. Ah, there it was! The glass came spinning down the bar, and then rocked to a halt directly in front of him. If this were not the true Olaf Bjornsen, it was surely his reincarnation—Olaf with a twentieth-century tongue.

He poured his drink, raised it, and remembered to toss it off at a single gulp. Remembering again, he pushed the chaser scornfully away. A chaser for a fellow from the mines? Bah!

"New to town, ain't you?" inquired Olaf, eyeing the untasted chaser.

Ed watched him with incredulous disgust. According to his father, no questions were ever asked in Sierra Padre. A man talked of his own volition, or else the town waited to know him by his actions.

"Kind of," he snapped.

He turned to glance out the window over a lordly prospect of rocks and mountains and calling distance, when the doors swung wide and an unsteady figure stepped within them. He was a tall man somewhere between fifty and sixty, and a generation of hard living had whitened his head and seamed his face as weather and a million years have wrinkled the front of Bald Eagle Peak itself.

But he was dressed like a youngster who has lately struck gold, perfect from his new hat to the dark yellow of his Napatan boots. His years sat easily upon him; his step was elastic and quick; his eyes danced as he looked around the barroom, and his body was still as light and gaunt as the body of a youngster in his prime. His working days were far from over but, as he stood there, Ed Raleigh noted an unsteadiness about the fellow which was not the unsteadiness of age.

"It's old Martin," observed Olaf Bjornsen, "and he's starting ag'in."

"He's finishin', you mean," nodded a bystander at the bar. "He's jest about gone."

Old Martin strode to the bar with fumbling steps and leaned his elbows upon it at the side of Ed.

"Whiskey," he said hoarsely to Olaf Bjornsen. "Whiskey, lad."

Olaf, turning for the bottle, winked broadly at the others. A tide of anger swelled in the breast of Ed Raleigh. They were mocking the old man. He watched sternly, with a bright eye. If this mockery went too far, there were ways of putting a period to it. He tightened his formidable right hand tentatively and loosed the grip again. The knowing grin, in the meantime, traveled up and down the bar.

Martin raised his brimming glass. His hand was shaking the moment before, but now it was perfectly steady—rock-like, as the hand of a crack shot when he draws his bead.

"Gents," he said in a deep voice with a little quiver of pathos at the bottom of it, "look at what I got in my hand."

"We see it, Jim," said the bartender sarcastically. "You was always able to keep more in a glass than anyone in town."

"That's my reputation," answered Martin proudly. "Well, boys, this is the last drop of liquor that I drink in Sierra Padre! I'm wishin' you all luck. Here's to you."

He downed the glass, and then turned a watery eye of sorrow on the others.

"Are you swearin' off?" queried Ed Raleigh sympathetically.

The old man looked at him and then started. "You give me a touch, partner," he said, still keeping a keen glance on Ed Raleigh. "But, no, he won't look like you by this time. No, lad, I ain't swearin' off, but I'm leavin' Sierra Padre."

"Never comin' back?" asked Ed kindly. "Where you goin'?"

"To make the honor of Jim Martin clean . . . the honor of Jim Martin!"

The slight quaver grew more pronounced. From the corner of his eye Ed watched the open grins of the others, and he set his teeth.

"Someone been doin' you dirt, partner?" he asked, and his glance threatened the rest and wiped away their mirth.

"It has been did," sighed Martin. He straightened. He struck the bar with his bony fist, and the glasses danced and jingled. "It has been did!"

"But where you goin'?" persisted Ed. "Ain't they nobody to help you?"

"Nobody," said Martin solemnly. "This here thing lies between me and my Maker. Maybe under the stars I'll meet him and shoot him like a dog, and God will understand." He looked about him, sighing. "Joe," he said to the man with the stately beard, "it ain't easy to leave all you boys. Joe"—he approached the other and clasped his hand—"I know what's goin' to happen to me. I know that after I've killed him, they'll get me. Yessir, I'll give myself up. After finishin' him, they ain't nothin' left for me in life. But I'll die happy."

Joe attempted to draw away, but Martin took it for a gesture of persuasion.

"Don't try to talk me out of it, Joe. My mind's

sot on it like a rock. I'm goin' out to get me a gun, and then I'm goin' down and get the train. I got only half an hour to make that train. And I got to get me some decent clothes. I ain't goin' to face him lookin' like a bum. Joe, I got the money. I got the time. He's as good as dead. But it hurts me, Joe, to leave you boys. It sure do. And to the end I'll be thinkin' of you . . . thinkin'. . . ."

He choked and covered his face with a shaking hand. Ed Raleigh felt stinging tears in his eyes.

"Before I go," said the old man faintly, "I got to break my vow and have one more drink . . . with you, Joe."

The bartender, as if he read Martin's mind, was already opposite them with a bottle and two glasses.

"Here's to a quick trip, Jim," said the stately man. He winked cruelly at Olaf. "Are you goin' to give him a chance to draw?"

"Chance? Me? Him?" Martin finished his whiskey hurriedly and smote the bar, coughing. When he could speak again, he cried: "What chance did he give me? No, he played me a dog's trick, and I'm goin' to shoot him down like a dog and stamp in his face when he's dead! But even that won't bring her . . . back . . . to me."

Big Ed Raleigh shuddered, for he saw a sob swell the throat of Martin, and he had never seen a grown man weep before. But old Jim mastered himself even as his eyes grew dim.

"She's gone," he whispered to himself sadly, faintly. "Young man," and here he whirled and pointed a gaunt arm at Raleigh, "beware of women, like you'd be keerful of a pizen-mad dog. Beware of 'em! They sink teeth in you . . . here!" He touched his heart and then struck it with his fist. "A woman has made me all hollow in here. That's what she's done."

His voice changed. It shook him like a leaf that trembles on the quaking aspen before the coming of the storm. It rumbled from his chest like distant thunder on the mountains.

"But the gent that done me wrong is goin' to die before the sun rises. He's goin' to eat dirt, and die, and watch me laughin' while his eyes get dark." He struck the bar again with his fist. "Olaf," he called. "More whiskey. I got to drink with this young gent. I got to drink to his health. I got to break my vow about not drinkin ag'in in Sierra Padre. I got to make sure he's been warned plenty."

When the glasses were poured, he raised his own brimming potion.

"Think of the whisper of a woman like it was the hiss of a snake," he said to Ed Raleigh. "Think of her promises like they was spoke by a Mex . . . a yaller-hided Mexican greaser. Drink to me, lad, and tell me you won't forget!"

"I won't forget," promised Ed Raleigh, his eyes very wide.

They drank solemnly together.

"And now, boys," said Martin, turning to the others, "I'm sayin' good bye and God bless ye before I go on my last trail. I'm prospectin' for death." He raised a forbidding hand, though no one had moved to speak. "Don't argufy. Don't be persuadin' me. Nothin' between heaven and the Rio Grande can stop me. And, boys, if you got womenfolk to home, bid 'em say a prayer for the soul of poor old Jim Martin when he's hangin' on the gallows."

He started for the door with long, wobbly strides, his body wavering.

"Good God!" cried Ed Raleigh. "Are you men going to let him go out and commit murder like this?"

He sprang after Jim Martin and caught his shoulder.

"Partner," he said earnestly, "no matter what you got ag'in that gent, you be thinkin' twice. You ain't spry enough to get away from a marshal after you've pulled your gun. Where you goin'?"

"Down in yonder valley, lad. Leave go my shoulder."

"And what's the name of this man?"

"Pete Raleigh! And he's goin' to die before mornin'."

Ed Raleigh's hand fell, as though paralyzed, from the shoulder of the revenger. He gaped; he tried to speak; and before he could regain his self-control Jim Martin had staggered side-long through the swinging doors.

When Raleigh came to life, half a dozen men blocked his way and drew him back. And—what curdled his blood—they were laughing.

"Let me go, you fools!" shouted Ed Raleigh. "Let me go, or there'll be some busted heads in here. Lemme go. He's heading down the valley to murder my old man."

"Hold on!" urged the white-bearded man, wiping tears of pleasure from his eyes. "Old Martin has been startin' down the valley after your dad's hide for twenty-five years and more, and he's never got away from Sierra Padre more'n once."

Ed Raleigh stopped struggling.

The amusement on all the faces around him was too genuine for a bluff.

The Consuming Fire

"But what in the name of God does it all mean?" he gasped, bewildered.

"Are you Pete Raleigh's boy?" queried the stately elder, stepping closer. "By the Lord, I think you are. You have the look of Pete as I remember him. Same dark, thin face. So you're Pete Raleigh's boy! I'm Patrick Swanson."

"Pat Swanson!" breathed Ed. "Why you're the sheriff. . . ."

"Not for twenty years," chuckled the old man. "I see your dad ain't quite forgot me, now he's rich'n all that. Still remembers the sheriff and. . . ."

"And the Taliaferro gang."

"Righto!"

"And how you fought Bud Jackson on the. . . ."

"Morgan claim."

"Yes, yes!"

"Sheriff, it's sure great to meet you, but ain't there really no danger from old Martin? He sure talked like death and killin' and gun play."

"Didn't he, though? He's been talkin' like that, off'n on, for these twenty-five years . . . ever since your pa pulled his stakes out of Sierra Padre."

"But what's he mean about a woman? Dad was always straight, as far as I know."

"He's talkin' about Bess Devine."

"My mother! The infernal old fool, I'll. . . ."

"Easy, lad. They ain't no harm in him. So Bess is your mother, eh? Last we seen of her was when she eloped with your pa."

Ed Raleigh scratched his massive head, frowning. "But what does Martin mean by this rotten talk?" he frowned.

"It's always this way. I'll tell you the yarn. Back there in the old days when Sierra Padre was first boomin', after gold was struck in the Bald Eagle,

Bess Devine was the prettiest girl in the town. For a minin' camp, she was almost too pretty to be good. Mind you, I don't mean your ma wasn't the straightest, finest girl that ever stepped, but you take the finest kind of girl and put her down in a gang of men, without no competition to speak of, and she gets a lot of funny ways with her eyes.

"Speakin' in general, Bess played tag with the whole camp. She could pick a man up with her eyes, and make him drunk with a smile, and then she slipped away to the next man. They was considerable Irish in Bess, which they's some in me, too. I understood, but they was a pile that didn't.

"When we give a dance, mostly the men was dancin' with each other. We'd tie a red string around the arm of some of the gents, and they was the ladies and the others danced with 'em. But Bess was an honest-to-God girl, and they was always a crowd around her. She could pick and choose from a hundred, always. And she did do her pickin', right enough.

"She had her favorites, and she danced with 'em, but she always give the ones she left behind her best smile and her best look under the lashes of her eyes. Gives me a thrill yet to think how Bess used to handle us. She always made the ones she didn't dance with feel like she really *wanted* to dance with 'em more'n with anyone else in the room . . . but they just hadn't happened to ask her first.

"She was the kind of girl, lad, that a man would see jest once and then keep dreamin' about her for a year or so afterward. That's the kind of girl she was. I can see her yet driftin' through a crowd, shakin' hands with newcomers, smilin' right and left, and sowin' the seeds of hell-raisin' all around her.

"Her eyes was as blue as the sky and her hair was as black as midnight, and they was a ripple like runnin' water in her laugh that started at your head and wound up in a shiver at your feet. That was Bess Devine . . . your mother.

"Well, among the other suckers who couldn't read Bess's mind, along come this Jim Martin. He seen her in the street and stopped and gaped at her like she was a fish out of water. And then he went to the dance and seen her again. And some-how . . . I think they'd been a fight between Bess and your pa . . . somehow Jim got the bid to take her home after the dance, and he was so proud he couldn't hardly see a step in front of him.

"The next day he started off straight for the mountains. He had his outfit, and he was goin' to find gold. Couple of months later on, your pa ups one day and elopes with Bess and goes away, down into the valley. He had his stake, and the only thing that'd kep' him in Sierra Padre some weeks had been Bess.

"Well, about the next day, down comes Jim Martin out of the mountains with sixty days' whiskers on his face and his saddlebags loaded with ore. Whiskers and all, he goes straight for the cabin of Bess, and learns out from her pa that she's gone. And her pa didn't spare no words when he was talkin' about Pete Raleigh. I know, because I was sort of lingerin' around, and I heard, and what be-tween old man Devine and young Jim Martin it was the most outcussin'est time I ever heard. It laid over anything the Taliaferro boys ever done after I got 'em rounded up.

"After a while Jim comes back to the saloon and

starts drinkin' and tellin' the boys that he was going down into the valley to catch the gent that run off with his girl. First he allowed that he'd get fixed up. He was goin' to look his best when he went down there. Because he wanted to kill your dad and then let Bess see what she'd missed by not takin' Jim Martin.

"Them was the days when I packed a star inside my vest and a forty-four . . . old style . . . on my hip and I hung around promiscuous, waitin' to land on Martin before he left town. He'd cashed in with his gold and was loaded with yaller boys, and he spent the whole day throwin' money away. The saloon got a lot of it, and his hand got so shaky that he couldn't handle his razor, so he hired a gent to shave him and give him a round hundred for the job. Then he went over to the store and got the best they have in the line of clothes. When he comes out of that store, he was about the slickest thing we ever see here in Sierra Padre.

"Next he comes down the street and buys him a six-shooter. It was a beauty, and in them days it was a treat to watch Martin handle a gun. "After that he comes back here to Olaf's place, all lit up already, and starts sayin' good bye to the boys. It took him a long time because all the boys was fond of Pete Raleigh, and they tried to persuade Jim to stay quiet. But Jim Martin kept right on, and every time he said good bye he said it was the last drop of liquor that would pass down his gullet until he'd dropped Pete Raleigh in the dirt and stepped on his face. But every time he'd see some other friend of his and have to have jest one more drink.

"And every time he had another drink, he set 'em up for the house and didn't ask for no change. Takin' it all around, it was a pretty fair payin' after-

The Consuming Fire

noon for Olaf's place. And Jim's money kept goin'
like water. Pretty soon down the street he heard
the train whistle, and that was the train that Jim
wanted to catch to get down into the valley. So he
lets out a holler for the engineer to stop for him
. . . like he coulda been heard . . . and starts runnin'.

"But he was overbalanced with red-eye and,
when he got outside the door, he doubled up on
the steps and puts his head on the floor and went
to sleep, peaceful as a kid. The train pulled out and
Jim Martin wasn't in the coaches. The next mornin' he woke up broke. Somebody'd rolled him for
his wad, what he hadn't spent. All he had was his
fine clothes and his gun. Well, he wasn't goin' to
be able to walk down in them boots, a three-day
trip and, besides, his clothes was sort of messed
up from lyin' on the steps of the saloon. And he
wasn't goin' to go down and do that killin' without
bein' able to show himself all dressed up fit to kill
to Bess afterward.

"The end was Jim Martin traded his gun and
clothes in, and borrowed a stake, and started out
prospectin' again. It was two years, pretty near,
before he come back, and then he come back with
a nice lot of stuff and cashed it in proper. We'd all
forgot about Bess and Pete by that time, but Jim
Martin hadn't. He'd been off there in the hills
swinging a pick and cursin' Pete in time with the
swing of it.

"He started right in on the same program. He
was jest burnin' up with hate for Pete. It was a sort
of consumin' fire in him, like the sky-pilot says. He
began spendin' money real liberal. He bought fine
clothes again, got him a gun, and then he bought
him a ticket for the valley.

"I wasn't the sheriff no more then, so it wasn't no trouble of mine. Besides, I didn't have no hankerin' to mix things with him without it bein' my own fight. I jest sat back on my haunches with the rest of the boys, and Jim kept on swearin' that not another drop of red-eye would flow down his throat, and then havin' another drink, and gettin' real sad, and weepin' over the boys, because he wasn't never goin' to see them again.

"We begun makin' bets about whether he'd be too drunk to get to the train when it come in, but the boys that bet against him lost their money. He jest lasted to the train and got inside and done a flop in his seat. "They was considerable excitement, and the boys sent for the sheriff. But before he got there the mornin' train come through the next day, and off of it stepped Jim Martin bilin' mad.

"After a while we found out what had happened. Before his train got to the station down in the valley, Jim was sleepin' sweet and soft and peaceful with his head on the arm of his seat. When he got to the station, the conductor threw him off and left him on the platform.

"That was late in the evenin', and they wasn't nobody jest then in the station house. When the station agent come out in the early mornin', he seen Jim Martin still lyin' on the platform, smilin' in his sleep like a newborn baby, and he jest nacherally figured that Jim had come to the station to get a train and had been too drunk to quite make it. He seen how much money they was in Jim's pocket, and it was jest enough to take him up the line to Sierra Padre. Believe he kept Jim's gun for a souvenir.

"The agent got him a ticket and took the money

and put Jim Martin aboard the first train to the cut. Jim come to on the way, and after a while it sort of soaked in on him that he was travelin' toward the mountains, when he should have been travelin' away from 'em. He wanted the train stopped, but the conductor wouldn't do it. Then Jim was goin' to kill the conductor, and a lot of the gents on the train draped themselves over Jim to keep him quiet. They wasn't none too gentle and, when they got through with him, Jim looked like he'd been fightin' a mountain lion, he was that tore up.

"Well, for a couple of days he went stompin' around town, cussin' his luck. Then he settled down when he couldn't bum no more drinks offen Olaf. He got another stake and hiked for the hills again. That's been goin' on ever since. This makes about the sixth time he's come down to town. Every time he goes back up to the hills and works away in the mines. Then, when he has a little stake, he takes it and goes off prospectin' by himself. Usually he makes some sort of a strike and stays with it till he gets out the easy pay.

"Then he comes down here rampin' and ravin' and cursin' Pete Raleigh and makin' lectures about what women ought to be and what they are. He always starts drinkin'. He always starts throwin' his money away, because they ain't anybody more generous than old Jim Martin. But after that second time he ain't never got as far as buyin' his gun."

The door opened. Peter Raleigh stood in the entrance. He was a very big man by nature, but with the light behind him he looked to his son like some biblical giant. That shaggy beard which was the despair of Mrs. Raleigh now flared out a little on either side, clotted with the dust and sweat of long riding, so that he looked as if a strong wind were still blowing against his face.

His coming made a little pause through the barroom and, when he thudded heavily across the room, all eyes jerked after him, stride by stride. He came to a pause before his son.

"Well, my fine young snapper," he roared, "what in hell might be the meanin' of this?"

His voice was made for the open; it raged and echoed through even the big bar. Ed Raleigh screwed up his courage and tried to match that volume.

"I'm starting for myself," he answered.

"You are, eh?"

"I sure am!"

"You're goin' to loot the mountains, maybe, and come back with a million inside a year, eh? You young fool," snorted Peter Raleigh, gathering head, "I tell you, you're going to hit the trail home with me."

As a rule he had his way with his family, and he would have had his way again had they been alone, but it seemed to Ed Raleigh, staring miserably past the shoulder of his father, that he surprised a meager, inward smile just twitching at the lips of Olaf, the bartender. It maddened him.

"Where you start for ain't my worry," he said quietly. "You go down into the valley or keep on into the hills. I won't stop you. No more will you stop me where I want to go."

There was a certain acid in the cool tone of this announcement that shocked Peter Raleigh back to good judgment. His wife had the same quality of voice when she was driven into a corner on some subject near to her heart.

146

"Don't you be sayin' things you'll be sorry for later on, Eddie," he said more gently. "You and me are goin' to walk outside and talk things over. Come along."

But once more Ed Raleigh saw a smile pass between Olaf and one of the others, and he grew hot to his hat brim.

"What you got to say," he declared, "you can say right here. This was a good enough place for you to start talkin', and it's good enough for you to finish in. I can stand it if you can."

Anger always made Peter Raleigh half devil. He stood swaying with sudden passion.

"Now, by God!" he thundered. "You hear me, young gent, you start for that door or from this minute you ain't no. . . ."

The door swung wide. A gust of voices rolled in from the porch, and then the loud tones of Martin.

"Come on in, boys, and have a drink. You'll need liquor before you come to the end of this here story. It's sad and ornery."

He came first, a trifle unsteady, and behind him were several who obviously had just come down from the mines.

"Dad," whispered Ed Raleigh, the color rushing from his face, "for God's sake, make your getaway. This is Martin, and he's lookin' for you with a gun."

"Martin?" Big Raleigh wavered, and then shrugged back his shoulders. "I've never sneaked away from any man, and I ain't goin' to begin now."

Ed, knowing this was irrevocable, stepped back and prepared for the fight.

"Are you still plannin' for that train?" said Olaf to Martin.

"And I'm goin' to get it. Olaf, I want you to know my friend, Bud Hendrix." He waved forward a huge, black-bearded man. Bud has guaranteed to get me to that train." He turned. "Step up, boys, all of you. My dust ain't run out yet by a hell of a long ways."

Here his eye fell upon Big Raleigh. He halted, and then walked straight across the room and paused a pace away from Peter. With his hand on his gun, Ed waited for the lightening move, the flash of steel. In his heart he had never admired his father as he did at this moment, for the big man did not stir a hand. He waited for the other to make the decisive move.

"Stranger," said Martin suddenly, "you might as well know what's comin' off. Come and liquor up and hear a story what every man ought to know."

He waved toward the bar, and Pete Raleigh, after an instant of hesitation, smiled quietly and followed. As for Ed, he was ready for the trouble which he thought must come.

"Got your eye on the time, Bud?" asked Martin.

The other exposed a huge gold watch. "I'm watchin' every minute. If what you say is right, that gent ought to die, and I'll help you on your way."

"If I'm right?" roared Martin. "Don't the whole town know how Pete Raleigh done me dirt and sneaked away my girl and married her?"

By his side Pete Raleigh straightened and, for a moment Ed thought that the dénouement was about to come, but then he saw his father relax and watch Martin with an odd smile.

"For twenty years," said Martin, "I been hungerin' to get at him. For twenty years I been burnin' up with fire to see this gent face to face. And now the time has come."

Ed Raleigh shuddered, but his father had not stirred. He still stood there at the side of Martin, looking at the avenger with the quiet, reminiscent smile. Everyone had taken his drink, and it was Pete Raleigh who proposed the toast.

"Martin," he said, "here's hopin' that you meet Pete Raleigh face to face . . . as close as I'm standin' to you now."

"Ah!" groaned Martin, and tossed off his drink. "Stranger," he went on, laying a hand on Raleigh's arm, "I like you. You got a straight look about your eyes. Well, so long. I got to go down and kill Pete Raleigh. This is my last try and, if I don't get him this time in the valley, I'm goin' to call the deal off. When I come back, partner, I want to see more of you."

"Thanks," said Pete Raleigh. "Go get him."

"Time's up!" barked Bud Hendrix.

"Wait a minute," pleaded Martin. "I got a gent here that can understand, and I want him to know. . . ."

"Don't you hear the train whistlin'?"

"Damn the train! Partner. . . ."

But Bud Hendrix was a man of his word. Far away the train hooted around the bend and Bud, fixing one brawny arm under the shoulder of Martin, caught him with the other hand on the opposite side and fairly lifted him toward the door.

"When he's dead and buried," shouted Martin over his shoulder, "I'll come back and see you again, stranger."

Pete Raleigh waved his thanks.

"Set 'em up, Olaf," called Martin as he was borne through the door. "Set 'em up for all the boys, and I'll pay when I get back from makin' Missus Pete Raleigh a widow."

It was some time later that Peter Raleigh remembered the mission which had brought him to Sierra Padre but, when he turned, his son was not in the saloon. He went hurriedly into the street and peered up and down, but there was still no sign of Ed Raleigh. For far up the side of Bald Eagle Peak, steering his course through the ears of his burro, Ed Raleigh was voyaging into the old land of his father.

In the meantime, notwithstanding the assistance of Bud Hendrix and his gold watch, Jim Martin again missed the train.

THE MAN WHO FORGOT

Faust's first appearance in Street & Smith's *Western Story Magazine* was "Jerry Peyton's Notched Inheritance," a serial that began in the issue dated 11/15/20. This serial was published under a new pseudonym—George Owen Baxter—and in succeeding years Faust would add to his string numerous other *noms des plumes*. He was so prolific an author that during the 1920s he might have a serial by David Manning, a serial by George Owen Baxter, and a novelette by Max Brand all running in the same issue of *Western Story Magazine*, and this remained the case as late as the issue dated 4/2/32. Frank E. Blackwell, editor of the magazine for all the years Faust was a contributor, once recalled: "How did I get hold of Faust? Bob Davis was over-bought. Munsey found it out, told Bob he'd have to shut off buying for as long as six months, and use up some of the stuff in the safe. Faust, always in need of money, no matter how much he made, came to me with a story. I bought it. He was mine, and mine only from there on." This wasn't completely true. Faust did write for other magazines as well. But for nearly fifteen years he did write better than a million words annually for Blackwell. A short novel Faust titled "The Man Who Forgot" marked his second appearance in *Western Story Magazine*. It was published in the Christmas issue dated 12/25/20 as by John Frederick. This new byline was necessary because the same issue carried the final installment of George Owen Baxter's "Jerry Peyton's Notched Inheritance."

The Man Who Forgot

I
"A FRESH START"

It was snowing. A northwester was rushing over the mountains. As the storm wind shifted a few points west and east, the mountains cut it away, so that one valley lay in a lull of quiet air, with the snow dropping in perpendicular lines; or else the mountains caught the wind in a funnel and poured a venomous blast, in which the snow hardened and became cold teeth.

The two men lying in a covert saw Skinner Mountain, due south of them, withdraw into the mist of white and again jump out at them, blocking half the sky. The weather and the sudden appearances of Mount Skinner troubled Lou Alp. In his own way and in his own time, Alp was a successful sneak thief. He had been known to take chances enough; but that was in Manhattan, where the millions walk the street and where mere numbers offer a refuge. That was in Manhattan, where a man may slip into twisting side streets with a dozen issues through alleys and cellars. That was in Manhattan, where a fugitive turning a corner is as far away as though he had dropped to the other side of the world

Far different here. Of man there was not a trace, and the huge and brutal face of nature pressed upon the sensitive mind of Lou Alp; the chill air numbed his finger tips and made his only useful weapons helpless. Lou Alp depended upon sleight of hand and agility rather than upon strength. This whirl and rush of snow baffled him and irritated him. He kept repeating to his companion: "Is this your sunshine? Is this your happy country? I say, to hell with it!"

His companion, who lay by his side in the bushes and kept a sharp lookout up the road at such times as the drive of the snow made it possible to see fifty yards, would answer: "It's a freak storm, Lou. Never saw it come so thick and fast so early in December as this. Give the country a chance. It's all right."

Alp would stare at him in amazement. From the time of their first intimacy Jack Chapel had continually amazed him. That was in the shoe shop of the penitentiary where they had sat side by side on their stools. The rule was silence and, though there were many opportunities for speech from the side of the mouth in the carefully gauged whispers which state prisoners learn to use so soon, Chapel had never taken advantage of the chances. Lou would never forget the man as he had first seen him, the clean-cut features, the rather square effect given by the size of his jaw muscles, the prison pallor which made his dark eyes seem darker. On the whole he was a handsome chap, but he had something about him more arresting than his good looks.

For the most part the prisoners pined or found resignation. Their eyes became pathetic or dull, as Lou's eyes became after the first three months. But the eyes of Jack Chapel held a spark which bespoke neither resignation nor inertia. He had a way of sitting forward on his stool all day long, giving the impression of one ready to start to his feet and spring into action. When one of the trusties spoke to him, he did not stare straight before him, as the other prisoners did, but his eyes first looked his questioner full in the face and flashed, then he made his answer. He gave an effect, indeed, of one who bides a day.

These things Lou Alp noted, for there were few things about faces which he missed. He had learned early to read human nature from his life as a gutter urchin who must know which face means a dime, which means a cent, and which means no gift to charity at all. But what lay behind the fire in Jack Chapel's eyes he could not say. Alp was cunning, but he lacked imagination. He knew the existence of some devouring emotion, but what that emotion was he could not tell.

He was not the only one to sense a danger in Chapel. The trusty in charge of the shop guessed it at the end of the first week, and he started to break Chapel. It was not hard to find an opening. Chapel had little skill with his hands, and presently job after job was turned back to him. He had sewed clumsily; he had put in too many nails; he had built up the heel awry. After a time, he began to be punished for his clumsiness. It was at this point that Alp interfered. He had no great liking for Chapel, but he hated the trusty with the hatred of a weasel for a badger. To help Chapel was to get in an indirect dig at the trusty.

Because Lou Alp could do almost anything with his agile fingers, he began to instruct Chapel in the fine points of shoemaking. It was a simple matter. He had only to wait until Chapel was in difficulty, and then Lou would start the same piece of work on one of his own shoes. He would catch the eye of Chapel and work slowly, painstakingly, so that his neighbor could follow the idea. Before long, Chapel was an expert and even the carping trusty could find no fault.

Now charity warms the heart; a gift is more pleasant to him who gives than to him who takes. Lou Alp, having for once in his life performed a good deed, was amazed by the gradual unlocking of his heart that followed. He had lived a friendless life; vaguely, delightfully, he felt the growth of a new emotion.

When the time came, he had leaned over to pick something from the floor and had whispered sidewise: "What's the charge?"

The other had made no attempt to reply guardedly. His glance held boldly on the face of the sneak thief, as the latter straightened again on his stool. There was a slight tightening of his jaw muscles, and then Chapel said: "Murder!"

The word knocked at the heart of Lou Alp and made him tremble. Murder! Looking at the strong, capable, but rather clumsy hands of Chapel, he saw how all that strength could have been applied. Suppose those square-tipped fingers had clutched someone by the throat—an ache went down the windpipe of the thief.

If Lou had been interested before, he was fascinated now. In all their weeks of labor side by

side, only four words had been interchanged between them, and here he was in the soul of his
companion. He was not horrified. Rather, he felt
a thrill of dog-like admiration. He, Lou Alp, had
wished to kill more than one man. There was the
"flatty" who ran him down in "Mug" McIntyre's
place. He had wanted to bump that man off. There
were others. But fear, which was the presiding de-
ity in the life of the sneak thief, had warded him
away from the cardinal sin. He respected Chapel;
he was glad he had helped his neighbor; he felt
even a touch of reverence for the boy.

And later on he had said: "How?"

"It was a frame," answered Chapel. "A dirty
frame!"

And then Alp knew the meaning of the spark
behind those eyes. It took some of the thrill from
his feeling for Chapel, but now he understood that
undying alertness, for it sprang out of the hate of
a man who has been wronged. After all, it is almost as exciting to be seated beside a man who
has been wrongly convicted of murder as it is to
sit beside a man who is really guilty.

A little later Chapel put his first question.

"And you?" he said.

"They framed me, too," said Alp, and with marvelous skill he was able to put a touch of a whine
even in his whisper. "The dirty dogs framed me,
too!"

He hardened his face in lines of sadness, prepared to meet unbelief in the eyes of the other, but
there was no questioning in Jack Chapel's mind.
Instead, he sat rigid on his stool and his eyes
flamed at his companion. Then he smiled. The last
bar was down between them; he admitted the
sneak thief into his friendship.

Events came swiftly to a head. About his past Chapel was reticent. He had come from the West and he was going back to some part of his own great country when he was out. He was not going to attempt to get even for the double-cross which in the first place had brought him East and then lodged him in prison for a ten-year term. His vengeance was barred, for it was a girl who had engineered the whole scheme to save her lover. Alp learned of this reticence with amazement. If a strong man had injured him in a similar manner, he might well have postponed his vengeance as he had often postponed it in times past; but to withhold the heavy hand from a woman, this was a thing which he could not comprehend. As always when a thing passed his understanding, he remained silent. In the future he was to find that silence was often necessary when he talked with the falsely accused murderer.

A new event came. Chapel was planning an escape and he confided his plan to the sneak thief. That night Lou sat in his cell and brooded. If he took part in the attempt, it meant a probable recapture and a far heavier sentence for breaking jail. The other alternative was to tell the prison authorities everything. They would make him a trusty at once, lighten his service, and cut his term as short as was possible. On the other hand a still, small voice kept assuring him that if he betrayed Chapel, he would sooner or later die by the hand of that man. There was a third possibility, to remain quietly in the prison, say nothing, and take no part in the attempted escape.

Lou Alp had not sufficient moral courage to be reticent. As a result he found himself dragged into the plan. On the appointed night, after five minutes of quiet work and murderous suspense, he stood outside the black walls a free man, with Jack Chapel at his side. Instinct told him, as strongly as it tells the homing pigeon, safety lay in the slide across country to the all-sheltering labyrinth of Manhattan, but the voice of Jack Chapel was stronger than instinct and Alp started West with his friend. They had aimed for a district safely north of Jack Chapel's home, had ridden the beams as far as the railroad would take them, and then plunged into the wilderness of mountains on a road that led them here. The night before they had spent in a small village and there, with his usual ferretlike skill, Lou learned of the payroll which was to go the next day from the village up to the mine in the hills under charge of two armed men. He had told Chapel, and the latter insisted on a holdup.

"I'll take what's coming to me, and no more," he said. "What's my time worth for two years? I don't count in the pain or the work or the dirty disgrace, but write me down for a thousand a year. That's two thousand. Then you come in. A year and a half at the same rate. That's thirty-five hundred the world owes us and here's where we collect. Thirty-five hundred, no more and no less. We use that to make a new start. Tell me straight, is that square? And we take it from old Purvis's payroll. God knows Purvis can afford to spare the coin. He's so crooked he can't lie in bed. How'd he get his mines? By beating out poor devils who hit hard times. So he's our paymaster. Something is coming to us. We're both innocent. We've both been hit between the eyes. Now we can get something back. Is that logic?"

There had been a sort of appeal in his voice as

he made the proposition to Alp early that morning.

"Sure it's justice," nodded Lou.

Then Chapel drew a little breath and his eyes flashed from one side to the other. "I ain't much on a holdup," he faltered.

"You never stuck 'em up before?" cried Lou, horrified by such rash inexperience.

"Sure I never did. That doesn't make any difference. I know how holdups go. You step out and shove a gun under the nose of somebody. He jerks his hands over his head. You go through his pockets or whatever he has the coin in. You take his guns. He rides into town like a shot. A posse starts out after you. You go one way and they go the other way. Haven't I seen it work out that way a hundred times? I tell you there's nothing to it, Lou."

Once more Lou had been drawn into the dragnet of the other's commanding will.

II
"WITH A TWIG"

Alp did not like it, no matter from what angle he looked at it. It was foreign to him. The game was not his. He was used to playing a lone hand and now he lay like a rabbit in a covert, not knowing what was expected of him, or if he would have courage to carry through the part assigned him. If it had been spring weather, he kept saying to himself, with a good, clear sky to pour content through the mind of a man and air through which one could see, things would have been very different with him. His one comfort was the bright eye

GET YOUR 4 FREE BOOKS NOW—
A VALUE BETWEEN $16 AND $20

Mail the Free Book Certificate Today!

FREE BOOKS CERTIFICATE!

YES! I want to subscribe to the Leisure Western Book Club. Please send my 4 FREE BOOKS. Then, each month, I'll receive the four newest Leisure Western Selections to preview FREE for 10 days. If I decide to keep them, I will pay the Special Members Only discounted price of just $3.36 each, a total of $13.44. This saves me between $3 and $6 off the bookstore price. There are no shipping, handling or other charges. There is no minimum number of books I must buy and I may cancel the program at any time. In any case, the 4 FREE BOOKS are mine to keep—at a value of between $17 and $20! Offer valid only in the USA.

Name_____

Address_____

City_____ State_____

Zip_____ Phone_____

Biggest Savings Offer!

For those of you who would like to pay us in advance by check or credit card—we've got an even bigger savings in mind. Interested? Check here. ☐

If under 18, parent or guardian must sign.
Terms, prices and conditions subject to change. Subscription subject to acceptance. Leisure Books reserves the right to reject any order or cancel any subscription.

GET FOUR BOOKS TOTALLY *FREE*—A VALUE BETWEEN $16 AND $20

of his companion. Cold had turned the fingers of Jack Chapel purple around the knuckles, but for some reason Alp could not imagine him stopped or even seriously embarrassed by such a thing as cold.

Yet he asked to make assurance doubly sure: "Pretty smooth with a gun?"

"Me? Smooth with a gun?" asked the heavy-shouldered young fellow. "Why, Lou, I couldn't hit the side of a barn with a rifle, let alone a revolver."

The terror which had been reined up in Lou Alp's vitals now burst loose and flooded him. The chill which swept through him was a mortal cold that had nothing to do with either wind or snow. It was fear, horrible, strength-devouring fear. He could not even speak, as he heard his companion continue carelessly.

"But what does gun work have to do with it? I wouldn't hurt those two fellows if I could. Their boss is a skunk. He deserves anything that comes his way, but I don't hold any grudge against those two fellows. Not me! But there'll be no shooting. No, all you need for a game like this is a little bluff and some sand."

He followed his statement with his usual chuckle. Alp was seized in a fresh amazement. There were qualities about this man which never grew old. There was a surprising freshness, a nearness to the soil. Two things about him spoke the two sides of his nature. There were the bright, steady, and dangerous eyes. Lou Alp had been among the defiers of society long enough to recognize that glance. On the other hand, there was that ready chuckle. It came deeply out of his throat; it was musical, changing, and redolent with good nature. It was a laugh which instantly made a roomful of people smile and turn around. It was a laugh which never offended because there was not the slightest suggestion of mockery or derision or self complacency in it.

Yet it failed to warm the trembling heart of the thief at this juncture. He continued to stare as though at a revelation of madness.

"But for heaven's sake . . . " was all he could say. Then: "I've been wonderin' about your gun, where you been keepin' it all this time?"

"Here," said the other and, reaching above him, he snapped off a twig, shook the snow from it, and presented to Lou Alp the frost-blackened, curved fragment of wood. The sneak thief threw back his head and began to laugh wildly. The sound came up through his slender throat cackling. It was singularly like the wind-shaken scream of some bird of prey.

"That!" he cried. "Man, don't you know that you got two armed men to handle? Don't you know that they're lookin' for trouble? That's why they're with the coin! And even if you had a gun . . . " he broke off, unable to continue. Then: "Let's get out of this. I'm froze clear through."

"What's the matter?" asked Chapel. "Don't you trust me?"

Again Alp was staggered. He had dragged his cold-cramped body to his knees and now he paused, agape. He was about to say, "What has trust got to do with powder and lead?" but he checked himself. It occurred to him that this singular fellow might be angered by any doubts cast upon him; already there was the queer, thoughtful flicker in his eyes, and Alp dropped back into his bed of leaves and snow. It came to him that much as he dreaded the storm and the coming of the armed men, he dreaded Jack Chapel even more. He knew now why the twelve good men and true had looked into the face of this man and had believed all too readily, with only the most circumstantial evidence to back their belief, that he had been guilty of a murder. Aside from the escape from the prison he had never seen Chapel meet danger or perform any violent act, and yet he was ready to premise the most tremendous things of this bright-eyed man.

He lay back in the snow without a word and began to massage his lips with his knuckles, so as to be able to speak when he had mentally framed his argument. He must prevent this incipient act of madness that would destroy them both. His agile brain began to turn and twist around the subject, looking back on a score of arguments; but, when he was on the verge of beginning, there was a low exclamation from Jack Chapel.

"They're here!"

He cast one wild glance down the road, but a whirl of snow rose and closed the way before him. Then, like the coward that he was, he looked to his companion, prepared with the protest, prepared with the plea, to let the danger and the money pass. He was stopped by the singular expression of happiness in the face of his companion. Somewhere he had seen such a look. Now he remembered. It was when he had taken a girl out of the slums to the theater; when the curtain slipped up, in the dim glow from the stage, he had turned and watched the face of the girl, her lips parted, her eyes at once dreaming, wistful, and eager.

Such was the face of Jack Chapel. The same hushed expectancy, the same trembling alertness,

Max Brand

the same love of the unknown that lay before him.
Now, through the curtain of the snow, the heads
of two horses thrust out, powdered and unreal.
Instantly the whole of the buckboard and the two
men who rode in it came out upon Lou Alp. They
were humped into bunches of flesh, shrinking
from the cold, made numb and sleepy by it. Looking up at them they seemed huge and formidable
to Alp. A shudder went through his meager body
when he thought of a single man, armed with a
bent twig, trying to halt that on-sweeping force of
horses and wagon and fighting men.

Chapel was on his hands and feet like a runner
at the mark. The wagon rushed nearer, rattling
above the hum of wind and the soft crushing of
the snow among the naked trees. Suddenly the
man leaped out from behind his screen with a
deep shout.

The horses stopped and veered to one side,
cramping the wagon dangerously. The men in the
wagon sat and stared stupidly at the apparition.
There stood Jack Chapel before them, crouched a
little, with the twig in his hand not extended at full
arm's length, but drawn back close to his breast.
For the moment Alp forgot that it was simply a
crooked piece of wood. He expected to see fire
flash from the end of it.

The guards must have expected the same thing.
For they made no attempt at resistance, but
slowly—or was it the feverish activity of Lou's
mind that made it seem slow—they put their
hands up to their shoulders and then, inch by
inch, above their heads.

Chapel was barking orders. Obediently they
climbed down and turned their backs, still with
hands above their heads. Jack went to them at a

run, still speaking swiftly, cautioning them not to make a suspicious move. He jerked a revolver out of the holster that hung at the hip of one of them and tossed his twig away.

Lou Alp stood up. The blood was beginning to run freely again in his veins. A spot of red stood out in the hollow of each sallow, thin cheek. For the madman was turning his madness into sane matter of fact. With his twig he had rendered two stalwart men helpless. With a cry of encouragement, Lou was about to step out and render such help as he was capable of when the second of the guards, whose revolver had not yet been taken, jerked down his arms, whirled, and fired.

It happened with incredible suddenness. Lou felt his left leg go numb, but he forgot that, giving his whole attention on Chapel. He expected to see that broad, strong form topple to the earth. Instead, his friend smashed the fist that carried the revolver into the face of the man who had just fired. The fellow tossed up both arms, staggered back, and sank slowly into the snow. His companion, turning at the shot, grappled the bandit. For a moment they swayed and twisted and then were torn apart. The guard came close again, his arms reaching out. He was met by the lunging fist of Chapel and dropped loosely upon his face.

By the time Alp's brain began to work, he felt the numbness in his leg give place to a sharp pain, as though a red-hot knife had been thrust into his calf and left there to burn the flesh. Not until then did he realize that he had been shot through the leg by that first wild bullet from the gun of the guard. A red trickle was running out over his trousers. He watched it, fascinated.

Chapel was tying the fallen guards. Now that

the danger was past, Lou attempted to go to him, but his left leg crumbled beneath his weight. Lying on his side, he saw his friend climb into the buckboard, take up a box, smash the lock with a bullet, and then drop to the snow with a stack of what he knew to be money. Chapel was counting it. Was it possible that the fool was only taking the thirty-five hundred? There must be at least twelve thousand in that payroll!

He dragged himself out from the covert at the same time that the other finished dumping his loot into a sack. Chapel was instantly beside him with an exclamation while tears of self-pity rose into the eyes of Alp.

"The dirty swine," he moaned. "Look what they done to me? Will you? And what harm was I doin' 'em?"

Before he answered, Chapel knelt beside Lou, ripped up the leg of his trousers, and examined the wound. "It's an easy one," he said. He was tearing away his own coat as he spoke, and now he ripped his undershirt into strips and made a swift and skillful bandage. "Clean as a whistle, Lou," he went on reassuringly. "You won't lose a tablespoonful of blood hardly. Keep your chin up, will you?"

A hot rage sent a mist across the vision of Lou. "Pump 'em full of lead !" he said through his teeth.

"Why?" asked Jack Chapel.

"Didn't they do this? You ask me why?"

Something in the face of his companion cleared Alp's eyes again. He saw that Chapel was looking at him with a curiously cold glance.

"It was just a chance that you got hurt," he said. "Besides, do you blame 'em for tryin' to protect the stuff they were sent out to guard? No, they showed they had . . . courage. I like 'em all the better for it, but the luck was against 'em. And that's the only reason why we're not blown full of lead, the way you want me to fix them now that they got their hands tied."

Lou Alp forgot the pain of his wound as he met the new glance of Chapel.

"Say, Bo," he grinned feebly. "You don't think I meant it, do you? The leg was hurting like fire and it peeved me for a minute."

"Sure," said Jack Chapel slowly, "I know what you mean. Only. . . ." He did not finish the sentence.

III
"WHITE VS. YELLOW"

Somehow that incomplete sentence tied the tongue of the sneak thief even when he saw Jack Chapel take up the box with the gold coin and drop it in the snow beside the guards. There went close to ten thousand dollars perhaps. Yet Lou Alp merely writhed in silence. He dared not speak.

Lou was lifted in the strong arms of Jack Chapel and placed in the rear of the buckboard. Looking over the side, he saw Chapel search the two guards for weapons, and then in amazement he saw him cut the bonds of his enemies. Such faulty procedure took the breath of Lou Alp. Still he attempted no advice, and even flattened himself on the bottom of the buckboard.

He felt quite sure that up to this point his presence had not been noted. He had not issued from his hiding place until after both guards had been stunned by the blows of Jack Chapel and, as they lay face downward in the snow, there was small reason to think that they had heard his voice over the screaming of the storm, or that they had seen him during the very brief interim before he was placed in the bed of the wagon. He lay still and said nothing while the two struggled to their feet and went with uncertain steps down the road. The circling, thick eddies of the snow covered them from view quickly. Jack climbed up to his place in the driver's seat. He turned and looked down to Lou Alp, bedded in feed sacks with his injured leg cocked up to break the jar of the bumps. As he turned, Lou saw Chapel's right hand laid on the rail of the seat, with the knuckles scraped bare and bleeding. The blows which knocked down the guards had done that work, he knew, and he felt once more that surprise, tinged with fear, with which he had already discovered so many unsuspected accomplishments in his companion. He knew enough about boxing to recognize the snapping, straight-armed power of the blows which had stunned the guards. He felt again that there was more to Jack Chapel than appeared on the surface. The man was hiding something.

"Are you going to be all right, there?" asked Jack.

His voice was cold, and Alp winced under it. "I can stand it, pal," he said conciliatingly.

He watched to see the face of the other soften, but with a curt nod Chapel turned and started the horses on. He swung the wagon about and sent it along the valley with the storm at their backs. They made good time up the road, jogging steadily on for the better part of three or four hours. Before the end of that time Lou Alp had squirmed into a dozen positions and was finding ease in none.

The Man Who Forgot

How fervently he blessed the moment when the buckboard was brought to a halt. Chapel climbed down from the seat and stood over his companion.

"We've come to the end of the road," he said.

"This wilderness? Where in the name of heaven can we put up? Jack, I can't stand much more!"

"Look over there."

Lou strained his feverish eyes and made out the vague form of a house ghost-like in the storm, a big house of which he saw more the longer he stared.

"But how'll I get there?" he groaned. "Must be half a mile, Jack."

"I'll get you there."

Something of restraint in his voice made Lou wince again. He broached the vital question. "Will . . . will you be safe there?" he asked. "Suppose the posse turns along this road?"

"I dunno," replied the other. He turned as he spoke and looked into the teeth of the storm as though danger were at that moment riding upon him out of it. "I dunno. But I've got to get you to that house before you get a cold in your wound."

Lou could see his friend hesitating, and that hesitation drove him into a panic. Would he be abandoned here in the snow on the meager chance that someone from the house should happen on him, or that he could drag himself to the shelter? He was on the verge of breaking into a frantic appeal when he checked himself and thought of new tactics.

"Jack," he said, "listen to me. I've done you no good. First to last you've started everything and finished everything all by yourself. You got me out of jail. You brought me West. You planned the job down the road. You pulled it off. And all I've done

169

is to clog up the works and gum the cards." He paused a little to study the effect of his words. It was hard to read Jack Chapel with the wind turning up his hat behind and the snow spattering on his shoulders. He seemed so self-reliant and self-possessed that again the shivering took Lou Alp. Yet he persisted in his singular appeal.

"Leave me be where I am, Jack," he went on, his voice shaking. "If you come up there to the house with me, they'll have you sure. Before ten hours somebody'll come along this way and the folks at the house'll tell 'em that you been there to leave me."

The larger man grunted. "What'll you do without me?" he asked harshly. "You don't know these folks around here. You don't know their ways. You ain't like 'em and they'll see the difference. They'll start askin' questions and you'll be fool enough to start tellin' 'em lies. Inside of five days they'll have the sheriff out here to look you over as a queer one."

The sneak thief looked into his wretched soul and shook in acknowledgment of the truth. "Let them come and get me," he said hoarsely. "Let 'em come. But if they get me, I'll have this one satisfaction, that I didn't drag you into it. Jack, pal, you take the horses and go on. I'll take my own chances."

Through a heart-breaking pause he saw the other hesitate, and even turn partly away; but at the very moment, when a wild and craven appeal was about to break from the lips of Lou Alp, Chapel turned again and caught the meager hand of the thief.

"I thought you were bluffin' me," he said with emotion. "I thought you were yellow and were just bluffin' me. But now I see you're straight, partner, and I'll tell you where I stand. Back there when you were peeved and wanted me to bump off those two gents, I figured that you meant it, and it sort of riled me a little. Speakin' man to man, I thought you were a skunk, Lou. Been thinkin' so all this time right up to now. But a gent that plays square once, can't play crooked the next minute. Here you lie, helpless, but not thinkin' once about yourself."

The emotion in his voice had a powerful effect upon Lou Alp. Tears of self-pity for the sacrifice which he had shammed began to gather.

"And now I feel like a skunk," said Jack Chapel. "If you can take my hand and call it square in spite of what I been thinkin' about you, here it is. If you're still mad at me, why, when you get on your feet again, we'll fight it out. What say?"

Lou Alp, trembling at the narrowness of his escape, clutched the proffered hand eagerly and wrung it.

"That's good," said Jack Chapel simply. "That's mighty good!" He seemed to brush away the remnants of the situation and turned to new things. "Give me your arms and I'll get you on my back," he directed.

"But what about the wagon and the horses?"

"Don't you see what'll become of 'em? With this storm at their backs, they'll drift straight down the road. I don't know a whole pile about this country, but I know there ain't more'n one road for 'em to take down this valley. As long as the wind blows, they'll keep moving and they may wind up fifty miles from here. The posse, if they start one out right away, will go straight for the place where the horses and wagon, or what's left of the wagon, are picked up. They'll start combing the hills for me around that place. They'll never think to look for me in a house. Even if they find me, they won't know me because I had my handkerchief over the lower part of my face and my hat pretty well down over my eyes. And it's a cinch that they'll never dream of lookin' for two of us!"

It was all so logically reasoned that the sneak thief nodded in admiration. The fever which had been gathering in him, and the waves of weakness, began to make his head swim. Yet he followed Jack Chapel's voice.

"First thing they'll do will be to look over the list of their old employees. Why? Because I only took part of the coin. On account of that the big boss will think that somebody he'd wronged, or somebody with a debt he wouldn't pay, tuned up a gun and came out to take what belonged to him by rights. And I'll tell you what they'll do. They'll be apt to send the posse right to the house of the first man around these parts that the big boss owes around thirty-five hundred dollars to. When they get all through with that sort of lookin' . . . then, and not till then . . . they'll take the back trail. By that time anything may have happened. Ten days ought to make you fit for a saddle, and most likely it'll be ten days before anybody bothers us here."

"And so?" queried Lou Alp.

"And so I'm goin' to take you up to that house, and I'm goin' to stay there with you. I dunno who lives there. But if it's white folks, and you don't talk too much, we won't be bothered. You hear me talk?"

The sneak thief smiled feebly as he was raised into the arms of Jack Chapel. "Jack," he said, "you're riskin' your life for me. I know you could make a getaway into the hills if you wanted to.

You're riskin' everything to save me. You're givin' me everything. Some day I'll give it all back in a chunk!"

"Forget it," answered Chapel. "You talk a pile too much, partner."

Again he began to breathe hard as the strain of the steep hillside told on his legs and the weight of the limp body told on his arms.

IV
"GOOD SAMARITANS"

The half mile up that grade was no easy walk under any circumstances. With a staggering storm from one side, with the rocks slippery from snow, and with the burden of another man weighting him, it was a terrific task for Jack Chapel. Looking up into his face, Alp saw the fighting jaw thrust out and the muscles over the angles of the jaw harden. Yet he took the half mile with only three brief pauses for rest. Finally, just a brief distance from the house, he deposited the wounded man in a bank of snow and leaned over him, panting.

"I don't know what our story is going to be till I see the people of the house," he said. "The thing for you to do is to keep your ears open and your eyes shut. You understand?"

"You want me to faint?" grinned Lou Alp.

"Sure. Soon as I come close up to the door, I'll give you the word and you go limp. That'll bring me to the door with an unconscious man. As soon as I go in, they'll rush around until your senses come back. I'll have a chance that way to size up the gang in that house and frame a story. I'll tell the story so you can hear it. It won't be long, and you hang on to what I say. Will you do that?"

"I'll turn a flop," said the sneak thief, "that'll
have the real thing beat a mile. Lead on!"

Where it was a mere matter of stratagem, Alp
felt at home. His head cleared and his pulse
strengthened as matters approached this new crisis. Once more he was taken up and they came in
full view of a square-built ranch house whose tall
windows promised capacious rooms within.

"Now!" cautioned Jack Chapel, and the thief
made himself limp.

He became so perfectly inert that his left arm
dangled toward the ground, his head dropped
back and allowed his hat to fall off, while his long
black hair blew in the wind. He heard a grunt of
satisfaction from Jack Chapel that was music in
his ears. Then he closed his eyes.

He was too much of an artist to attempt to look
through the lashes at what passed around him. He
remained in darkness, his mouth agape, his head
dangling, his whole weight utterly inert. He felt
Jack prop him up on one knee and then heard the
clatter of knuckles against the front door; it was
opened. Warm air rushed out around them.

"Hello, there! What you got? Not dead, man?"

It was a deep, strong bass voice.

"No. But drilled through the leg. Accident.
Hunting." The reply of Jack Chapel was a tum-
bling mass of words panted out. "Lemme get him
to a bed, will you?"

"Of course. Let me carry him."

"No, I'll manage him. Not serious, but he's
played out. Lost a lot of blood."

"Up this way, then, son. Hello! Mother! Kate!
Come here. Hurry up. Hurry, I say!"

A scurry of voices and footsteps in the distance,

and then Lou felt himself being carried up a flight of stairs. The feminine rustling and voices came from behind and below and poured up around him. A young, pleasant voice had cried: "Poor fellow!" The voice of an older woman had screamed.

"Now, none of that foolishness," said the man who led the way. "Keep your head, Mother. He ain't goin' to die. Just a scratch. Lost a little blood. Kate, I want you to stand by to help. Get some water and bandages."

They reached level flooring, turned, and a door was opened. Lou could tell by the changed temperature of the air.

"I'll have a fire going in a jiffy," said the big man's voice. "Kate, get that hot water. But how did you get him here? How far'd you carry him?"

Lou felt himself laid upon a bed and then Jack Chapel was answering: "Not so far. We'd been hunting through the mountains. The storm got us, and we started down for lower levels. Coming along fine when this accident happened just in the hills, there above your house. And mighty lucky we were so close. Barbed wire is a curse, sir. Climbing through a fence got my holster caught . . . tried to get it loose . . . reached to pull my gun out . . . and somehow the thing went off and drilled Lou through the calf of his leg."

All the time he talked brokenly, he was working swiftly, taking off Lou's clothes. Presently Lou Alp found himself slipped in between chilly sheets. In the meantime, a pair of massive fingers closed over his wrist.

"He'll come along all right," said the deep voice after a moment. "Lucky it wasn't higher. Lucky it didn't hit the bone. Men of this generation don't know how to handle guns any more. No sense for 'em. Don't mean to hurt your feelin's, my young friend. By the way, my name's Moore, Roger Moore."

"My name is Jack Chandler and this is Louis Angus."

"Glad to know you. He ain't one of the Barr County Angus family, is he?"

"Might be related. I dunno."

"No, he ain't got bone enough to be one of 'em. Well, son, lucky you landed here. And you're welcome as long as you'll stay, and that'll be ten days anyway before he's on his feet. Come on in, Kate. Meet Jack Chandler. This is my daughter. Put that basin down over here, Kate. There's a good girl. Nothin' to be white about. The gent ain't goin' to die. Got a .45 through the calf of his leg, though. Was it a .45?"

"A .32," said Jack Chandler.

"What! Never seen a .32 tear things up like that, but bullets are as tricky as guns. Never know what they'll do. Look at that scar on my wrist. Bullet went in there, twisted clean around my forearm, and come out by the elbow. Didn't break a bone or tear a tendon and my arm was as good as ever inside three weeks. That's one of the queer things a bullet'll do. Luck, eh? Hello! He's comin' to!"

Alp had felt a covert nudge from the knee of his companion and he took it as a signal to open his eyes. He did it very well. First he blinked. Then he glared up at the ceiling and murmured: "It's all right, Jack. You couldn't help it."

"Delirious a little," muttered the deep voice.

Alp sat bolt upright in the bed and stared wildly around him. "What the devil!" he exclaimed.

His words met a pleased chuckle from half a dozen faces, and each with shining, kindly eyes.

The Man Who Forgot

"The snow," said Lou vaguely, rubbing his eyes. "The wind . . . I. . . ."

A silver-haired woman with a youthful, beautiful face came beside him and laid her hand gently on his shoulder.

"You lie down, my boy," she said. "The snow and the wind and the trouble are all left outside. And now we're goin' to take care of you."

He allowed himself to be pressed back into the bed, but still his eyes went the rounds of the room. He saw Jack Chapel standing over him, his face grave with well-simulated trouble. He saw behind the woman the owner of the deep, bass voice. From the hand and the voice, he had expected a giant. Instead, he saw a stubby fellow, middle-aged, with a prodigious pair of shoulders and a not over large head set between them. His arms were very long, and the hands in exact proportion to the shoulders. Yet the small face which topped off this clumsy body was so filled with energy and penetration that Lou Alp forgot the lack of proportion.

Rattling at the fireplace at one side of the big bedroom was evidently a woman servant, and close to her stood a girl with sunny hair and earnest blue eyes, still darkened with the shadow of her recent fright. Her head was framed by the snow-crusted window beyond, and against that cold background the brown of her hair seemed golden and the olive skin took on tints of rich life. Upon Lou Alp she broke as light breaks upon deep darkness. Only the knee of Jack Chapel, striking his ribs, made him rouse himself enough to turn his glance.

"You'll have this room to yourself," the rancher was saying to Alp. "And you can take that smaller room next door, Mister Chandler. I suppose you'll want to be handy to your partner, eh? That way he can call you plumb easy."

He accepted the thanks which Jack Chapel proffered with a negligent wave of his massive arm.

"It ain't a thing," he said. "We're glad to have you. Lonely life we lead out here. Need company. Take Kate in particular, over there. She gets blue from bein' alone so much. Don't blame her. You try to cheer her up and I'll thank you for it."

The girl flushed and parted her lips to protest, but her father, laughing uproariously, drove her and the others out of the room.

"You boys make yourselves to home," he said from the door. "I'll see that you're kept quiet. If you need anything, just holler. We chow in about half an hour. We'll send up some broth and chicken for Mister Angus. S'long, boys."

He banged the door after him and went down the hall with a thunderous step.

The moment he was assured that there was no danger of being overheard, Lou Alp cried: "Did you see?"

His companion turned moodily. "See what?"

"The girl!"

"Huh?"

"The girl, blockhead!"

"Forget the girl."

Chapel began to pace the floor slowly. Once he stopped and kicked at the fire so that a shower of sparks went snapping up the chimney.

"Don't cuss women," said Alp, his face darkening. He was a good-looking fellow in his lean, dark way but, when he frowned, his face became savage to the point of venom.

"Cuss women?" said the other with a start. "Who cussed them? I didn't mean to."

"What a girl," sighed Alp. He looked hungrily at Chapel but, seeing that he could not confide in the larger man, he changed the topic reluctantly. "I guess we landed on our feet well enough."

"I guess we did."

"You don't seem terrible cheerful about it."

"Maybe I don't," growled Chapel.

"What's wrong?"

"They're clean," said Jack. He straightened, and took a deep breath. "They're clean!"

The sneak thief gathered the bed clothes a little closer around his throat. "But ain't . . . ain't you clean yourself, Jack? Wasn't it a frame that put you in jail?"

There was a sort of acid eagerness in his query, a bitter longing to hold his head as high as his companion's.

"I s'pose I'm all right," said the big man dubiously. "But I've been in jail, and I bring the scent of it with me. I've been in the shadow, and now I don't feel right. Understand?"

The thief merely stared. His mind came near enough to comprehension to be disturbed, but no more.

In the meantime Jack Chapel paced up and down the floor thoughtfully. "Did you notice their eyes?" he kept repeating "Nothing behind them. Did you notice their eyes? Straight as a string. You can look a mile into eyes like that. Nothing to hide in 'em."

"What have you got to hide?" asked Lou, rather viciously.

"Nothin' much. I'm just a supposed murderer and an uncaught highway robber. I'm a jail breaker and a bum. Outside of them little things, I guess the doctor'll give me a clean bill of health."

He began to laugh in an ugly manner. Then the laughter broke off short, and he stood beside the fire with his elbow resting on the mantel. Over his downcast face the light tossed up bursts of yellow and bursts of red. It made the lines deeper and the strong jaw became a cruel, dominant feature. Lou Alp, looking on, saw as from a distance there was some inner struggle going on in the man. But he did not speak. He could not even silently name the trouble to himself.

"Nobody'll ever get anything on you," he ventured at length.

"But what about myself?" cried Jack Chapel. He threw out his hand, but there was no oratorical suggestion in the gesture. It was simply the appeal of one seeking aid. "They took us in and didn't ask any questions. Why, if the old man had asked questions, he could have punched my story full of holes. But he's so honest, he doesn't bother himself doubting. Well. . . ." He stopped.

The sneak thief once more huddled deeper into the clothes. "Well?" he echoed faintly.

"Don't talk. I'm filled full of something . . . deviltry, I guess. I'm about ready to bust, Alp!"

V
"VICARIOUS VIRTUES"

A still small voice warned Lou Alp to be silent and let the mind of his companion work by itself. As one sees lights through a fog and cannot tell whether they mean ships or land or danger, so he stared at the gloomy face of Jack Chapel and wondered what passed behind his eyes. Secretly he rather despised Jack. Such exhibitions of emotion seemed ludicrous to Lou Alp.

Only one thing could extract any great display of his own inner self, and that was his overlord: fear. Yet, at the end of the chase when he found himself hopelessly lost, he could display the stoicism of an Indian. No third degree could make him betray the secrets of himself or of a confederate. Nothing under heaven could make him talk when he was helpless. The consequence was that each arrest was for a new and different crime, and not once had the police been able to link together a complete record of his doings from his testimony.

That day, for instance, up to the time when he was shot he was a coward, a trembling, rank coward. But the moment the bullet plowed through his flesh and made him helpless, he became brave. He had endured the torture of the ride with few murmurs, and only the new danger of Chapel's imminent desertion had shattered his nerves.

He was, indeed, the exact opposite of Chapel. To Lou Alp the exciting moment was the approach to this house where they knew no one, and where they might be betrayed and exposed. Once they were inside the place, helpless, hopelessly consigned to one course of action, fear departed from Lou Alp just as the fear which made the Indian flee in battle left him when he was in the hands of his enemy. On the other hand, Jack Chapel was perfectly at home meeting active danger, but this house closed around him like a new prison. The storm had been nothing except sound and fury, against which one could battle; but the silence of the house lay heavily on him. He was tormented by thoughts which could never enter the cramped forehead of Lou Alp. Under the sting of those thoughts he writhed. One room held the two men, but a world separated them.

In a few moments there was a tap at the door, which Jack Chapel answered. Katherine Moore entered with a steaming tray of food and her glance went pleasantly toward the wounded man, so that Lou Alp raised himself on one elbow, expectantly, and smiled back. Chapel took the tray.

"Thanks," he said. "But I'll take care of Lou."

The girl glanced at him in bewilderment, his tone had been so sharp. She apparently struggled against a touch of irritation, and then the feeling of a hostess overcame her scruple of anger.

"We'll see that he's comfortable," she suggested, "and then we'll both have to go down to dinner. Everything's about ready."

Chapel, on the way to the bed, turned back on her. "I'd better stay here till he's through. He might want something."

She paused, then, "We can leave the door open and hear him if he calls."

"If you don't mind, I'll bring a tray up for myself and stay with Lou."

This stark bluntness astonished Lou. It was almost as if Jack Chapel considered the girl an enemy. Katherine Moore continued to examine their strange guest in silent surprise. She said at last, laughing a little: "It will be a terrible disappointment to Dad. He's been congratulating himself on having someone to talk to. As a matter of fact, he's waiting for you now in the front room."

"Then I'll go," said Jack sullenly. He eyed his companion with a hopeless eye. "Get along without me, Lou?"

The Man Who Forgot

"Sure," said the other. "Sure, I can get along without you. 'S a matter of fact, I'd kind of like to be alone, not meanin' no offense to you, Jack."

Jack favored him with a brief glare and turned on his heel. The girl took the tray and placed it on the table beside the bed while she stacked pillows behind Alp. He watched the movements of her hands in a happy trance. Sometimes as she leaned her hair came close to his eyes, and the firelight was in it. She hummed a little, working over him, and the sound completed the charm for Lou. It seemed to him that he was swept outside of himself and carried away. Something was taken from him, and in its place a light and heady happiness began to run into him. She built up the pillows behind him; she took him under the shoulders and helped him to sit up higher; she put the tray across his knees.

"Are you comfortable?"

"Yes."

"Need anything more?"

"Nope."

"You must eat as well as you can. Mother says that's the thing for you. Have to build up lots of blood, you know, to take the place of what you lost."

Under his eyes she uncovered the dishes. The fragrance spoke strongly to the famished Lou Alp, and still he could not eat.

"Let me see you start," she was saying.

The sneak thief folded his hands and smiled vaguely at her. "Somehow, I can't," he murmured.

"It's the pain," nodded the girl. "I know how it works on one's appetite. You're mighty brave not to complain about it. Never a word all this time."

Lou Alp was dazed. He, brave? Since his earliest

Max Brand

recollection he had been kicked about by stronger men. Brave? One flash of fire in the eyes of another man had always made him sick at heart. Brave? He looked sadly at the girl, for she seemed so bright, so clean eyed, so beautiful, that the old rhythm ran into his head: "None but the brave deserve the fair."

"Oh," said Lou Alp, "I don't mind the pain, hardly. I'm kind of used to it, you know?"

A little impulse of sympathy moved the girl to lay her hand over his and press it warmly. "You're the sort of man my father likes," she declared, and her smile went through the eyes of Lou Alp and embraced his whole soul with warmth. Something akin to fear was in him and an enormous happiness wavered in front of him. A dream-happiness, and he trembled for fear the delicate illusion should vanish. The world-shattering truth came home to him. He, Lou Alp, was respected and admired as a brave man.

She was speaking of something else. What she said did not matter. The important thing was to keep her talking.

"Your friend is a little shaken up, I guess. Must have been an awful shock to hear that gun explode and see you fall!"

"Him? Shaken up?" gasped Lou Alp. He laughed faint and shrill. "Lady, you don't know him."

He observed that she was frowning thoughtfully, and began to regret what he had just said.

"He wasn't nervous?" she asked.

"He ain't got any nerves," declared Lou Alp.

"Hmm," said the girl.

Lou Alp gathered that in some cases she considered nerves a commendable possession. He felt that she was forming a strong prepossession

184

against Jack Chapel, and for some strange reason this fact pleased him greatly. Indeed, Lou Alp would gladly have destroyed her good opinion of every man in the world except one.

"I'll tell you how it is with Jack," he said. "He's hard. You see?"

"Ah?" said the girl.

It occurred to the thief that he must not go too far, for a suspicion of one would embrace them both.

"But he's square," added Lou. "He's terrible square in spite of the fact that he's hard."

"Terrible square is a good way to put it. He surely has a cold eye."

Lou Alp became alarmed. "You don't see under the surface," he declared. "In a pinch he's the best pal that ever stepped. No boastin', no braggin', but when the time comes he steps out and does his part. Steady as a rock, true as steel, honest as the day, that's the sort of a gent Jack is."

If he praised his friend, was he not removing the foundation of any suspicion she might have? Was he not, by allusion, strengthening his own safety and good repute in this household? "Birds of a feather," etc. Then he observed that readily as the girl had been prejudiced against Jack Chapel, she was equally ready to be prejudiced in his favor.

"Is he all those things? In fact, I guessed at part of them."

"Look at the way he done for me," went on Lou Alp. "It wasn't his fault I got shot. Then, when a lot of gents I know would of sat down and let me freeze to death, he starts right out to carry me and get me to some sort of help. Tears up his own shirt, makes a bandage, starts the long pull up that hill. . . ."

"Uphill?" echoed Kate Moore.

"Downhill, I mean. I got my tongue twisted. But he took me a long way. Most men would of buckled before they carried me half so far. Then he saw the house. Didn't leave me there in the snow to freeze while he went and got help, but he carried me right down, with his breath comin' more like a rasp every step. That's the sort of a gent. . . ."

His voice faltered and died away, for he looked more closely at her and saw that her eyes were on fire.

"It was a fine thing to do," declared the girl. "It was a fine thing. Sounds simple, but I know how hard it was. No wonder he was gruff after all that hard work. And he wanted to stay with you! Why, he has a lot of affection for you, Mister Angus."

"Him and me . . . pals," murmured Lou Alp.

He felt, miserably, that the light was gone for him. She stood up. "I'm going down, now. They'll be waiting for me."

"I'm sorry," said Lou.

"For what?"

"I'll explain later."

She went lightly out of the room, smiled back at him from the door, and was gone. A weight settled on the heart of the thief.

VI
"CHAPEL'S CHANGE OF HEART"

Alp had that surpassing mortification, the feeling that he had been defeated with his own weapons, that he had overreached himself. He had talked so hard to remove her dislike of Jack Chapel that he had overshot the mark and made her just as keen in an opposite direction. Before she left she had been looking at Lou through a film, and he knew perfectly well that on the other side of that film was the face of Jack Chapel.

He writhed in his bed and forgot the tray of food before him. If he had only dismissed Jack with a careless word of reassurance, but he had drawn a clear and strong portrait. Even now she would be downstairs studying the man. This thought led on to further misery, for Lou felt that there was much to be studied in Jack. If she once seriously turned her attention upon him it would be long before she finished the examination.

Turning restlessly in his bed, he saw that the last light of day was gone and the early winter evening, almost as black as night with the storm, had come. The window was white and sparkling with the crusted snow, but behind it was a field of dark. The fire, dying toward a bed of coals, no longer held the room in shadow but sent a steady glow over the opposite wall and kept the ceiling dim. It was a big, square, old-fashioned chamber with plenty of reach overhead, yet for all the solidity of the wall, the storm pried through crevices, perhaps around the window, and sent probing, cold fingers about the room. These icy touches of the air chilled the heart of the thief. He began to eat but without tasting his food.

Perhaps in all his life Alp had never seen a thing he desired to possess in another manner than taking it in his hands. The pinnacles of his life had been the moments when a weight of gold glided over the tips of his fingers, or when the cold surface of a rare jewel set the skin of his hand prickling with delight. He looked at those agile, lean, pale hands of his now with dumb lack of understanding. They were his weapons, his only weapons. They were his "open sesame" with which he set ajar the doors to his desires. They were his livelihood. They comprised his profundities and his subtleties. They were almost detached intelligences. They could glide over human skin without alarming the person he touched. They could gesture with the speed of a camera shutter, eluding the most trained and vigilant eye. The nerves of those sensitive finger tips informed him of the mechanism of a lock at the first turning of a knob. In the center of his palm a mind seemed to work.

Now Alp sat in his bed staring wistfully at the capable hands and realizing that the new thing which he desired was beyond the power of instruments ten times more gifted. In a word, it was something which could not be grasped, which eluded the usual methods of acquisition, which could not be bought or traded for, or stolen. Lifting his eyes again, Alp heard the storm go whining past the house, a lonely sound, and he felt here was music made to order for him.

What was the matter with him he did not know. Indeed, in all matters of emotion he was younger and less developed than a child. He knew fear from the ground up, but beyond that he was uneducated in matters of the soul. In a vague way he knew that the girl was at the root of his trouble; and yet in what way he could not tell. He had known other girls before. There was the one whom he had taken to the theater out of the slums, where she lived a soiled, small life bounded by the reaches of a dozen streets around one central place of noise, scrambling children, drunken men, scolding women. To that girl he had been a superior power, a voice of all knowledge. They had

had a few weeks of intimate companionship, but he soon tired of her and made it very plain to her that she had become an annoyance. The effect of this experience was the crushing of all her ideals and aspirations to lead a life of the better sort. If Alp had been told that he was connected with her failure, or even to blame for it, he would have been the most astonished man in Manhattan. But of such experiences his knowledge of women was built, and therefore it was no wonder that he found a new world in Katherine Moore. She possessed a combination which upset and startled him. He finally sank into broodings over his half finished tray of food.

How long he remained there without lifting his head he could not tell, but it must have been a long time. When he was roused by the entrance of Chapel, he felt as though he had been wakened from a deep sleep. He instantly straightened among his pillows. Into his thoughts of the moment before, the growing pain of his leg had entered, but now the pain was clean forgotten. An air of excitement had entered with the form of Chapel, and Alp, with his usual sensitiveness to changes, shared the unexpressed emotion.

It showed in the light, quick step of the larger man. It showed in the manner in which he walked swiftly back and forth through the room. Now and then he stopped in the midst of his pacing, and then went on again. Not gloomily, but as one rapt in a happy mood. Now and again a smile flashed on his lips and his eyes danced. The light murmur of his humming came to Alp in the bed. For some mysterious reason he connected that humming with the humming of the girl. He listened again.

It seemed to be the same tune. It went through the heart of Lou Alp with a bitter pang.

As a matter of fact for the first time in his life he was jealous. In his small soul each emotion was over-mastering. In his narrow heart every desire was a cloud-sweeping thing. Before Chapel spoke, the sneak thief knew that the girl was at the bottom of this sudden mood, just as he suddenly realized that she had been at the bottom of Chapel's previous depression.

Suddenly the larger man started and became aware of his companion. He hurried across to him and took the tray. He was filled with concern that his friend had been left alone so long. He apologized because he had not seen that the tray was still burdening his knees.

To all of this Lou listened in silence. He felt that something was beneath the rush of good feeling. It impressed him as penny alms thrown to a beggar by a newly-made millionaire. He had to cast a film over his eye to keep its coldness from being apparent. Chapel carried the tray out of the room and, when he had done that, he hurried back and sat down on the side of Lou's bed.

"Been lonely up here, old man?" he asked, and then without waiting for an answer: "Pretty clubby supper we had downstairs. These people are all to the good. Fine crowd. No dog. Plain, straight from the shoulder, don't turn corners when they talk. The old man is a world-beater outside of his stale yarns. His wife is a lady . . . a lady!"

He repeated the word with a singular softening of face and voice, but Lou Alp waited for something else, and presently it came.

"You dropped some pretty good words for me with the girl, didn't you?" he said, and his eyes were actually moist with gratitude. "Tell you what, Lou, you're such a silent gent that sometimes I hardly know how to make you out. About as noisy as a snake, not meaning that in an ugly way."

"'S all right," said Lou quietly.

He felt like a snake at that moment, and he would gladly have struck Jack Chapel with poison fangs.

"I made a fool of myself when I met her," went on Jack. He rocked back on the bed and gathered his knees within his strongly interlaced fingers. "But she dazed me a bit. I wasn't set for her, you see, and she made me feel that I'd been a skunk. You know how a good girl makes a gent feel?"

Lou did not know, but he kept his ignorance under a discreet veil. He knew only one thing now, and that was a raging hatred.

"I guess you made up for the way you met her later on," he suggested, and smiled for fear that he could not control a sneer.

Chapel flushed at the memory. "I dunno how it was," he said, nodding. "She seemed to sort of like me. Kept looking at me in a bright sort of way. You know?"

Alas, Lou Alp did know, and inwardly writhed in pain. "Go on," he said rather hoarsely.

"What's the matter?" asked Chapel.

"Matter? Nothin'. I've got a bit of a cold, that's all," replied Alp.

"Hmm!" murmured Chapel. Every now and then he forgot what he was about to say and sat smiling into space. "What a girl!" he said at length. "Anyway, she began talking after a while. Sat next to me at supper, you see? I ain't much at talking, and I had the handicap of knowing that I'd almost insulted her when we first met. But it don't take

any sense to talk to her. She leads the way and a
gent can just sort of follow along easy on the trail
she makes. She sure carried the lantern for me and
told me where to step. Right off she spilled out all
the nice things you said about me, partner. Mighty
decent of you, too. Fine of you to come out with a
bunch of stuff. Somehow," he paused, and his
glance flicked across the face of Lou with a shade
of its old coldness, "somehow I didn't expect anything like that out of you."

The sneak thief grunted.

"Well," said Chapel after a pause, in which he
appeared to be stumbling with incoherent mind
over the memories of that evening, "I wrote down
in red what you said about me, and I ain't going
to forget it. You're solid with me for life, Lou Alp."

Alp said nothing at all. Outside the window a
fresh gust of the storm went rattling and howling
by and, if he could have done so, Lou would gladly
have transformed his companion into a dead leaf
and thrown him to the mercies of that wind. He
began to ask questions and, though every answer
was a fresh probing of this new and acute inner
wound, he could not desist. He took a perverse
pleasure in torturing himself.

He learned that Kate and Jack had talked together a good deal during the supper. Old man
Moore had broken in for a few snatches of talk.
When he found that Jack had no pronounced po-
litical views, was not an expert cattleman, had no
intimate knowledge of guns and gunnery, he lost
interest. He confined his own share in the conversation to a few threadbare anecdotes at which the
family had faintly smiled, as at old, familiar faces,
and at which Jack had made an effort and had
been able to muster a laugh at the correct times.

"Kind of jokes my grandfather told," said Jack.

Then, after supper, they had drifted into a big, dark room with a fireplace of gigantic dimensions, filled with great logs that roared and snapped like musketry. Here Mr. Moore had fallen asleep in his easy-chair, Mrs. Moore had gone up to her room, and Jack and the girl had the time and the silence to themselves. He appeared to have made great progress in the direction of securing information. He knew the schools to which she had gone. He knew the names of her friends and particularly of one Ross Kirkpatrick, of whom Chapel spoke with a concentrated venom, which it was easy for Lou to understand. He was a wealthy mining man. He had built up his own fortune. He was an Eastern "college gent." Chapel referred to him with the polite endurance a Puritan would show for the devil. In the middle of this talk the door was suddenly flung open, and without any warning Katherine Moore flung into the room.

VII
"ENTER MARSHAL GAINES"

The rush of air from the opened door passed like a solemn sighing through the big room, but it did not need that sound to send the chill through Alp and Jack Chapel. The face of the girl was enough. She went straight to Chapel.

"Have you done anything wrong?" she whispered.

Why was all the concern for Jack Chapel? Was there not another man in the room? Through a haze of jealous agony Lou heard Jack answer: "In my time . . . things bad enough, I guess. Why?"

It was the grave and perfectly controlled voice which Alp envied. He was almost glad that the girl had not come so directly to him with that whispered alarm, for he knew that a sudden blanching of the face would have answered her. But Jack Chapel was quite controlled.

"I don't mean what you've done long ago, but lately . . . I haven't any time . . . a robbery. . . ."

There was a little pause—a heart-breaking little pause—and during that space of a second or so Alp stared intensely at the girl. She was without color. There seemed a cold film of blue shadow around her mouth, and her eyes were unnaturally dark and deep. There was accusation in the glance she fixed upon Chapel. It was rather a prayer for his good. It seemed impossible that Jack Chapel could lie to that face.

Then he heard Chapel's voice, rather stifled. "Robbery? I'll say this: that I've never taken a penny that I didn't feel was owing to me!"

Lou Alp sighed with relief. After all, had not the queer fool said something like this when he was about to commit the robbery? Had he not actually left part of the money behind, and the greater part at that? But he had no time for his own thoughts. There was a sobbing, small breath of relief from the girl.

"I knew . . . oh, I knew," she said. "But I had to ask you. And I had to . . . to tell you that Marshal Gaines is here, and that he's coming up to see you."

"Who?"

Lou could see that the name shook his companion.

"Marshal Gaines. But I'm so glad . . . so happy . . . that there's no trouble."

She was gone like a shadow and, as she went through the door, she looked back as she had looked at Lou once before, only this time the look was for Jack Chapel. And what a look it was! What a flash of eyes! What a tremulous smile! Bitterly Alp remembered that not once had she glanced at him this time. Her whole care was for Jack Chapel, and he, the wounded man, could fend for himself as best he might. His companion turned slowly toward the bed, smiling faintly.

"Who's Marshal Gaines?" asked Alp, leaning forward.

"She's got eyes like a man," was the singular answer of Chapel. "Eyes like a man's eyes. But her smiles! That's all woman. Have you noticed her smile, Lou?"

"Forget her smile," groaned the sneak thief. "Who's Marshal Gaines?"

"Marshal Gaines?" echoed Chapel carelessly. "Oh, he's just a gent that I know."

The words froze the trembling heart of the thief to motionlessness. "That you know?" he whispered at length. "Then, for heaven's sake, does he know you?"

"Better'n you do, a lot," replied Jack Chapel.

Lou Alp fell back in the pillows with a chalky face. "What does it mean?" he asked.

"It means we're done for," said Chapel.

"No, no, no," whined Lou. "No, no, no!" He began wringing his hands; then he stretched them out to Jack Chapel. "Gimme a lift out of the bed. I can't go back to the pen, pal. I can't go! Who got me into this? You did! Who tried to keep away from the whole thing? I did! You got to save me. You got to!"

"Shut up," said the larger man. He winced before this exhibition of cowardice and looked at the other with new eyes. "Is this the stuff you're made of? Shut up, or she'll hear you!"

"I don't care," gasped Alp. "Gimme a lift to the window. I can stand the drop to the ground. There's snow on it and it'll break the fall. Then, my leg's good enough. Gimme a help and I can wiggle along. I'll get away from this infernal trap."

"Shut up, will you?" snapped Chapel. "I got you into this. I'd get you out if I could, but I can't. Now stop whining. I told you who the gent is. It's Marshal Gaines. There's no hope."

"None?"

"None!"

A singular change came over Alp. He arranged the pillows behind his back. His natural color returned. "Pass me the makings, will you?" he demanded. "I thought there was a show but, if there ain't, let's see what the music's like."

The sudden change of front made Chapel blink. "You've got something, Lou," he admitted admiringly. He himself was gray about the mouth, and his jaw was set.

"Tell me about Gaines."

"It'd take all the rest of the night. I'll tell you this much. If I knew that Gaines was out on my trail, I'd stop runnin'. I'd turn around and go in and give myself up to him to save a lot of trouble for both him and me. That's the sort he is. He's so good that, if I had two guns and he didn't have nothin' but a knife, I'd throw up my hands and let him take me. Why, man, I ain't a gunfighter, and Gaines is a devil. He took 'Sandy' Crew. He took Gus Landers. He killed Peters and Galbright, and . . . I could reel 'em off by the yard. That's Gaines."

"Well," sighed the sneak thief, "it's something to

be taken by a bird like that. Thing that makes me sore is to be nabbed by some greasy cheap flatty, like's happened to me. Well, lead on your man-eater and let's have a look at his teeth."

He twisted his cigarette deftly into shape, lighted a match, and waited with a steady hand for the sulfur to burn away. Then he lighted his smoke and inhaled a deep breath.

"That's nerve," admitted Chapel, and brushed the perspiration from his own forehead. "That's nerve a-plenty. Here they come."

They heard the rhythm of footfalls coming un-hurriedly up the stairs. Once, and once only, the eyes of the sneak thief darkened as he glanced toward the window. Then his glance went back to the face of Chapel and lingered there with a hun-gry content. In this crisis he felt his superiority. The larger man was going through a torture.

"The girl," asked Chapel. "What'll she think?"

"Nothing," said Lou coldly. "After a day or two she'll brush us out of her mind. No trouble at all when they see they've made a mistake. Girls can forget anything."

"Do you think so?" said Jack through his teeth. "But not this girl. She'll remember. Lou, what'll we get for this?"

"Oh, about five more years for you, same for me, maybe, or less seeing you started everything and simply took me along."

"Five and ten . . . fifteen . . . forty-one," said the other, rather incoherently. "Too long! She. . . ."

He stopped, for the knob of the door turned slowly, then opened and Moore entered with a man behind him. Lou Alp prepared himself for a shock meeting the eye of this savage marshal, this man so terrible that even Jack Chapel gave up at

the mere thought of him. But what he saw was a
dusty little man with misty, long-distance eyes. He
carried his hat in an apologetic manner in both
hands, fingering the brim as though he felt that he
was out of place, but Lou was fascinated by the
action of those nervous broken hands. He recognized in them a quality of deft and easy precision.

"Here they are, Marshal," said Moore. "Here's
Jack Chandler and his partner, Louis Angus. Jack
and Lou, here's Marshal Gaines, my old friend. He
wants to talk to you boys. There's been an outrage.
Holdup down the valley. Thirty-five hundred dollars walked off by a holdup artist. Between you
and me, Marshal, I don't see what good this talk
will do you. That holdup was worked by one gent.
Here's two of 'em."

The marshal nodded. He stepped from behind
Moore and glanced at Chapel. Alp braced himself
for the shock of the recognition, the flash of steel,
as the marshal covered his man. He was stunned
by the difference between his expectation and
what actually happened. The marshal passed
Chapel over with a glance and turned at once to
Lou Alp, lying there helpless in the bed. It was em-
barrassing. Alp blinked and then smoothed his
face to a smile.

"How are you, Marshal," he said. It was always
a policy of his to be ingratiating with police. And
here was simply a new form of flattery.

"I'm doin' fairly well," said the marshal, advanc-
ing as far as the foot of the bed. "Got a touch of
rheumatism, though. Settled in my left hip a couple of years ago and I ain't much in the saddle
when these cold snaps come on."

"Oh, you'll do well enough," boomed Moore
from the background.

"Sorry to bother you boys," went on the marshal, "but I got to look over the strangers in these parts. I'd be sayin' that you're kind of new around here, Mister Angus?"

"Kind of," admitted Alp.

He observed a spark that came up behind the eye of the marshal, and the spark grew into a small and hungry fire. It made Alp feel distinctly ill at ease. The marshal's form was growing rapidly in his eyes.

"Well," said the marshal, "it ain't often that we get visitors around here in the cold spells. How long you think of staying on, partner?"

It occurred suddenly to Lou Alp that there was a double meaning in what the marshal was saying. He was addressing to the thief words apparently quite innocent in the ears of the other people in the room, but to Lou they might mean many things. At least he surmised that double meaning, and he decided to try out his theory.

"I dunno," he declared. "Maybe a month. Maybe a year. Maybe more."

The marshal shook his head. "I dunno," he said, "but I kind of feel maybe you're makin' a mistake. Take a gun wound like that, and it don't stand up none too well in stormy weather. I know."

Lou Alp shifted his eyes to the puzzled face of Jack Chapel. Plainly his companion was bewildered by this friendly dialogue and was waiting for the denouement.

"Know what I'd do if I was you?" went on the marshal.

"Well?" asked Alp seriously.

"I'd climb on a hoss as soon as that wound would let me and get away from here. I'd get down to some warmer climate. Otherwise you'll find rheumatism settlin' in your leg and making you lame, maybe for the rest of your life. Understand?"

"Maybe I do," said Lou, and his eyes grew larger. "Maybe I do."

"You look like an intelligent sort," said the marshal carelessly. "I wouldn't give that advice to everybody. Take your friend . . . Chandler"—and he turned to Chapel and looked him over—"if he had a wound like that in the leg, I'd leave it to his blood and good bones to bring him through safe and sound, even up here in the winter and in the mountains. Fact is, seems to me that some gents is all cut out for mountain life, winter or summer . . . and some ain't."

This statement of Gaines's was prompted by the fact that he had learned of Chapel's innocence of the crime with which he had been charged through letters from the prison authorities. The real murderer had confessed. Chapel understood.

Moore began to laugh thunderously. "There you go on your rheumatics," he said. "Get you on that and they ain't any means of pryin' you loose from it. Come on downstairs and have a drink, Gaines. I guess you've talked to these boys long enough?"

"Sure. I guess I have." The glance of the marshal went back and dwelt gently upon the face of Alp. The latter changed color. "I'm sure I have," continued the marshal.

"And you don't no ways think that they took the coin?" chuckled Moore.

"Nope. What I'm really lookin' for, Moore, is somebody that thought the big boss owed him some money, about thirty-five hundred of it. Well, glad to've met you boys. S'long."

Without another word he was gone. Chapel turned to Lou with a white face.

"He didn't know you, after all," said Alp cheerily. "Ain't that a load off? He didn't know you, the batty-eyed old fool. He missed you clean."

"He knew me," said Jack, "better'n you do. Why, three years ago I went on a hunting trip with the marshal. Not only knows me, but he knows that I ought to be in prison on a charge of murder."

"He can't know that. He'd . . . " began Alp.

"But he does. I got a letter from him while I was there."

"Then he's gone down to frame us!"

"That's not his way. And he seemed to take a fancy to you, Lou."

"You fool! Didn't you hear him plain as day tell me to get out of this country as soon as I could ride a hoss, and stay out?"

"You mean?"

"I mean that he knowed me. Heaven knows how. He's giving you a chance to make good, but he's letting me go to the devil."

VIII
"LOUIS'S LETTER"

However incredible the miracle was, yet it happened. Not only did the marshal leave the house of Moore, but he never returned. Afterward Lou and Jack heard frequent reports. The marshal let it be known throughout the countryside that he was going to get the daring outlaw or bust in the attempt. It was reported that he had brought several clues into the wind, and it was known that on two occasions he had made long rides through the mountains. But still the perpetrator of the outrage remained undiscovered.

What it was that urged the marshal toward this elaborate camouflage, Lou and Jack did not know, unless indeed it was that out of old friendship he had determined to give Jack another chance. One of the few failures which the marshal had ever made was being scored in this case, and people of the mountains wondered at it. Sheriff Meigs took a hand and followed separate clues, but those clues never brought him to the house of Moore, and Lou and Jack were safe.

The days went on with Alp improving by leaps and bounds. By the end of the first week the wound was only a red blur on the surface of the skin. In ten days he had taken his first careful step; within a fortnight he and Chapel were thinking of their departure.

Yet those days of recovery were by no means altogether happy days for Lou Alp. It was a period of storm and stress, with the storm composed of small things no louder than the laughter of a girl or the fall of a woman's foot. After that first day he saw the hopelessness of hope. Every morning, when he wakened, he made a firm resolve that that day he would bar her out of his heart. But before he had even seen her, at the first sound of her step or her voice, the hard lines in which he had set his face in preparation for the meeting dissolved, and invariably he smiled when he saw her.

If she had been oblivious of him, it would have been easier, but she paid him every attention. In fact, the girl and Jack Chapel were meeting, as it were, over his body. His welfare and the progress of his healing wound composed a topic which apparently possessed undying interest for them. He used to lie in his bed and read through the hypocritical warmth with which they made their inquiries. Always his condition was the starting point, and always the talk ended in something a thousand miles removed from him. Usually it brought both the talkers out of the room, and then a time of misery would begin for Lou Alp.

All day long, while he was bedridden, he found himself listening with terrific concentration for all sounds of life that passed through the walls of his room. When his door was left open, it was a double trial. Sometimes he could hear them talking, their voices reduced to an echoing murmur up the long hall. Sometimes the piano tinkled directly beneath him. Or again, and this more and more often, he caught the sound of their singing. They had learned some two-part songs. Jack Chapel had a strong, somewhat rough baritone, and the girl's voice was a light, sweet-toned soprano. It seemed that his strength covered the meagerness of her voice, and her quality smoothed the harshness of the man. The result was altogether pleasant. Lou Alp admitted that fact with the cruel and cold justice which had come to temper his mind more and more since the first day. But all things else were nothing compared to the sound of the girl's laughter. He could almost hear that even when the door was closed. He had a seventh sense for it. He could feel the rhythm of the sound before it was audible to his ear. He could tell it by a sudden quickening of the pulse and falling of the heart. Yet it was a mellow laughter, though it went through the heart of Lou Alp like a sword of fire.

It is very bad for a man to think of himself during any prolonged time. It is exceedingly evil for a man to set his heart on one desire, while his body is helpless to advance him toward his wish. A prisoner goes mad longing for green leaves. Yet the green may be on the other side of the wall, and half an hour in the sun would make him sick of the open day. Perhaps it is not the green of the leaves nor the yellow of the sun so much as the very thickness of the wall that torments the prisoner. Under ordinary conditions Lou would no doubt have cast the thought of the girl away or have pushed the memory of her into an obscure pain, recurring now and then.

Yet, perhaps, what a man once feels truly, he can never forget. Lou Alp was truly in love. Somewhere in that small, mean soul was fuel which fed the flame until it burned as brightly, as intensely as any noble passion in the heart of a noble man. The flame was too much for Lou. It crumbled that shell of a man. It tormented him. If he had been a poet, he could have translated his suffering into song and found relief. Or if he had been strong in manhood, he could have poured the truth frankly before the girl, and then roused himself with a muscular effort.

There was not a strong muscle in the body of Lou Alp. There was not a strong thought in his brain. She became to him what the drug is to the famished dope addict. He was in a fever, and the sight of her face was snow on his brow; his mind was filled with noises, and the sound of her voice brought him blessed peace. She fed the fire and she stacked it. If at times he blessed her as a devotee blesses his patron saint, at other times he writhed on his bed and cursed her with equal fervor.

There were not two possibilities. In the end there was only one result, and that result was a consuming, a devout hatred for Jack Chapel. Not that he really looked forward to winning the girl for himself if he could push Jack out of the way, but every time the girl smiled on Jack it cost Lou a pang, which he swore his companion should repay. Every time he heard them singing, every time the girl laughed in a high-hearted happiness, then Lou turned his face to the wall and begged God for a chance to blast this man, body and soul.

He did not reason on to final results. He only knew that Jack Chapel caused him pain, and therefore he wished to destroy the man. If it could be viewed abstractly, this devilish passion of Lou Alp's, was it not strange that such a girl as Katherine Moore, who had never in her life done as much evil as would give shading to a single day of an average man, was it not strange that she should have been the cause of such black viciousness?

She did not guess it, and Jack Chapel did not guess it. Once the sneak thief had determined that in some way or another he would destroy his former friend, he masked his purpose with truly fiendish cunning. At the very moment when he was closing his mind and his heart to all gentleness, he appeared to open his whole life to Jack. He told him stories of his childhood, and the dark, vicious days in the streets of Manhattan. He told him of adventures, some mean and all exciting. He told him things which would have caused an average man to turn away in loathing, but Jack was not average. He had on occasion called this fellow "partner," and in his Western eyes that was a sacred word, no more capable of recall than the fire of heaven. Moreover, a confession always subtly implies a reform and a change. Indeed, it is this hope of making the world believe him a better man or a man capable of better things, if he has the chance, that makes the suspected murderer make a clean breast of his past and sign his own death warrant. He will sign the paper that sends him to the gallows in the hope that his confession will draw one word of regret, one word of sympathy.

In this case the sneak thief was correct in his deductions. Jack answered the confidences of Lou with confessions of his own, and the two men seemed drawing close toward a true friendship. There was one bitterly sweet result of that. The more Lou wormed himself close to Jack, the more often the girl was with Lou. And to the man who is hungry, both the alms of charity and the alms of scorn are welcome. Lou accepted her presence with a deep joy and, knowing that her presence was due to Jack, he cursed Jack for it.

In the end, if he could have thought of no better way, Lou Alp would have stuck a knife into the back of Jack Chapel while his friend slept. But it did not turn out so. There was a better way, and Lou found it.

He had been searching his mind for days and days, hunting for some weapon which would strike down the larger man. One thing had repeatedly come home to him. The past of Jack, if it were known, would come like a wave and snatch him away to the prison as it withdrew. But if his prison record were known, the same danger that threatened one of them would threaten the other. Lou Alp was wanted, hardly less than Jack Chapel. He must find something that would overwhelm Chapel without scratching so much as a finger of the hand of he who struck him. Otherwise where was the satisfaction? Where would be the deep after-joy of seeing the girl in her despair, and re-

member her happiness of the past and all the pain
which she had poured into his brain?

And then it came to him. It was the robbery. In
that, at least, he had had no hand. Why could not
that be worked? There was the lightning which he
could direct at Chapel without singeing his own
skin.

Suppose, therefore, that someone were to
search the house for evidence of that crime. He
would find thirty-five hundred dollars in the bedroom which Chapel now occupied, for Alp had insisted that he keep all the money until they were
both well clear of the house. Also, the searcher
would find the two revolvers which Jack had taken
from the guards. Was not that proof enough?

But suppose that they then asked if he, Lou Alp,
were not mixed up in this crime? Very easily answered! He had been through the mountains with
Jack Chapel. He had met the man accidentally and
they had struck up a friendship without asking
about the past. On the trip they had stopped at a
village. There they had heard about the coming of
the payroll. The next day Jack had disappeared.
Lou waited for his return. Late in the afternoon
he had come, showing signs of having covered a
long distance in a short time. They had gone on
together in the storm. Then the accidental shooting occurred.

Or make it even stronger. After the return of his
companion, Lou protested against the robbery in
the first place and against keeping the money in
the second. He argued violently. Jack Chapel flew
into a rage, offered him part of the money for his
silence, was refused, and then deliberately drew
his revolver and shot down the unoffending Lou
whose passion for law and order had drawn him

to this dangerous pass. Thinking of this portion of the story, Alp felt tears of self-sympathy rise in his eyes. There he was on the ground, bleeding. Compassion seized the murderous robber as he saw his companion and late friend lying there in the snow. He felt remorse. He lifted the inert body. He carried his friend to the house of Moore and for a long time, filled with gratitude for that last act of grace, Lou refused to give the information. But at last the truth must be told, and he tells it. Surely that story would be smooth enough. Besides he would perfect it before it became necessary to tell it to the officer of the law.

To whom should he send the information? Not to Marshal Gaines, but rather to Sheriff Jesse Meigs who was the known rival of the marshal in that district, and who would consider it a choice morsel if he could take the man who had escaped the hands of the celebrated marshal. The plan had more and more good points which gradually unrolled themselves before the calm eyes of Lou Alp. There would not even be a whispered reproach from Jack Chapel until Jack was helpless in the hands of the law. He would make a bargain with the sheriff that his evidence should not be used against Jack until the last moment. In the meantime he would slip away and disappear, leaving behind him the money and the guns, sufficient evidence in itself to send Jack to prison for highway robbery, if not to bring out a lynching party to hang him up by the neck. The malice of Alp went even as far as this. Necessarily so, for if Jack survived, the day of reckoning sooner or later would come.

Yet for several reasons he decided to tell the marshal only enough to hint at the crime, only enough to bring the dogs of the law on the traces of Chapel. He wrote briefly:

> **If you want to find the dope on the holdup that fooled Marshal Gaines, come to Moore's house and look in the room where Jack Chandler sleeps. You'll find thirty-five hundred bucks and two guns.**

He addressed the envelope, writing the address as he had done the note with his left hand, for Jack Chapel knew his writing. Using the cane which Kate Moore had given him, he hobbled slowly down the stairs and then out the front door and into the wilderness of shining snow outside. It was only fifty feet to the road, and by the road was the mail box. He lifted the iron flap and dropped in the letter.

IX
"LEADEN SOLDIER"

The rest of that day passed smoothly. There was only one real task for Lou Alp, and that was to exaggerate his limp. For, of course, when his leg was entirely healed, he and Jack Chapel must go on together. Now it was above all things necessary that he keep Jack in the house until that letter reached the sheriff and brought the man of the law to the house of Roger Moore. How long it would require for that he had not been able exactly to deduce, but he imagined that at least two full days would be required, unless the sheriff left the town as soon as the letter reached him and rode at full speed with his men.

That thought gave Lou another qualm. He should have warned the sheriff that Jack Chapel was a dangerous man, that there might be more than one man's handful of work in taking him. He had prepared to submit meekly enough to the marshal, but that was because he knew Gaines. Driven to the wall, and particularly now that he had so much to hope from life, Jack Chapel would probably fight like a devil incarnate.

The worry of it held on into the night for Lou Alp. In the afternoon he had retired to his room, pretending a feverish aching in his leg. In reality his mind was on fire with doubts, and he sat before the fire which Jack Chapel had built for him and kept rubbing his hands. The rest of his body was warm, but his hands were moist and cold always these days. A continual tremor possessed them. This afternoon he heard much noise and bustling in the house. There was, to Lou, an appearance of stealth about the noise, but he laid that feeling to his uneasy nerves. Everyone in the house was smiling. Everyone seemed to have bright and misty eyes. Everyone had a loud voice and a gay manner. There was a sort of reckless happiness, so strong that it pervaded the atmosphere as keenly as the cold.

Lou Alp canted an ear toward these sounds and regarded them with keen suspicion. It even occurred to him that all the rejoicing was because the girl and Jack Chapel had let the others know of their engagement, and the rest of the house had kept the secret well from him. Why? Did they guess how he felt about Kate Moore? Had they penetrated beneath his bright, shifting glances? Was that the reason for their singular gentleness this day, and the kindliness of their eyes? The thought put a whip upon him and made him writhe.

Supper that night was a trial indeed. The merriment, which had gone ringing up and down the halls all day and which had seemed to cover itself stealthily, now burst out full-fledged. Roger Moore dug out his oldest and most musty stories. Mrs. Moore wore a flush in either cheek which made her seem ten years younger and turned her white hair into a mockery. Jack Chapel was continually laughing with everybody, at everybody. Once he slapped Lou on the back with a force that made the teeth of the sneak thief rattle. Joy was closed upon the world, and Lou Alp shuddered in its presence.

In some manner he got through that nightmare meal and was in his room again. He stirred the embers of his fire and roused it with fresh wood. There he sat, nodding over his plans until very late. Just after supper everyone downstairs had gathered in the big front room and Jack Chapel and Kate Moore came up to plead with him and bring him down.

"Don't you know what day it is?" they asked in one voice.

He stared at them with blank eyes.

"He doesn't know!" murmured Kate Moore to Jack Chapel, and then they laughed together musically, idiotically.

It seemed to Lou Alp that they were flaunting their joy in his face to torture him with it. Finally they gave up their pleading, cast him a word of commiseration for his leg like alms thrown to a dog, and were gone off down the hall. Hardly had the door closed on them when he caught the muffled peal of their laughter.

Fools!

Later still, while the fire was dying down, he thought that steps went up and down the hall and paused at his door. He thought he heard guarded whispers. His mind was still clear enough and strong enough to dismiss such absurd conjectures, and finally, quite late at night, he went to bed and was instantly asleep.

Dreams haunted him. People seemed to come to him. Once his eyes snapped open and he could have sworn that there had been someone leaning over him. He could almost have sworn, from the jumping of his heart and the tingling of his skin, that there was someone in the room at that very instant. He dismissed the illusion. What earthly reason could there be for stalking him?

When he wakened naturally after such a disturbed sleep, it was quite late. He lay looking up to the lofty ceiling. There was a fresh scent in the room, as if the window had been left wide open and the odor of evergreens had blown into the chamber. Lou Alp was no passionate lover of fresh air, and he certainly was never guilty of leaving the window open in winter. Then he was aware that he was hungry, and he hunched himself up in the bed, preparatory to getting up. Yet he did not slip from beneath the covers. He remained there with his elbows propping him and blinking.

For this was what he saw. On either side of the tall window leaned a great fir branch. From the mantelpiece over the fireplace dangled a long woman's stocking, bulged out of shape by its contents. On the table beside the bed there was a scattering of parcels large and small, wrapped in red paper and tied with gaudy green ribbon.

Lou Alp sat slowly erect in the bed. Then, like a

sleepwalker, he got carefully out of bed and walked across the floor, in bare feet which did not feel the cold. He took the long stocking from its hook. He opened it and drew forth the contents, one by one. A bag of sugar candies, red, green, yellow, purple, blue; a necktie of gaudy stripe; some animal cakes, gilded with the colors of life; and on and on, his hand reached down the bag until he found a card and drew it out.

A happy, happy Christmas to the man who forgot.

The card fluttered from his hand, and falling into the fireplace began to blacken with the heat of the dying embers. And yet he turned again to the stocking and continued to draw out the silly knickknacks. A jumping jack which squawked foolishly when one pressed the button.

They had given him the gifts they would give a child in the house. Why? Because he did not know? Yet he seemed to expect something different, something more, and finally, at the very bottom of the stocking, his reaching fingers closed over the last thing. He knew it before he drew it out, and the form of Lou Alp shook, and his face whitened.

At length he let the stocking fall to the floor and there in his hand was a leaden soldier with red coat and stiff back, a painted musket at his side. Upon this Lou Alp gazed with a sort of horror, and raising his hand slowly he brushed numb fingers across his forehead. He had forgotten, but now it came back to him, so many things out of the past. But how had they known about the lead soldiers which in the brief time of his child life at home had been an inevitable part of every Christmas stocking? For some reason it humbled him.

He went with the lead soldier still clutched in his hand and opened the packages on the table, the largest first. It was a fleece-lined leather coat with a card scrawled upon in a great, rough hand: **"To Lou from Roger Moore. Good luck."**

Then a bundle of home-knitted socks so soft and woolly that they crunched up in his hand and warmed his numb finger tips. **"To Lou from Mary Moore."**

Then a big box of cigarettes, his own favorite brand of tailor-mades. **"To Lou from Kate."**

Then a heavy little package, the smallest of them all. The heavy leather tore its own way out of the flimsy wrappings of its own accord. Lou took out of the holster a neat little automatic, such a gun as he had often praised to Jack Chapel as the king of weapons, rather than one of these clumsy, wrist-breaking .45s. It came apart under his deft fingers, and was assembled again. A perfect weapon!

Then the card: **"To my partner, Lou."**

No name to that. It came suddenly home to him that no name was needed, for probably Jack Chapel had never applied the term "partner" to any other man. Lou Alp, dry-throated, laid the weapon carefully down on the table. He took up the little case of cartridges and loaded the gun with familiar swiftness.

There is a personality in weapons. The little automatic was particularly fitted for the sneak thief. One would expect to find it on him, and certainly he had skill in its use. Many a dick in Manhattan could have testified that Lou, in spite of his cowardice, when pressed to the wall could fight with

tigerish ferocity. For there is nothing quite so terrible as the cornered coward. Under the surface
lay the claws, under the velvet touch the steel.

Laying aside the loaded weapon, he sank down
on the side of the bed. The chilly wind, prying
through the crevices of the room, set him shud-
dering as though with an ague, but Lou Alp paid
no heed to it. His face was buried in his hands,
and in one hand was the leaden soldier.

In that manner Jack Chapel found him sitting
when, a little later, he opened the door softly. He
shut it again, just as silently. The girl behind met
him with a glance of eager curiosity when he
turned away. Jack Chapel laid a finger against his
lips, and then whispered: "Hush! He's remembering."

"Poor fellow," said the girl, and her eyes misted.

"Poor devil," said Jack Chapel.

They had between them such a great happiness
that they felt they could give alms to all the world
and still have plenty left.

X
"A MAN WHO FORGOT CHRISTMAS"

Who knows what might have happened if Lou
Alp had heard nothing of what they said? But he
heard. The closing of the door, softly as it was
done, had roused him as whisper rouses a cat. Instantly he was beside the door, on his knees, and
this was what he heard:

"Poor fellow!"

"Poor devil!"

There is no man so low as to accept pity from a
successful rival. If a great tide of tenderness had

been rising in the heart of Lou Alp the moment before, it was now suddenly checked. He remembered that a treasure remained to Jack Chapel. The pity had a string to it that sent him reeling and gasping back into the room, as though a bullet had plowed through his vitals. He remained there in a silent frenzy, biting his hands, beating at his face.

Who has seen the frantic contortions of the cat that, playing with the mouse, loses the little creature? For such was the fury of Lou Alp. The fact that he despised himself for still hating Jack Chapel did not matter, it only intensified the hatred.

Going down for breakfast a little later, he found the old Negro servant hobbling up in the opposite direction. Lou nodded to him, and shrank aside, for he had an almost physical aversion for Negroes. But there was a great red-lipped smile, a flash of rolling eyes, and out of a deep throat the greeting: "Merry Christmas!"

The words came back from the lips of Lou Alp, but they came as a harsh and hardly whispered echo: "Merry Christmas."

That chance meeting prepared him for what was to follow. In the dining room the people were already gathering. Mrs. Moore had on a new dress and, from the manner in which she kept looking down at it and then across at her daughter, it was plain who had made the gift.

The bald head of Roger Moore was covered by a black silk skull cap which he touched now and then, as one will handle a novelty. But what Lou chiefly saw was the picture of Kate Moore and Jack Chapel in the corner. They were whispering together. They were almost holding each other's hands. Lou, shocked with surprise, realized that the parents of the girl must know what had been going on, that they actually approved of her affection for this unknown fellow, this chance acquaintance.

In the meantime all eyes had whipped across in his direction the moment he put foot through the door. There was a chorus of greetings.

"I dunno what to say," muttered Lou Alp.

"You don't have to say a thing."

"I forgot. . . ."

What a joyous laugh there was.

"The best joke I ever heard," cried Roger Moore in his enormous voice. "A man who forgot Christmas!"

The words remained ringing in the ears of Lou Alp all during the breakfast, all during the rest of the day. But, after all, what was Christmas? Weren't there other holidays? What about Washington's Birthday? What about New Year's? Certainly all those were holidays which closed banks and stores with as much definiteness as any Christmas that had ever happened. Yet no one would laugh at him for forgetting such days. And here was Roger Moore with a brand-new jest added to his stale collection, happy as a child with a new toy.

"Don't apologize," the old fellow said. "You made us all a present, without knowing it. I wouldn't have missed this for a year of life!"

Wherein was the day different? For it was different. It came tinglingly to Lou Alp himself. This was the one day in the year when the world forgot its taking and gave itself up to giving. Very strange! People gave things away and were happier because of the giving.

Here he sat, the sole member of that household who had not given away valuable things, and yet all the rest were happy and he was wrapped in gloom. It made him shake his head. How had it all begun, this giving away? Out of his childhood the old story came slowly back to him, the stable, the manger, and Mary with the child. The child who grew to manhood and gave everything and took nothing. The one perfect type of the selfless man, who lived for others and who died for others.

And what was the result of this giving, this senseless outpouring of effort? Buildings erected in His name around the world, and myriads carrying His thought and one day each year set aside for giving in some small measure as He had given. The thought burdened and bewildered Lou Alp who had lived with his hand in the pockets of others. These people had given, and yet they acted as if they had received. Kate Moore, Jack Chapel, Mrs. Moore, Roger Moore, they all met him with open eyes and open hearts as though he had conferred a favor on each by his mute acceptances.

A bee buzzing in a small, closed room fills it with sound to bursting, and one large thought crammed the narrow brain of Lou Alp until it reeled. The thought kept him occupied all that day. Automatically he spoke, answered questions, smiled vaguely, and lived on the edge of the happiness which flushed the others and raised their voices. Nothing mattered. When the cook dropped the platter and spoiled the dinner set, there was only laughter from Roger Moore, and a smiling shake of the head from Mrs. Moore. When a gust of snow rushed through an opened window and soaked the carpet, there was an outburst of merriment, and everyone set about repairing the damage.

One would have thought that the howling wind was the voice of a friend, to see these people and to hear them. One would have thought that each of them sat in expectation of a legacy. And was there not, perhaps, a legacy left them by that man who had died two thousand years before? Again the thought appalled Lou Alp.

They were seated around the dinner table. Roger Moore was at the head, Mrs. Moore at the foot, with her cheeks roses and her hair whiter than ever by contrast. Lou Alp sat at one side, and Jack Chapel and Kate Moore at the other. It was a large table, so heaped with food that the five people seemed utterly inadequate. The mountain of bittersweet in the center helped to separate one from another, so that Lou felt that a great distance lay between him and the two opposite.

Things came and went, plates were passed before him, and he ate mechanically, hardly tasting what he touched. Roger Moore was filling his glass with wine, a rare treat in the mountains.

"Watery stuff," Roger Moore said, "but it's sort of in style this time of year."

Lou Alp did not hear or, if he heard, he did not understand. For the great thought was still rising and ebbing through his mind and crowding all other things out. All other things except the loveliness of Kate Moore.

How beautiful she was! There was about her a perishable quality. One might have wished that she be transmuted to marble and color, so that she could neither grow old nor die. No, death was not so much to be dreaded as the withering years.

Lou Alp attempted to push the thought of her

beauty away by remembering what time accomplished. There was Belle Samson of Fourth Street near the Bowery. Belle at nineteen had been ravishing. The sort of girl people turned to look at and go on, half smiling and half sad. But Belle married Gandil, the saloon keeper, and at twenty-five her color was gone, the luster fled from her hair, her shoulders bowed, her fingers stubby. Still pretty, but without that other thing, that quality of a different world which stops the minds of men.

He could enumerate others. And then he squinted at Kate Moore across the table. It made no difference. He tried to dim those eyes with time. He tried to paint in the wrinkles on the brow and by the mouth. He tried to straighten the curve of the lips. But, when he had finished the picture which fifteen years would make of her, his hand fell away from the picture and his eyes saw the truth. No matter what she became, she would always remain, to him who loved her, what she was at this time. As if these young years alone truly expressed the soul within her. Afterward the husk of the body changed, but the spirit of beauty remained. Into the dark mind of the sneak thief the gentle thought made way, that love is an immortalizer, that time cannot undo that marvelous embalming.

XI
"THE GREATEST GIFT"

It had been an unfinished beauty, the face of Kate Moore, when he first saw her on the day of the shooting and the robbery. There had been lacking some master touch, and his weak hand had aspired, all unknowing, to supply the missing thing. But now the picture was completed. The room was lighted. There was nothing more to be wished. Every time she turned to Jack Chapel, the sneak thief remembered his first aspiration and knew that another hand had done what his own could not accomplish. Something as dry as soot choked him with hatred for Chapel.

They had come to mince pie and plum pudding when a knock was heard at the front door. The old Negro with a yellow face appeared at one of the two doors leading from the hall to the dining room, his lips parted to speak. He did not come to speech, for a hand brushed him roughly to one side and a big man, armed, stood in the doorway.

Lou Alp glanced to the other door. Immediately it was filled by a second man. Likewise he was tall and he was armed. There needed only one glance at either of them to know that these were trained man-hunters. The face of Roger Moore, starting up from his chair, would have supplied the information.

He choked down his morsel of pudding. "What the devil, Sheriff . . . ?"

The tall man who had first appeared raised his hand and took off his hat, which up to that time he had apparently forgotten.

"Maybe I look like the devil to you, Roger," he said genially, "and I'm a pile sorry that I have to break in on a party like this. I'll tell you how it is. I've got a little job to do here, and I've got to see that you folks all stay in your places while the job is bein' done. They ain't goin' to be no unpleasantness I hope. Jest you go right on eatin'. And then I'll slope and there you are. But don't nobody, man or woman, leave his chair till I get back!"

He disappeared, and a third man stepped up to fill the vacant place at the door. Neither he nor the other man offered a single offensive word or gesture, but it was plain from their shifting glances that they were keeping every member of that Christmas group in mind. But that was not what Lou Alp saw first of all. He saw Kate Moore, as she had sprung up, clutch the arm of Jack Chapel with both her hands, and the white, still face which she turned to her companion told Lou that she knew everything—everything. Jack Chapel had laid his past bare before the girl. Had he told her about Lou as well, curse him? But he had told her, and in spite of that she loved him. Once more the knife entered the flesh of Lou Alp, and he grinned in his agony.

Now another thing. They were settling back in their chairs, and Roger Moore was saying something about an outrage and that the sheriff couldn't run for dog catcher in that county after an affair like this, invading a private home at Christmas. But the big voice of Roger Moore was a blur in the ears of Lou Alp. He saw Jack Chapel sink back into his chair with a reassuring word to Kate that brought a tint into her cheeks again, and then the eyes of Jack went across the table, across the mountain of bittersweet, and dwelt steadily on the face of Lou Alp.

He knew! As sure as there was a God in heaven, he knew that he had been betrayed and who the Judas was. Lou Alp, with murder and horror in his heart, slipped his cold fingers over the butt of his automatic. Yet it did not come. The explosion hung fire, and then did not explode. There was death in the eyes of Jack Chapel and yet he did not lift his hand.

The Man Who Forgot

A vast wonder swept over Lou. Roger Moore was ordering everyone to fall to and enjoy the dinner in spite of the sheriff. Jack Chapel seemed to be obeying the order. He did not eat. He drained his wineglass, and then he turned to Kate Moore and began talking in a low, swift monotone. There was something almost fierce about his face, the set of his jaw, and the flare of his eyes, and Lou quaked with the thought that he was telling the girl the story of the betrayer.

But no. She raised her glance and gazed at Lou, and yet he knew that she did not see him. Her eyes were wide and starry with the look of distance. Her lips were parted as though she drank. Lou Alp knew that indeed she was drinking, drinking the words of the condemned man at her side. That was the reason, then, that Jack Chapel would not lift his hand for vengeance. That was the reason he let Judas sit unharmed across the very table. He needed those last, priceless moments to pour out his heart to the girl. The whisper became more than the rush of the storm past the windows, and like a storm it shook Lou Alp.

In a rush of inspiration he knew that man who sat opposite him for the first time, knew that Jack Chapel would let himself be taken without one word of accusation leveled at his confederate. What had the whole story of their relations been? It had been a giving by Jack and a taking by Lou. He had given Lou the very gun, which now threatened his life, if he made one hostile move.

Lou Alp closed his eyes and sagged forward in his chair but, in the darkness that swam before his vision, he saw a picture grow, a picture he had seen long before, forgotten, almost. It was a picture of one man among many at a table. There was light upon that single face. Lou Alp opened his eyes again and saw Jack Chapel's face. For the moment in the blur of his sight it seemed that there was a light upon the face of his companion.

Steps were coming heavily down the stairs from above, and the heart of Lou Alp beat steadily in unison with that sound. The form of the sheriff towered again at the door and, casting down a bag which he carried, it struck the floor with a clash of much metal within. Jack Chapel stood up by his chair. He laid his hand on the shoulder of the girl, but he sent his last glance across the table, and Lou knew that he was forgiven.

"Gents," said the sheriff, "I'm sorry to say it, but there's a thief in this house and his name is. . . ."

The explosion of a revolver tore the next word to rags. Lou Alp was on his feet with the automatic barking in his hands. Roger Moore, with an expression of dumb surprise, slid gently under the table. Kate Moore had shrunk back against the wall, carrying Jack with her and circling him with her entangling arms. Mrs. Moore sat stupefied.

Not one living soul would ever know what beautiful gun play was going on before them. For Lou Alp was a master hand, when his hand was steady, and today his hand was steadier than it had ever been before in his life. He did better than hit the bull's-eye. He chipped the edges of his target. He sent a slug through the shoulder of the sheriff's coat and trimmed the edge of the other fellow's long mustache with his first two shots. So lightning fast was his work that he had fired twice before the others, trained gunmen though they were, had their weapons out.

A bullet crashed through the left shoulder of Lou Alp and drove him back against the wall. He fired again, aiming nicely, and gave the hair of the sheriff a new part. Another slug struck him in the hip. Two guns roared at once, and Lou sank gently forward on his knees, still farther forward, and finally lay on his face.

The sheriff was the first to cease firing. His long legs brought him first to the side of Lou. He jerked him over upon his back.

"Yes," said Lou Alp, "I done the job. And then I shoved the coin in Jack's room, because I wanted to frame him. He didn't have nothin' to do with it."

Jack Chapel burst in between and gathered the shattered body in his arms. The whisper reached his ear only.

"My gift," said Lou Alp. "Be good to her."

THE FEAR OF MORGAN
THE FEARLESS

"The Fear of Morgan the Fearless" by Max Brand first appeared in *All-Story Weekly* (6/28/19). Some of Faust's most moving stories are narrated in the first person singular. Usually, as here, his young and callow narrators witness the clash of titans and from it learn something of the meaning of life. This is the first appearance of this story in book form.

The Fear of Morgan the Fearless

Pete's was different. That was why we liked to go there when the last copy was in and the press started. After one has footed it all over the city through the day, interviewed bored celebrities and listened to the barking of a city editor, quiet is a blessing. Pete's was quiet.

Of course there was the roar of the Elevated where it turned down from the Bowery just outside the door, and there was the rattling and rumble of the surface traffic as well. But for all that, Pete's was quiet. The lights were rather dim and yellowish. The hissing of frying meat in the little kitchen at the end of the room was a soothing sound, and the feel of the sawdust under one's foot was pleasant beyond words.

Holmes discovered the place. Holmes was fat and subdued from a long career as a copy reader, but he was always discovering things. He mentioned the place to Crosby and me, and after that the three of us rarely missed our early morning half hour at Pete's. I don't know why he chose Crosby and me. I was only a cub and hardly knew him. Crosby was a star. I suppose it was because both Crosby and I came from the West and Pete's was decidedly Western in atmosphere. A lariat sagged over the coat hangers the length of the room on one side. On the facing wall, high out of reach, hung a richly ornamented Mexican sombrero. Near it was a pair of silver spurs in a glass case. The spurs had belonged to Morgan.

In fact Morgan was almost like an invisible personality in the room. Pete talked of him constantly. We loved to hear the big chap tell tales of his favorite desperado, and almost every night he gave us a new chapter.

Morgan the Fearless had performed as many heroic actions as there are pages in a book. He had bullied saloons full of gunfighters. He had held up stagecoaches. He had plundered the safes of crossroad general merchandise stores. He had shot up whole towns. The day was not finished until we had heard of an exploit of Morgan's. We were rarely disappointed.

At that hour there were few customers in the place. Pete used to bring us our order and then come and take the other chair at our table. He never gave until he received. He was curiously hungry for melodramatic bits of news and, among the three of us, we always managed to give him some choice tidbits. Crosby had stored away a thousand stories of revolting crimes. After a while we fell back upon him altogether.

Pete would listen with both elbows spread out on the table and his big fingers running through his drooping mustache, and in his eyes would come a peculiar dreaminess. Then, he would talk of Morgan the Fearless, stimulating his memory or his imagination from time to time with noisy sips from his cup of coffee. His language was a singular mixture of Western and New York slang.

But an end came to both Pete and Morgan the Fearless. It was all on account of Holmes who asked the foolish question. Holmes had an almost feminine curiosity. Even his years of copy reading had not killed his hunger for news. He asked Pete to tell us what had finally become of Morgan. Afterward we held it against Holmes, but that night I suppose Crosby and I were equally curious. After all, it was a natural question for, according to Pete, the fearless Morgan had already passed through enough adventures to make the fame of a dozen ordinary desperadoes.

"The end of Morgan?" said Pete rather vaguely, running his pale glance from one face to the other, for he had a peculiar way of failing to meet your eye.

"He did have an end, didn't he?" queried Holmes. "Or is he still at large shooting up towns in the wild West?"

"He sure had an end," said Pete slowly.

But he advanced no further but set to stirring his coffee vigorously and frowning at the brownish scum of milk which had gathered on top.

"This is a special occasion, you know," insisted Holmes. "Crosby is going out to Chicago tomorrow and I think Morgan ought to finish his last installment before Crosby leaves, don't you, Pete?"

The force of this appeal was manifest at once in another roving of Pete's eyes. Crosby was his favorite of the three of us. There was no doubt of that. It was from Crosby that he heard most of his favorite tidbits of sanguinary news.

"All right," said Holmes, spreading his elbows out on the table in a restful attitude of attention, "let's have the death scene of Morgan."

Pete's eye wandered to a corner of the room and stayed there a moment, and his spoon stopped in its incessant circling.

"Morgan didn't die," he said at last.

"Ah," said Holmes, rubbing his hands in anticipation, "I get you now. Better than a death scene. Enter the lady. She saved the soul of Morgan, eh? Crosby, I'll lay you ten to one she was a blonde. Did she have dimples, Pete?"

Pete sighed. "There wasn't no woman," he said.

It was apparent enough to me that the memory of the thing was torturing Pete. I would have stopped Holmes if I could, but he disregarded my frantic winking with a careless shrug of his shoulders.

"No woman?" he cried. "That's rotten luck, Pete, eh? I had a picture of her stowed away in my brain. Even got as far as the dimples."

"Shut up, Holmes," broke in Crosby, "this isn't your story."

"But what do you make out of it?" growled Holmes. "Pete says that Morgan ended up with a bang, and yet he didn't meet a woman and get saved, and he didn't die."

Here Pete fortified himself with an exclamatory sip of coffee and cleared his throat noisily as he set down his cup. We waited with a curious intentness, knowing that the story was about to come. I could see Pete's plump face wrinkling a little with pain, or perhaps it was from the mere effort of memory.

"I don't know as I said that there," he volunteered. "In a way he didn't die, but in a lot of other ways he did die. Yep, I got a hunch that he died, all right."

He dropped his head and scowled as he drew a scroll on the tablecloth with the handle end of his knife. We exchanged glances of wonder, but no one spoke.

"It was down in Barclay's," he went on. "I think I've told you a lot about Barclay's already, haven't I?"

"Sure," said Holmes cheerily, "this begins to look up. Barclay's was the road inn, wasn't it?"

"Yep," agreed Pete.

"That was the place where Morgan drank a quart of fire water one night on a bet, wasn't it?"

"Yep," said Pete, growing more cheerful as he thought back to his older tales.

"Some tank!" exclaimed Crosby. "Well, go ahead, old-timer. A saloon was a good place for Morgan to wind up in."

"The death! The death!" exclaimed Holmes, who was irritatingly eager for the story.

"Remember the goose and the golden eggs, Holmes," I said.

"They had stood for Morgan a long time," went on Pete as if he had not heard the comments. "He'd never done no murder. He'd shot a couple of men, but fair fightin' always. That was the way it lay for a while. Sometimes they'd get up posses and chase him through the hills. All they got was a sight of him duckin' around a curve a long ways ahead or maybe some bullets kickin' up dust just in front of them and tellin' them to keep back, sort of polite. That was the way things stood for a long time. But Bridgewater was gettin' bigger an' bigger an' finally they got to be a city and had their own mayor an' all that. That was how it started."

He shrugged his fat shoulders and frowned over his coffee again. It seemed as though he hated to come to the point of his tale.

"Well," he went on, "one night this guy Morgan holds up a stage comin' into Bridgewater on the Caswell Road. It was the first stage he'd stuck up for nigh onto two months. That was the funny part of it. He just did it sort of for fun because excitement was gettin' kind of low around there an' you can all buy in on the fact that Morgan sure enough loved excitement."

"We gathered that, all right," grinned Crosby.

"I thought his finish came in a saloon, not holding up a stage?" queried Holmes.

Pete regarded him with equal parts of sadness and vexation. "I'm tryin' to tell it from the start," he said, "because, if there hadn't been no hold up, there wouldn't have been no finish to Morgan in the saloon. You see, when he stuck up the stage, all he got was a couple of watches which stopped runnin' in a few days an' a handful of silver money with a couple of fivers. That was all he got an' all he did, except to shoot the ear off the near leader as the stage was coming around the bend and to throw a fright into the mayor's daughter. That was how the trouble began, that throwing a fright into the mayor's daughter."

"Ah," said Holmes, "I knew there'd be a woman in it. Was she a blonde, Pete?"

"She wasn't much of anything," said Pete, in his slow voice, "her hair was light and her skin was dark and the most she had in the way of variety was a string of freckles runnin' across the bridge of her nose. Nobody ever looked twice at her in her life, I reckon, exceptin' her father . . . an' her father was mayor of Bridgewater."

He stopped again for his noisy recourse to the coffee cup.

"Her father was built bulgin', like a wheat sack that ain't filled tight an' sags in the middle. That was what old man Craig looked like. He ought to have been good natured, he was that fat. But he wasn't. He was the kind of guy who keeps hammering the hollow of one hand with his other fist while he's talkin' to you. That was how he got elected mayor of Bridgewater. He talked them out of their votes. He talked so much nobody else got a chance to be heard. Well, as I was sayin', he was fat enough to have been good natured, but he wasn't. He had a sort of ingrown grudge against the world. First thing he did when he got into office was to get them to raise the price of the liquor licenses. I leave it to you, what kind of a guy is that?"

Pete threw out his hands palm up in a gesture of appeal. One after another we shook our heads in solemn agreement that such a mayor was not a man at all. He seemed to be mollified by our agreement.

"Yep," he went on, "he sure had a grudge against everything in the world except his daughter, and his daughter was the one who got scared and squealed and fainted like a young fool when Morgan held up the stage as quiet and gentleman-like as any stage was ever held up in the Rockies. So she come home and she had hysterics all the way into Bridgewater. That was ten miles, but it didn't use her up none. She still had plenty of strength left to cry and holler around her dad. An' the old man got terrible sore.

"The next day he fired into the sheriff and told him he was no good. He wasn't no good as a sheriff, but he had a winnin' way with him an' the mayor got more unpopular than ever after he done it. But there wasn't hardly no way of disputin' the mayor. He was right. The sheriff let Morgan keep cavortin' around the country and, when he went out an' chased him with a posse, everyone knew that the only reason Morgan didn't stop an' hold up the sheriff an' his posse was because he had a sense of humor.

"Well, the mayor, he got some of the leadin' citizens of Bridgewater together, leavin' out the saloon-keepers, and he told them that these things would have to stop and, when they asked him what, he said: 'Morgan!' They all agreed with him and then they asked him how? But the mayor was mad. He was so mad that he was willin' to pry himself loose from some of his tin. He said he was goin' to send away for the best gunfighter in the United States and get him up there to corral Morgan. The prominent citizens, they all laughed and said there wasn't no man in the world could round up Morgan and that the gunfighter had better be measured for a coffin before he started to work.

"But the mayor, he was so fat and bull-headed he couldn't get more than one idea at a time into his head. The next thing folks knew they heard that the mayor had dug down in his jeans and sent to Austin, down in Texas, for a sure-enough gunpuller, a guy that was known all through northern Mexico as the best livin' imitation of the devil. Buck Christy was his name.

"I don't know how much the mayor guaranteed to Christy if he'd come up and corral Morgan, but anyway one day a little skinny runt with a pale face and a manner that said 'Excuse me!' before he opened his mouth, this here guy got off the stage at Bridgewater an' went up to the mayor's office. The mayor was sittin' in his office, with his feet on top of the roll-top desk. He was all through his day's work and was trimmin' his fingernails.

" 'Are you the mayor?' asks this strange guy.

"The mayor slants an eye at the guy an' spits liberal into the place where the spittoon ought to have been an' wasn't.

" 'I am,' says he.

" 'And I'm Buck Christy,' said the stranger an' held out his hand.

"The mayor, he didn't make any move to meet his hand. He just sat there and popped his eyes.

" 'You're what?' says he.

" 'I'm Buck Christy,' says this guy with the pale face.

" 'You're hell,' says the mayor, sort of comin' to life. 'Buck Christy'd eat three or four guys like you before breakfast, sort of as an appetizer.'

"Now the mayor was a big man an' this guy was small, an' there was a couple of clerks in the outer office who heard an' saw all this. But they didn't see anything more because this little guy, he turned around an' locked the door. Afterward they heard a tolerable lot of noise in the office. Pretty soon the noise stopped an' before the clerks could batter down the door to rescue the mayor, the door opens an' the little guy comes out lookin' as pale an' sad as ever. Behind him was the mayor. He was kind of red in the face an' his collar was missin', also a large part of his right sleeve.

" 'Boys,' says he, speakin' sort of cheerful, 'this here stranger is Buck Christy that I reckon all of you've heard a lot about.'

"Christy, he just stood there an' looked around at them an' somehow they all forgot to grin. They all come up and said how glad they was to meet him, an' Christy just looked at them with a sort of silly grin an' a kind of 'excuse me' look around the eyes."

Pete sighed deeply. "That was how Buck Christy came to Bridgewater," he went on, "an' that was the beginnin' of the end of Morgan."

"Do you mean to say that little guy licked Morgan?" queried Holmes. "I thought Morgan was a big guy, as big as you are, Pete?"

"He was," said Pete.

"And Christy licked him?" asked Holmes again.

Pete shrugged his shoulders and frowned.

"Go ahead, Pete," broke in Crosby, "an' you shut up, Holmes. You're doing your best to spoil the best story we've heard."

Holmes relaxed into silence and Pete took up his narrative.

"Of course everyone around these parts heard about it right away. All the men out of Bridgewater started bettin' on it like it was a horse race. Harry Everett . . . he was the guy that Morgan found in the blizzard an' carried home . . . Harry Everett, he rode into Bridgewater an' offered twenty-to-one that Morgan would make a fool of Christy.

"Christy, he heard what was happenin', an' he went down to Barclay's where Harry was hangin' out.

" 'How much do you want to bet ag'in Christy,' says he, goin' up to Harry.

" 'Anything you got to offer,' says Harry as quick as a flash, he bein' a real sport with an awful comeback when he was called.

" 'Well,' says Christy, 'I got a thousand that ain't

doin' a thing an' I don't know anything I'd rather do with it than this.'

"So they made the bet regular, an' they wrote it down an' got the mayor to come an' witness it. That was the first time the mayor ever come into Barclay's. I reckon it was the last.

"Well, if there was considerable excitement about this guy Christy before, it didn't let down none after that there twenty-thousand-dollar bet was laid. Nobody talked of nothing else. But Christy, he didn't do nothin'. Then people got to askin' questions. They say the mayor went to Christy one day an' told him that he had to do something quick because everybody includin' himself expected him to do something besides layin' bets on himself.

" 'There ain't nothing for me to do right now,' says Christy in his soft sort of voice. 'Pretty soon this guy Morgan will come in to me. So why should I go out to him?'

" 'How do you mean Morgan will come to you?' says the mayor, maybe thinkin' that Christy was goin' nutty, or something.

" 'He'll come to me because he's proud,' says Christy. 'That's what Morgan'll do, he'll come to me because he's proud!' "

"And did Morgan come to him?" burst out Holmes.

I choked him with one hand and dragged him back into his seat with the other.

Pete included us with one of his vague-eyed glances. "He did," said Pete. "Morgan came to him, all right." He stopped again to drain the last of his long-suffering coffee.

"Christy spent all the time he was awake in Barclay's," he resumed. "When anyone asked him why he spent so much time there he said that he was keepin' long office hours for the sake of Morgan.

" 'For the sake of Morgan?' they would ask.

" 'Sure,' he'd say, 'this is where Morgan is goin' to call on me before long an' I want to be in when he comes.'

" 'Do you really think Morgan'll come in here where there's always a crowd?' they'd go on to ask Christy.

" 'Sure,' Christy would say, 'the crowd won't stop Morgan any. He's proud, that's what's the matter with Morgan. He'll hear after a while that I'm waitin' for him here an' then he'll come in. Why should I ride way out in the desert when I might as well meet Morgan here among friends?' "

"And Morgan came in?" We said it all three together in a sort of awed whisper. The thing was beginning to grow ghostly.

"He came in," said Pete. "It was pretty near twelve o'clock at night. There were about fifteen or twenty fellows in Barclay's big room." He paused and looked around the room. "It wasn't any longer than this room," he said critically, as if it were necessary that he be absolutely accurate now, "but it was some wider, I guess.

"The boys, they sat around and played cards and maybe some of them now and then went up to the bar an' got a drink at the end of a hand because there was a lot of money goin' about an' the winners was treatin' pretty general. They was all getting pretty quiet because most of them had been playin' all evenin'. They was sort of tired outside an' heated up inside, the way you get when you've been playin' cards a long time. Nothin' seems to happen except what comes in the game, an' the rest of the world, it just sort of fades away and doesn't matter. Maybe you fellows know, what?"

"We sure do," said Crosby, with feeling, who had lost half a week's pay at stud the night before.

"There was one funny thing about that room," went on Pete in a solemn voice. "I never noticed it before that night, but afterward I never forgot. There was a big gasoline lamp that hung from the center of the wall right over the bar. It was a mighty bright light, all right, but right under it where the body of the lamp came there was a sort of shadow that fell on the floor and made rings there of different kinds of light. But all the rest of the room was lighted up as bright as day, almost.

"Well, the boys was there all playin' and drinkin' as I said, when all at once the door opens quick and there stands Morgan with his two guns out and coverin' the crowd. There wasn't anything said. Somebody looked around and then got right up with his hands over his head. Then one by one everyone else got up and put their hands over their heads. But Morgan, he wasn't watchin' none of them. He just had his eyes on Christy and he made a little move up with the barrel of one of his guns. Then Christy, he put up his hands.

" 'Boys,' said Morgan, 'I hope I ain't disturbin' you much an' I won't make you uncomfortable with no long call. I ain't here to rob anybody, not even you, Mister Barclay. All I want is this guy Christy who was betting a thousand dollars that he would make a fool of me. Which of you is Christy?'

"He knew who Christy was, but he wanted to hear Christy announce himself.

" 'I'm Christy,' says the little guy, an' with that he stepped out of the circle and walked a bit closer

241

to Morgan. He stopped in the circle of the shadow under the lamp.

" 'Don't come no closer, Mister Christy,' says Morgan very slow an' with his hand tightenin' around the butt of his gun.

" 'I don't have any idea of comin' closer to you,' says Christy. 'This here spot is pretty comfortable to me. But my arms get terrible tired of stayin' up here in the air. Will you mind tellin' me short an' simple just what you want of me, Morgan?'

" 'I want you to come with me,' said Morgan. 'I got a trick that I want to show you.'

"Now right there was where the first funny thing happened. I know you boys won't believe me, but I'm tellin' this with my hand on my heart. When Morgan said that, Christy started to take both his hands down out of the air. He didn't do it sudden. Morgan could have shot him three times while he was takin' his arms down. He could have shot him six times while he was drawin' his gun, he was that slow and careful. But Morgan didn't shoot. It would have been murder because Christy was movin' that slow that he might have well told Morgan in words just what he was goin' to do next.

" 'If you make a move to raise that gun, you're worse'n dead,' said Morgan.

" 'Of course I am,' said Christy, an' his voice was just soft an' apologetic as it usually was, they say.

" 'Then you turn about an' follow me,' said Morgan, 'all I got to say to you now can be put short an' simple.'

"An' Christy's gun was hangin' down limp at his side the full length of his arm, an' both of Morgan's guns was lookin' him right in the face.

" 'Sure I'll go with you,' says Christy, 'if you really want me to go, but you want to be tolerably sure of that first, eh, Morgan?'

" 'I reckon I know my mind,' says Morgan, with a sort of a grin, 'an' I reckon you'll know it, too, before long.'

" 'There ain't no possible doubt of that,' says Christy, 'but before I go with you I got something to say to you, Morgan, an' I think it's only fair to the boys here that they should hear what I've got to say.'

" 'Well?' says Morgan, wonderin' what was comin' next but willin' to listen, he was that pleased to have the drop on his man out of both barrels. 'Make it short,' says Morgan.

" 'There ain't nothin' that needs a lot of talkin',' says Christy. 'I just want to tell you an' the boys that you ain't no bad man, Morgan.'

"I guess that sort of stunned Morgan an' everyone else in the room.

" 'You ain't no bad man,' said Christy. 'You've just been kiddin' yourself an' the rest of these here innocent people along, Morgan. Understand?'

"Morgan didn't understand. Nobody else did understand. They wouldn't have understood if they had heard it read to them in the same words out of the Bible. They saw that Christy was pullin' some sort of a game, but they couldn't make out what it was.

" 'You've done some pretty nice little jobs,' went on Christy, 'I ain't denying that. Yes you've done some pretty nice jobs, all right, but it wasn't because you was any bad man, Morgan. Why, you ain't got any more heart than a woman.'

"Morgan, he just stood there and made his eyes bigger so he could look at him better. He couldn't understand yet. He thought maybe this man,

Christy, was tryin' some sort of new humor on him. So he waited a little while longer and, when he got through waitin', it was too late!"

Somewhat to our horror Pete broke off suddenly and dropped his face into his hands with a groan.

"Steady, man," said Crosby, leaning over and putting a hand on Pete's shoulder, "we know Morgan was your friend, but let's hear the rest of it."

Pete raised his face and began again, but his voice was unsteady. "There they stood," he went on. "There was Christy with his gun hangin' at his side and there was Morgan with both sights full on Christy's face . . . like this!"

He stretched both his hands before him with the elbows resting on the table and his hands took shape as if they were quivering strongly about the handles of two revolvers. And his face changed, too. It grew harder, and he scowled steadily into space as if he were narrowing his eyes to take a careful bead through the sights.

"An' Christy went on talkin' in a soft voice," said Pete, his own words dropping into a singular drawling monotone which made my flesh creep.

" 'You been doin' a lot of things more than you've got the heart for, Morgan.' he says, an' he was lookin' Morgan straight in the eye all the time.

"Now he had a mighty pale face, but as he stood there lookin', Morgan forgot the face. All he could see was them eyes burnin' at him out of the shadow under that there gasoline lamp, an' he kept lookin' an' lookin' an' the eyes kept getting bigger an' brighter through the sights of his guns.

" 'You got the heart to do a wild thing on the spur of the minute,' says Christy, 'an' sometimes you do it pretty well, but you ain't got no heart to stand up to a man face to face an' get away with a big thing.'

"He went silent for a minute, just lookin' steady at Morgan an' then Morgan, lookin' through the sights of his guns, could see the sights beginnin' to waver just a little from side to side an' then up and down. It wasn't much of a waver. Maybe holdin' the guns steady in one position had made his hands begin to sort of get unsteady.

"Anyway the guns began to stir, though they never stirred enough to get the bead off of Christy's face but, when Morgan tried to steady them down, he found that he couldn't do it.

" 'For instance,' went on Christy, 'you're goin' to fail with me tonight for the first time in your life, Morgan, because tonight for the first time in your life you're up against a real man, understand? Yes, you do understand, Morgan, you're beginning to weaken now. I can see it. Everybody in this here room can see it. You're beginning to weaken.'

"An' as he said it, sure enough Morgan began to think to himself: 'What if I don't get away with this? What if these guns won't work? I didn't look at them tonight! What if they're on the blink?'

"That's the way he began to think to himself, an' all the room was quiet as if someone was expectin' something from him an' he couldn't make up his mind what it might be. An' still Christy's voice went on in that damned monotone like.

" 'You never dreamed that you could ever fall down on a job, did you, Morgan? But tonight you're fallin' down. You're gettin' weak. You ain't sure of yourself, what? You don't find it very nice to stand here an' look a man in the eye, what? Why, you ain't got the heart of a woman, Morgan, not the heart of a screamin' squallin' girl of six-teen, not you!'

"An' somehow Morgan got to sayin' those words over an' over to himself."

Pete turned suddenly on me, and I jumped when he touched my shoulder. "Did you ever get a tune in your head and try to get rid of it an' have it come back in your mind all the time?" he asked.

"Yes, yes," I said, "don't scare me to death, man!"

"That's the way it was in Morgan's mind," he said dully. "He kept sayin' those words over an' over in his mind: 'You ain't got no more heart than a woman!'

"An' then another funny thing happened, because those two guns of Morgan's, they began to drop little by little down Christy's face. An' they dropped to his chin and stayed a little, but Morgan couldn't raise them any higher. An' they dropped to his breast and they stayed a long time over his heart, an' then they dropped until they was pointin' at Christy's feet.

"So there they was, them two men, Morgan big an' Christy little, with Christy's eyes holdin' on to Morgan's and Morgan's eyes waverin' but stickin' to Christy's eyes that was burnin' into him out of the shadow. I don't know how long they stood there, an' there wasn't a sound in the whole room.

"But pretty soon there was someone in the corner who began to whisper sort of hoarse like, he was sayin' his prayers: 'My God!' an' then over again 'My God!' 'My God!' If you ever heard the sound of water drippin' regular into a well, that's the way those words came into Morgan's ear.

"An' then something began to come up in his

throat an' choke him an' he felt his eyes gettin' dizzy and dim.

"Then came another strange thing, for Christy, he laid his own gun over on the bar, slow, without ever movin' his eyes from Morgan's and then he made one slow step and then he took Morgan's guns out of his hands one after the other very slow and careful, an' Morgan just stood there an' didn't make a move, with his hands still out in front of him as if he was still holdin' the guns in them.

"Then Christy, he spoke again at last.

" 'It wasn't all fair, Morgan,' he said. 'The light was shinin' in your eyes and I was in the shadow. But the work's done now. You won't do harm again.'

"Then Morgan, he sort of woke up with a start an' all the room got bright to him all at once. He saw what had happened an' his own guns in Christy's hands. He made a sort of jump for them, but Christy, he didn't shoot, he just made a step back an' to the side and swung one gun so that the muzzle of it hit Morgan over the temple. It didn't knock him down, but it cut him bad over the forehead, an' it was enough to stop him and send him back another pace. That's how Morgan died. He wasn't never no sort of a man after that."

He dropped his face to his hands again. He had grown deadly white, a sick pallor like the belly of a fish, and as he went pale I saw a little irregular scar which traced itself across the corner of his forehead. I looked across at Crosby. He had seen, too, and his eyes were big with horror. He was almost as pale as Pete. But Holmes did not see.

"But what became of him?" he insisted. "Did they arrest him then? Did he serve a term?"

"I don't know what became of him," said Pete.

"That's when he died. They tried to arrest him, the other boys in the room. Christy wouldn't let them. He held them off, an' I think Morgan went outside an' got on his horse an' rode away."

I think Holmes must have been drunk or crazy that night. "Where did he ride?" he queried eagerly.

"To hell!" cried Pete, and he stood up at the table and threw his hands up into the air.

We got up and went silently and hastily out of the room. The doors closed behind us as if they were shutting on a death.

I never have spoken with Holmes again. Once I passed down the street with Crosby and went by Pete's old place. He might still have been in it, and I hesitated a little as I passed, but Crosby took me by the arm and we walked on together down the street and into the night. Crosby was sickly pale and I was feeling queer inside, myself.

THE SACKING OF EL DORADO

"The Sacking of El Dorado" by Max Brand first appeared in *All-Story Weekly* (10/11/19). It weaves several elements from other stories into a more perfect form. The next month in *The Argosy*, also published by the Frank A. Munsey Company, the installments of one of Max Brand's finest early novels, "Trailin'," would be featured. Thus this novelette, which appears here for the first time in book form, falls between publication of the serials "Luck" and "Trailin'," a period of striking creativity and originality for its author. It has all the magic of a story set in that land of the mountain desert, a place for Faust as timeless as the plains of Troy in the hexameters of his beloved Homer and as vivid as the worlds Shakespeare's imagery projected from the bare stages of the Globe.

The Sacking of El Dorado

I
"A CORNERED RAT"

The heart of Blinky Meyers warmed. He had long played poker with more admiration than competition. The tales of his skill as a conjurer with cards had spread too far for his financial welfare.

It was known that he could "break" a new pack in the accustomed manner and "set it up" at the same time. It was further credited that he could "run up" a pack three times on his next deal. These feats were always sufficient to attract an admiring group around his table, but they discouraged opposition.

For six weeks now he had finished each night a paltry five or seven dollars to the good at Harris's. It was disheartening. He had even contemplated changing his hunting ground. But familiarity drew him back to Harris's night after night.

It had once been the back room of a saloon and

there was still a scattering of sawdust on the floor to grit comfortably underfoot. It had been enlarged to take in several adjoining rooms, but it still carried the attraction of a place of mirth. Blinky Meyers so loved mirth that on night after night he was found under the dirty yellow flare of the gaslights, saying: "holding two," or "gimme two," and tapping his cigarette softly on the table to shake out the dust before lighting.

But tonight his heart was warmed. For he had found a green pea, a sucker of the first water, an innocent with just enough knowledge of the ancient game to make him easy meat. It was a large-handed farmer from upstate who had come to New York to expand his already swollen bankroll at the expense of the Manhattan gamblers.

Evidently he had found some success. Perhaps he had fallen in with more of the innocents on his first nights in the city. Certainly he had never encountered a card magician of the skill of Blinky.

Indeed, he had a certain skill, as Blinky discovered when he found a crimp in the pack on the stranger's first deal. The upstater could run up a pack once. He did it well. He knew the lay of the cards under his cut with a prophetic accuracy. So the heart of Blinky warmed.

The crowd which circled the table to watch the game was sympathetic. They were curious, not as to the extent to which the upstater would fall, but just how great his fall would be. Blinky laid the tracks gradually and carefully before putting the skids under his opponent.

By the fourth hand he had marked every honor card in the pack by skilful little markings with his dexterous thumbnails. They were faint incisions in the upper right-hand corner of each card, and it would have troubled a man with a microscope to discover them. But Blinky could read them across the table without trouble. He need not have gone to the trouble of the marking, but he wished to make doubly sure of this fish before he landed him.

It was only after the stranger had won four pots that Blinky began to use his real skill. He began by winning one and losing two, but each time his losses were several times smaller than his single winning. The pressure of the crisp roll of bills in his inside vest pocket was infinitely assuring to him. He was playing carefully.

The crowd about the table was full of attention and admiration. They ventured careless remarks from time to time, full of significance to the initiated. Every time they spoke, Blinky turned his head toward the speaker, but he never moved his steady, pale eyes from his opponent, and his thin little smile never varied.

There was something singular in that gaze. It surely could not have been through that he had won the title of Blinky, for his glance was always fixed and unwavering. It was not challenging. The faint apology of the smile robbed it of offense. One could search in many sections of the world before he would find another expression like Blinky's. But let him go into one of the saloons along the lower bend of the Bowery where the Elevated thunders around toward the City Hall, and he would find many a duplicate of it, men with the same apologetic steadiness of eyes, a humble searching of the gaze as if exploring the character of the men in the barrooms, and deciding which one might be approached for a drink.

To those not familiar with this type, the gaze

might indeed have been found sinister, suggestive of infinite reserve and ominous self-possession. To the initiate it is the last sign of the Manhattan gutter rat.

The game was progressing more rapidly now. The upstate man was beginning to sweat under his losses, but he was also beginning to remember his former successes. He sat hunched forward in his chair with a nervous smile on his lips and in his face the hungry expectancy of the gambler who waits for his "luck to change." The cards were "running against him." He turned from time to time toward the spectators to call them to witness how much the cards were against him, and each time he was met with the noncommittal shrugging of shoulders from men who exchanged half smiles when his head was turned.

Finally he commenced to call for drinks, Scotch and seltzer. After each loss he called, and each time the whiskey was a little taller in the glass, the seltzer a little shorter. His mood changed as he drank. He was cursing now, and each time more loudly. Blinky Meyers watched and judged with infinite care.

To be sure there was a little flat automatic pressing comfortably under his armpit. He had flashed that gun many a time before, but he had never fired it. He knew his men and he knew well enough that this customer was not a man to be bluffed out. He could not be frightened away with the mere show of weapons. Therefore, the one thing that remained in the mind of Blinky was to cut and run when things came to a showdown.

He had no doubt that he could make his getaway should the stranger become obstreperous. He knew the rooms like a book. There was the electric switch to the left entrance over there. He could make for the door, running low, and switch out the lights as he passed, then double back across the room and make down the opposite stairs to the street. In the confusion of darkness there was not a chance in a million that he would be caught. The stranger would follow down the stairs toward which he had headed.

All this was merely in case the upstater pressed things to an extremity and, as the game progressed, Blinky had less and less doubt that this would be the case. The stranger was beginning to accept his losses with a savage silence, and he kept a sulky eye upon Blinky's motions as he dealt the cards. He had already discovered that Blinky was running up the pack. Beyond a doubt he had noticed the first crimp in the cards, but he never could suspect either the second or the third run-up, and consequently he repeatedly was banging into the other crimps. So he sat, stirring now and then viciously, and clearing his throat and rolling his eyes as if he were rehearsing his outburst.

It never came. There was an unexpected interruption which surprised them all in the shape of a number of soft footsteps on the stairs, a sudden opening of the door, and the call of: "Don't move, any of you!"

The place was pinched.

For a second no one moved. All eyes turned toward the doors which were blocked with plain-clothes men. All doors save one, and Blinky was the only one to notice this. Unquestionably, if he had not previously figured on a quick getaway, he would never have had the courage to make the move. But the pressure of the roll of bills over his heart urged on his courage. Furthermore, there was the weight of the gun under his armpit. It occurred to him now that if he were caught with that gun, it would go hard with him. And there were several little affairs in his past which would hardly bear the investigating light the police were almost certain to turn on his life.

There was a shout of warning from one of the officers as he leaped from his seat, and, running low, made toward the door. He saw the detectives grouped there, braced to receive him. But they were not the object in Blinky's eyes. He swerved as he came to the door. His hand reached out and touched the switch. At once the place was dark, and Blinky swerved again and made toward the door which he had seen unguarded.

The room was full of outcry and confusion. He stumbled across several prone figures on his way. Twice a pocket bull's-eye was flashed and these helped him toward his goal. In another moment he was through the door and running swiftly down the stairs.

He hardly noticed the shadow at the first landing until it resolved itself into the figure of a man who sprang on him suddenly. As the body struck him, Blinky fought back. He knew that detectives were not idly to be tampered with, but this man appeared no larger than his own meager proportions. Moreover, there was that pressure beneath his armpit warning him that in case he were caught he could expect no mercy from the law. He struggled desperately.

But, as happens sometimes to the best of men, he struggled vainly. In some mysterious manner he landed sprawling on his knees upon the floor and the next moment he found his neck bent down and his arms up in a merciless half-nelson.

"'Nough!" groaned Blinky. "You got me all right."

His captor chuckled softly. "Now, damn you," he said, his voice breaking from the low laugh into sudden fierceness, "are you through, or will I have to wring your miserable neck before I let you up?"

"You're breaking it now," gasped Blinky. "For God's sake, let me breathe!"

The other laughed again, somewhat breathlessly, and slowly released his grip. Blinky rose to his feet and surveyed his captor, rubbing his aching neck the while. The light from the gas jet farther up the stairs fell full on his own face but made a shadow of his captor's. All he could make out was a figure proportioned about like his own, but with a suggestive bulging of the coat over each shoulder that took the heart out of him.

"Blinky, you yellow dog," said the detective. "I'm going to get a raise at your expense. Stand still there, or I'll bust you in two. That's better. Bah, don't make any starts at *me!*"

As Blinky showed signs of restiveness, the detective swung his hand like a flash and slapped his captive smartly across the face. Blinky shrank back against the railing of the stairs, and cowered. His heart was sinking rapidly.

"Hey, you," muttered Blinky. "Look here. I got two-fifty. I'll split it half and half. What say?"

The detective grinned. Even in the shadow Blinky could see it, and his heart fell.

"None o' that stuff," said the officer, his expression changing suddenly. "I'll take it all in the name of the law."

Blinky stared at him dully.

"Turn around here," continued the mild little detective, "or I'll knock your block off, hear me?"

Blinky turned obediently with his hands still in the air and the pressure of the roll of bills heavy over his heart. Perhaps it was this pressure and still more the weight of the automatic under his arm which nerved him to action now. For he felt the patting of the detective's hands along his hips. To be found with a concealed weapon in his possession meant more than the money which was on him. A long term confronted him. He thought of Sing Sing and he thought of Blackwell's Island.

"I'm a family man, Blinky," the detective was saying. "This means something to me. Turn a bit to the left. Left! Ha! None of . . . *damn you!*" cried the detective, and his hand flew to his pocket.

Blinky fired. A short outcry answered his shot. He did not wait to make sure of his game but fled down the stairs and into the street. He paused a crouching instant at the door to make sure that there was no bar of waiting detectives in sight. Then he raced directly across the street and down the opposite alley.

Before he reached the next street he recollected himself. He stopped, took off his hat and smoothed his hair, arranged his necktie and settled his clothes. Then he stepped out jauntily enough into the penetrating light of the street lamps.

His mind was fully made up. Within a few hours the call would be out for him. He remembered Blackwell's Island under the swart shadow of the Queensboro Bridge, and his blood went cold.

He turned back now toward the Bowery and caught a Fourth Avenue car. At Forty-Second Street and Madison Avenue he got off and went into Grand Central Station. It seemed to him that when he asked for the New York to Chicago timetable the man at the information stand looked at him sharply. All the world would seem to have sharp eyes upon him now, thought Blinky, and he shivered slightly.

The train would not leave for an hour. He went out of the station and crossed the street to the Belmont Bar. He sat at a table with the timetable clutched in one hand. As the waiter took the order, once more Blinky felt the surveillance of keen eyes. He drank his first brandy straight and hardly felt the burn of it. The second he filled to the brim with seltzer and sipped to kill time. He dared not befuddle his brain with alcohol at a time like this.

At last he sat in the train, heard the last call, and the train pulled roaring down the subway.

II
"IN THE WILDS"

It was to Blinky as if he had left his native land for a foreign shore. With a typical New Yorker's sense, Chicago was to him merely "somewhere in the West," a vague city of smoke, overhung with the souls of slaughtered cattle. Further than Chicago his thought could not strike. As he sat in the seat, he turned sadly in his mind the various periods and episodes of his life.

It had all been bounded by Manhattan, the East River on one side and the Hudson on the other. Once in a long while during the hot months he had taken a girl for a long boat ride up the Hudson, but these were daring voyages of adventure and discovery, vying with the exploits of those old Vikings who forestalled Columbus half a millennium.

Now he was venturing into those wilds where the hills had hardly forgotten the war cries of the Indians. Blinky Meyers was sad indeed. By the time he reached Chicago, his gloom had become a crying homesickness. He had no care where he went now. He wandered idly through the streets until he came to the first policeman.

This sight startled Blinky. He had almost forgotten that there might be policemen in far-away Chicago. He changed his course and, after a time, managed to hunt out a resort whose doors swung continually with the entering and outgoing stream of pleasure seekers. There were sailors, soldiers, longshoremen in the crowd. They were pleasant to the familiar eye of Blinky. Here he could lose himself among his fellows.

The sense of relief was too much for his overstrained nerves. He had not slept on the train that night, nor in the morning. Now he relaxed all care. He found a table in a corner and commenced on his favorite brandy. The rattling of an electric piano lulled and lured him. His guard fell lower and lower. Now the drinks called strongly for repetition. He kept his glass filled constantly.

There is something in the oily substance of old brandy which makes it slow of effect, but its effect is no less sure and, consequently, the time came oversoon when Blinky Meyers, pale and vacant of eye, stared at the piano, wondered whence this heavenly music could come, and uttered his order slowly and with careful lips.

It was in such a state that a fellow of his own order found him. He sat at Blinky's table after asking if his company were permissible. It was more than that. It was vastly welcome, according to Blinky. So the stranger sat down. He too, it seemed, was partial to brandy and, if the drinks he poured for himself were strangely small, they were made large at once with seltzer and they were drunk with a gusto which equaled Blinky's. Furthermore, if these drinks were paid for from Blinky's roll, why, that was only just. The best of good fellows have their low moments.

So Blinky grew mellow and mellower, and confident and more confiding, and he talked of Manhattan, and of the procession of bridges over the East River, and of the Woolworth at night, and of the crossing of Forty-Second Street and Fifth Avenue in the day, and always he was met with sympathetic gutturals. The stranger had little to say, but he seemed to understand, and understanding was all that Blinky's soul craved. The understanding, in fact, became so perfect that the last Blinky knew he was making an uncertain progress over a sidewalk which shifted and wavered as strangely as a sea in a storm, leaning upon the arm of his new-found friend who was urging and supporting him toward a haven of rest.

He awoke in the haven of rest the next day at noon. His head was dizzy from the sun which slanted through a cracked window. The buzzing of flies filled his brain with delirium. He woke further enough to raise his sick head. He was lying with all his clothes on. The sight brought him to the realization that his clothes were irking him with a thousand itching and rubbing wrinkles. He rose with a swimming sickness and ventured as far as the washstand. The water in the flowered pitcher was tepid and dirty but, when he dipped an end of the wrinkled towel in it, it was heaven to his forehead and sweeter heaven to his throat and the back of his neck. He reeled now before the mirror.

The sight of the unshaven and flushed face which looked back at him was disconcerting. Then, as the memory of the past evening returned, he went with a doubt to search his clothes. His premonitions were sadly fulfilled. The roll of bills from his vest pocket had disappeared. In his trouser pockets he found a little over a dollar in change. His automatic was safe, however. Probably the thief had been afraid to keep it.

In New York the loss of his money would have made him more angry than sad. In Chicago it made him feel like a mariner stranded on a desert island. Through his head fleeted prospects of labor at the docks, of shoveling coal, of various sad and distasteful sights which he had seen. The soul of Blinky Meyers shrank like an apple under the summer sun. He grew flabby.

It served at least to sober him somewhat, and as he sobered his mind began to work more actively. Joined to the activity of his mind was his depression, both physical and mental, the aftermath of too much liquor from the day before. The first thing that bore in upon him was the consciousness that he was the object of the law's anger. The thought suggested further flight.

The idea came to fill his mind more and more. He consulted the meager change in his pocket and his heart fell again. He even thought of appealing to the police to apprehend the man who had filched his money. The thought on reconsideration made him laugh aloud, and the laughter in turn made his head ache.

He went down into the street and invested in the first saloon in a gin fizz. This stimulus encouraged him toward a breakfast which he made for twenty-five cents in a lunch room on a couple of boiled eggs and coffee. The soul of Blinky Meyers commenced to revive, but his fears revived at the same time, with surprising violence. The fact that he had made the journey from New York to Chicago in a day made the distance seem to him a mere step. He must move on.

"Westward, the course of empire. . . ." Blinky Meyers boarded a west-bound freight.

Half a day out a braky discovered him. He demanded a dollar for the privilege of riding the train on that section. Blinky dug miserably into his pocket and found little better than half that sum. The braky received it with manifest scorn and, after pocketing the sum, kicked Blinky ignominiously off the grade. The train had just started and Blinky rolled a great way down the cinders, cut and scraped and bruised by his fall.

He rose sick at heart and went back to the station to wait his fortunes with the next freight. He sat upon a pile of tiles near the station, pulling his derby deeply over his eyes.

He succeeded in catching that freight, but the next two days were merely variations of hell for him. Brakies on Western divisions are apt to be harsh. Blinky was a proper object for their harshness. To their words he responded with silence. From their blows he cringed, which is not the way of a proper tramp. They enjoyed the novelty to the full of their strong vocabularies and their still more wonderfully strong good right toes.

So it chanced that Blinky, bruised, shaken, and sore in a thousand places, reached Weatherby Gap and was booted farther than common by a braky of most uncommon vocabulary and leg power. He wiped the cinders from his cut cheek and scraped eyebrows before he rose and looked upon the wilderness around him.

It was a singularly bleak country: bald, scalped mountains shot up on all sides with a struggling growth of evergreen climbing their sides. Flags of mist whipped from the peaks and a low wind hummed through the shrubbery. It was as sad as death to Blinky, but death itself was not so sad as the toes of the angered brakies. Blinky turned his back upon the railroad station and surveyed the scene gloomily. What lay in the wilderness he had not the least idea. There was a road, and the road promised human habitation sooner or later.

The idea of physical labor was still mightily distasteful to him but not so distasteful as the journeying hell of freight trains. A virtuous resolve filled Blinky's mind, and he turned resolutely down the road and into the shades of the trees.

It was late in the afternoon. The shadows began to slip, cool and splotchy, through the trees and the gnats and flies, which had gone zipping through the warmer air all day, settled now in sleepy droves close to the ground but roused themselves at the presence of Blinky to follow him steadfastly along the road.

He had to cut a twig from a tree and, as he marched, he kept the twig playing about his face to brush away the annoyance. As he walked, the grime and grit accumulated from his days in the boxcars bothered him more and more. So that when he saw the glint of water through the trees, it was a most pleasing sight to him.

He stopped a moment to enjoy the gray-green shimmer of the water between the tree trunks. Then he stepped from the road and into the forest.

The Sacking of El Dorado

He found the pool a few rods deep in the wood. It was formed by the angle of an inconsiderable brook, which kept up a continual chattering through the afternoon hush. Blinky stooped to try the water with his hand. Lo! It was as mild and warm as the air of that summer day.

What with the flies and the grit, his mind was made up on the spot. He threw off his clothes hastily and stepped into the water. Gathering courage, he made a long dive. He came up safely, and then he started paddling about. The water caught and slid on his shoulders pleasantly. He tried floating on his back for a while and managed it passably well, though the fresh water did not buoy him as the salt water to which he was accustomed. He had to paddle hard with the extended hands to keep afloat.

Perhaps it was the noise of this paddling that covered the approach of the other man. At any rate, as Blinky floated and paddled, he started at the sound of a voice behind him.

"Ah, there, partner!"

III
"MARKSMANSHIP"

Blinky quite forgot that he was in the water and started erect. Luckily the water was shallow, and he stood with the cool waves lapping about his breast. Through the patched filtering of the sunlight he made out the figure of a man on a horse. Very gross and huge it seemed to Blinky as he stood in the pool.

The water chilled him all at once. Perhaps this was some messenger of the law come thus upon his trail. For the law was to Blinky a fearsome and mysterious agent whose arms reached everywhere and whose heads were more numerous than chimera.

"Are you dumb?" repeated the voice, a little sharply this time.

"Dumb?" said Blinky. "Sure, I ain't."

"Come on out then and talk to me," said the forbidding horseman. "I'm lonely and want company."

Blinky paddled obediently out from the water and, as he did so, the horseman dismounted. Blinky stood shivering in the chill air with his arms wrapped vainly around him.

"How'n hell d'you come here?" inquired the rider.

Blinky swallowed before he could answer. "I dunno," he said, "I just happened along."

The horseman chuckled. "I reckon you did," he said in his heavy voice. "Better put on your clothes before you freeze. Are these yours?" He leaned over the heap at his feet. "Hallo!" he cried a moment later. "What's this?"

The stranger held the bundle of Binky's clothes at arms' length. Then he dropped them all save the trousers.

"Look here, pardner," he grinned to Blinky. "Are these sure enough pants? Why, the legs ain't much bigger'n the sleeves of my shirt!"

The trousers were sadly wrinkled and soiled, but they still showed the latest slender New York cut. Blinky shrugged his shoulders and said nothing.

"And this here," continued the rider, abandoning the trousers and picking up Blinky's battered derby. "Say, Billy, where'd you come from that they let you wander around in things like this? Is this a hat?"

Blinky flushed under the scorn of the question. "Of course it is," he said angrily. "Of course it's a hat!"

"Aw, go on," grinned the rider, "it ain't more'n a grapefruit skin with a rim. What?"

He dropped the hat and picked up the coat, letting one hand fall down the cut in line of the side. As he did so, he started with a different interest.

"H-m," said the horseman, fumbling through the coat. "You carry your badge with you, what?"

Blinky saw the glint of metal in his hand. His heart sank. His automatic had been discovered. He cursed himself inwardly for not throwing it away long ago.

"What's this here?" continued the stranger. "Is it a toy gun?"

Blinky took up his clothes and started to dress. "It's a gun, I guess," he admitted.

The other spread the gun on the palm of his hand, and Blinky could see that his weapon was the object of a long and careful scrutiny.

"Yes," said the stranger, "I reckon it's a gun all right, but does it really shoot?"

An enforced silence followed as Blinky struggled his head through his shirt. He hadn't much idea as to whether it would still shoot or not. He had only used it once since he possessed it, and that once was the cause of his sudden exodus into these parts unknown.

"I guess it shoots all right," he said.

The stranger sighed deeply. "It's sure strange," he observed at last. "I reckon this here science is a pretty wonderful thing, all right. But, say, could this here little gun really hurt a man?"

Blinky shuddered in reminiscence. "It can do that," he said.

"I ain't disputin' you," said the other, "but speakin' of guns. . . ." As he spoke, he reached a hand behind him, and it came forth again bearing a long, blue-barreled Colt. "Speakin' of guns," he went on, "this here is what I've always called a man-killer, an' I didn't know there was any other brand goin' that would really do the work."

Blinky was sitting on a log tying his shoes, but he looked up at this remark and watched with fascinated eyes as the rider whirled his big gun on his forefinger. He felt that he was before the denizen of another world in the presence of this big-shouldered man with the broad-brimmed hat slouched far back on his head. His mustache thrust out straight from the end of his nose and then dropped at a sharp angle toward his chin. He was framed by the equally brawny horse which loomed behind.

"Still," said the stranger, "here's what looks to be a barrel and, though it's a pretty small caliber, it might do damage. Here's what looks to be a handle, though it fits mighty small in a man's hand." He remained a moment studying the automatic. "How'd you come by such a gun as this here one?" he asked sharply.

Blinky Meyers winced. "I just come across it," he said slowly.

"And how do you happen to be along here?" continued the other. "You ain't got any deputy sheriff badge about you. What?" There was no mistaking the ominous touch in his voice as he said this.

"Sheriff badge?" queried Blinky tremulously. "No, I'm afraid I haven't."

The big man strode to him and tilted his head

back with one ponderous hand. Then he chuckled. "No," he said, "I reckon you ain't no deputy."

"Is it forbidden to carry guns out here?" continued Blinky humbly, thinking that he might plead ignorance of the laws.

"Aw, I don't know," growled the other, but there was a hint of good nature in his voice now. "I never seen one carried the place you got it in. Under the armpit, huh?"

"Yes," said Blinky, "I thought that was the place to carry it."

The rider pushed his hat still further back on his head as he scratched his head in his thoughtfulness. "It may be the right place to carry it in some sections but not out here, not that I've seen much," he said. "Say, how'd you get it out for a quick draw? Suppose a man was ridin' up on you from behind, and you wanted to get him quick as soon as you heard him, and you didn't hear him none too soon, how'd you get him with a gun stowed away under there?" He gestured toward the pit of his arm.

"I don't know," said Blinky, quite awe-stricken. "I never tried to get a man that way."

The stranger watched him a moment and then burst into a heavy laugh. "No," he said, "I reckon you never did. Wal, this is sure the funniest gun I ever seen. You don't mean to tell me it shoots straight, huh?"

"I think it does," said Blinky, and sighed at the memory.

The other looked at him a bit uncertainly. "I'm thinkin' of stayin' here a while tonight, maybe campin' here till mornin'," he said. "I been travelin' a long while already. I reckon you'll stay with me. What?"

It was more a decision of his own than a question, and the explosive violence of his last queried word somewhat shocked Blinky.

"Camping here?" asked Blinky in amazement. "Why, there ain't any bed here, is there?"

The stranger laughed shortly. "Sure, there ain't," he said, "but I got the makin' of a sort of a meal behind my saddle there. I reckon horse blankets will keep us warm. What?"

The novelty of the proposal and the rather strangely decided manner of the big man were too much for Blinky. "Me?" he said at last. "No, I guess I'll move on. There must be a town around here, ain't there?"

The rider greeted this remark with a short silence. "I reckon there is," he said at last.

"Then I think I'll be moving on," said Blinky, who was beginning to feel more and more uncomfortable.

He rose from the log as he spoke and started casting about in his mind for the proper adieus to his singular companion.

"Wait a minute," said the other, stretching out his arm, though not touching Blinky. "Here we are leavin' one another, and not knowin' each other's names. That's hardly companionable, is it? What?"

"I guess not," said Blinky.

"Then what might be your name, partner?" asked the rider bluntly.

"It might be Meyers," said Blinky cautiously. "Does that mean anything to you?"

The stranger pondered the name. "Not a thing," he said at last with apparent relief in his voice. Then he leaned forward toward Blinky. "And supposin' my name was Donahue," he went on, "would that mean anything to you?"

"Nothing at all," said Blinky cheerfully, for he began to feel that he had to do with one of his own feather. "Not a thing, pal." He waited for a response, but got none. "If I could bother you for my little gun . . . " he began tentatively.

"There's one more thing," said the other, "not that I have any hankerin' for the gun but, say, what sort of a color would you say that there horse of mine is?"

"That horse?" queried Blinky. "I suppose I'd call him a big, raw-boned roan, eh?"

The stranger shook his head with emphasis. "And you're lookin' for the town tonight . . . maybe for El Dorado?"

"The nearest one, whatever it is," assented Blinky.

"I reckon it wouldn't do for you to go into that town and say you met a man who rode a big roan horse," said the rider. "You see, there's a lot of folks in that there town of El Dorado that are a lot more curious than what's good for them to be. If you told them that, they might just naturally start out and look for that there horse. You see?"

Blinky stared at him vaguely, a glimmer of comprehension beginning to come to him.

"Besides," said the stranger more pleasantly, "I'd kind of like to have company tonight, it bein' powerful lonesome 'way out here in the forest and the mountains. What?"

"I suppose it is," said Blinky politely.

"And you suppose right," said Donahue, "so I have an idea that you'll stay here with me and have supper with me, which I'll cook. And afterward we'll talk maybe about this little gun of yours which has sort of took my eye, so to speak."

There was no doubting his intentions by this time, and Blinky, with an inward tremor, resigned himself to his fate. Beyond the fact that the rider kept the automatic stowed away in his hip pocket, his actions were wholly cordial toward Blinky. He himself cut the first dried branches into slivers and lighted them with a match. It was he who fanned them carefully to a blaze and then piled twigs and branches until a cozy little fire burned up. It was he who produced a large piece of bacon and sliced it deftly with a pocket knife; he, again, who brought forth a heavy loaf of bread and then a tin and coffee. The only commission which was left for Blinky to execute was to bring the water for the coffee.

Blinky forgot a large portion of his fears while the fire was burning, and while the odor of the broiling bacon, which sizzled on the point of a stick, filled the air, and still more when the steam of the coffee joined the other fragrances. The rider made no fearsome moves and even sang snatches of popular songs in a broken voice—songs which Blinky had heard years before in the theaters of New York. They touched him to the heart, and a thousand tender memories of old Manhattan choked him while the big man sang.

He himself made other offerings later on. They were later songs, and they were sung in a somewhat mellower voice. The rider listened in fascinated attention. After they had eaten sandwiches of bread and bacon, the bread sadly old and tough and the bacon sadly burned, and drunk their portion of bitter coffee, Blinky gave himself wholly to the spirit of music, for he had lost much of his awe of the rider by this time. He lay back with his head pillowed on a small log, watched the leap and shimmer of the last sunlight on the water beyond, and how the smoke shook up in swift jags of blue-white past the stiff-shafted pine trees. So he sang and whistled a score of tunes he had heard and danced to in New York, and the larger man leaned with his elbow fallen on his knees and beat time with a ponderous hand to the rhythm of the tunes.

Afterward there came a little silence, and Blinky Meyers found himself lying back with wondering eyes, studying the swart trees and over their spear-pointing tops the pink-tinted blue of the sky. A silver wraith of mist blew over the eastern pines, and after it came the moon, round and white with the mist dissolving from its face.

"There's one thing I still got to talk about," broke in Donahue at last.

Blinky drew himself up on one elbow and frowned at his companion, half irritated and half frightened.

"It's about this here shootin' iron," said Donahue. "Leastwise, you claim it shoots. What?"

"Sure it does," assented Blinky.

"Huh," grunted Donahue. "Any objection to me tryin' it out?"

"Where?" grinned Blinky. "On these trees?"

Donahue regarded him with compassion. "Naw," he said. "Look at these here pebbles all around. They're white and bright. Suppose you throw 'em up in the air, and I'll try what this here gun of yours can do."

Blinky sat up to stare at him. "Why," he cried, "these pebbles wouldn't be no more than little points of light to shoot at."

Donahue cleared his throat modestly and covered his face with his hand to hide his smile.

273

"That's all I need to shoot at, partner," he said. "You try me out and, if I miss, it'll be your gun's fault, not mine."

He fondled the gun as he spoke and balanced the handle in the palm of his hand.

"All right," answered Blinky. "Here's for you." But he stopped with the pebble in his hand and pointed suddenly. "Look!" he said. "There's something worth shooting at. Can you hit that?"

Slipping with furtive movements from the roots of a tree toward the edge of the pool came a chipmunk a short distance away.

"Wall, damn me," whispered the rider, "the little feller's come down to get a drink. What?"

He made no move toward pointing the gun.

"Give it to me," said Blinky, his thin face hardening and a strange smile coming on his lips. "I think I could hit it. Let me try. Let me try!"

He kept his eyes hungrily on the chipmunk as he stretched out his hand toward the gun. Consequently he did not note the sudden curling of the rider's mouth.

"Not a hope," said the rider softly. "Why, that there poor little devil may have a family stowed away in these here trees somewhere. Maybe he's come a long ways for that drink. What?"

"Are you going to shoot?" demanded Blinky impatiently, turning toward his companion.

"Nor you ain't, neither," said the larger man. "I done a lot of shootin' in my day, maybe, but I ain't never done it yet for the fun of killin'. What?"

Blinky stared at him without a flicker of understanding in his eyes. The face of the rider had softened, and his eyes moved away from Blinky.

"There," he said, "he's gone back to his mammy and his kids."

Blinky turned and saw a disappearing stir of brown fur among the roots of the trees. "Well," he sighed, "you're sure a funny guy, all right. Want to try on these pebbles now?"

"All right," assented the rider. "I'll use the Colt first and get my eye. Haven't done much shootin' lately."

He laid aside the automatic and picked up the long-barreled revolver.

Blinky tossed a pebble into the air. As it started on its downward course, the gun exploded in Donahue's hand and the pebble disappeared.

"That was luck!" cried Blinky, unable to believe the testimony of his eyes. "You can't do it again."

Donahue merely smiled. "Throw again," he said and, when the pebble was tossed, he fired again, and once more the pebble disappeared.

Donahue was beginning to grow interested. He rose to his feet, and Blinky did the same. He had quite forgotten his fear in his admiration for this superhuman marksmanship. Pebble after pebble he tossed in the air, and every time Donahue struck his mark. Five times he repeated this, and on the last shot he turned and cried to Blinky: "Watch this whirl, partner!"

As Blinky tossed up the pebble, the gunman threw his revolver into the air. It flashed in a couple of rapid circles and, as it struck in the hand of the marksman, it exploded. Again the pebble disappeared.

Blinky shivered in the earnestness of his interest. "My God," he said softly, after a moment of pause, "that's not human. I can't believe that!"

The gunman grinned. "Nothin' at all," he said. "Now, let's see what your toy gun can do." He dropped the Colt and picked up the automatic, fingering it cautiously. "Fits snug in the hollow of the hand, all right, doesn't it?" he said. He made the gesture of drawing and aiming it half a dozen times. "Throw a pebble," he directed.

Blinky tossed the pebble, and again the pebble disappeared as the gun exploded.

"By God!" cried the gunman in admiration as he looked down to the shining little weapon. "She shoots true, all right. Nice clean kick, too. Try again!"

Again he struck the pebble.

"And now what'll she do on the flip, eh?"

"Try it," said Blinky.

"I ain't much used to the hang of it yet," said the gunman dubiously, "but here's where I learn."

He tossed the automatic high as Blinky threw the pebble, and the gun exploded as it reached his hand again. But to Blinky's astonishment the pebble fell untouched. He saw it rattle on a stone a few yards away. Then he turned his worried eye to the marksman.

Donahue had staggered back against a tree, and stood with his head strained back and his hands clutching at his breast. Blinky shrank close to the ground.

IV
"DEAD OR ALIVE"

Donahue reeled a bit forward and fell horribly near the fire. Blinky Meyers reached him at a leap and dragged the heavy body a foot or more away with infinite labor. Then he managed to turn him on his back, and the soiled and leaf-straggled face looked up to him, grimacing with pain.

The Sacking of El Dorado

"Scragged on my oldest an' my best stunt," moaned Donahue with a painful breath between each word, "an' all because o' your damned new gun. It sure can shoot. I'm the everlastin' witness o' that."

A fresh contortion of pain silenced him, and he closed his eyes, fighting against the desire to cry out.

Blinky began fumbling clumsily at Donahue's breast. The latter cursed and thrust him strongly away.

"No use," he said. "I'm through, all right. What a hell of a place to die in! I thought it'd be a barroom, anyway, with the odds ag'in me. What a hell of a place to die in, here, with the stars watchin'. What?" He broke off to laugh. The sound broke and bubbled horribly. "Think of it, will you?" he demanded in a hoarse whisper when he had recovered. "They're electin' a constable at El Dorado tomorrow to go out an' catch me, an' I reckon they'll be a powerful few that'll want the job. Think where they'll find me . . . what a hell of a place to have to die in."

The words trailed into a groan, and he lay for a moment with closed eyes.

"Water," he said after a moment without opening his eyes. "Damn you, don't you see I'm burnin' up?"

Blinky grabbed the coffee pot and rushed to the edge of the pool, where he hastily emptied the grounds, rinsed the can, and started back with it full of tepid water. Halfway back he stopped short, for he saw the big roan, which Donahue had unsaddled and tethered by the lariat to a tree, rear back on his tether. There was a sharp, gritting sound as the rope knot slipped and then came free, and the big roan turned and walked with pausing feet toward his master's fallen body.

It came over Blinky with a rush of horror that perhaps the charger would trample the fallen body. He could not move but waited to watch. For how could he stand against this giant beast? But when the horse came to Donahue, he dropped his head, with the ears flattened close to his neck, and stood with his forelegs spread and his nostrils hardly an inch from the fallen man's face. He drew back a pace or two after that and stamped and tossed his head to break into a whinny that rang through the trees.

Blinky remembered his mission and ran toward Donahue. He found the wounded man muttering continually like a dreamer in his sleep, for his eyes were still closed.

"Partner," he said, opening his eyes as the can touched his lips, "if I was goin' to live, I'd stake you rich for doin' this."

He drank deeply, Blinky supporting his head.

He fell back rather contentedly after that, his eyes opening and closing between breaths as if he were fighting against an overpowering sleepiness. "Where's Sammy?" he asked. "Him and me's been pals a long while."

A step came behind Blinky, and a great head thrust past his shoulder. It was the roan.

"Hello, Sammy!" muttered the gunman. "Ain't this a hell of a place for me to die in . . . what? Think of all the places you an' me has been!"

The roan leaned his head still closer, and his ears pricked as if he were intent on hearing every word. So the man and horse stood side by side to watch the coming of death. Once Blinky turned toward the roan with almost a feeling of fear, for it seemed to him that a human personality was watching there at his side and looking out of the round, bright eyes.

The wounded man stirred again and moved out one hand to touch the velvety nose of the roan, which was standing just above him.

"Sammy . . . ," he began and then broke off, and his hand dropped. He was quiet for another moment. "Partner," he said after a little, and his voice was faint but quite clear, "do I know you well enough to ask you a favor? What?"

Blinky knelt suddenly, and his voice choked. "Anything this side of hell," he whispered with sudden emotion.

"All right," said the gunman, "it ain't anything much, except that I sort of hate to have 'em find me in this hell of a hole, me that has lived so wide and free, sort of . . . what? Well, I want you to drag me off somewhere through the trees here, an' scrape out a bit of a hole in the dirt an' roll me in there where they'll never find me. What? You could sink me in the pool, but that'd poison the water when some poor devil comes here wantin' a drink. Will you do this?"

"I will," said Blinky tremulously.

"Say it again," said the gunman insistently.

"So help me, God," murmured Blinky.

Donahue smiled and then groaned. In the flicker of the fire Blinky could see the glisten of the sweat that stood on the dying man's forehead. It filled him with awe to see this courage in the face of death. He thought back into his own pale soul and shuddered.

"One more thing," said Donahue. "This here roan . . . this here Sammy . . . you c'n see him, can't you? My eyes are gettin' pretty thick. Hey, Sammy!"

The head of the big roan stooped close over Donahue, and his hand moved up uncertainly and touched the wide-spreading nostrils. Then he sighed, and his hand fell again.

"Sammy an' me has been pals," he said. "Seems a sort of shame that any other man should back him savin' me. I broke him when none of the rest of them could. I lassoed him. I saddled him. All by myself. He was a hell-bender, was Sammy, then. He was four that spring. You should have seen him. What?" He closed his eyes and smiled. The thought was pleasant. "Shame that any one else should ride him. What?" he went on feebly. "Shame that any one should spur him after he gets old, me being dead. What?"

"Yes, yes," muttered Blinky, stammering, for the tears, despite himself, were running fast down his face and tickled on his chin.

"It ain't much that I want you to do, seein' that you see that. What?" said the gunman.

"No," said Blinky miserably.

"I'd ask you to shoot Sammy so's no one else could ever back him," went on Donahue, his voice growing more and more uncertain, "but I know you'd lose heart for it when you seen him lookin' down the line of your barrel with his ears stuck forward. But use him well, pal. What?"

Blinky turned and looked into the big eyes near him. "Yes," he said after a moment of pause, and then repeated the order to himself. "Sure I will."

Donahue raised his hand slightly, and Blinky slipped his own more tremulous fingers within it. The pressure in return was cold and feeble.

"Partner," said the gunman, "you're O.K. So long."

After that he was quiet for a long time. Blinky thought once that he had died, but he remembered that when men die their eyes open. So he waited on. It would be a fearful time, he thought, when this big man's eyes should open at last and look to the stars. At the thought he raised his head to note what they would see in that last long glance. There were the stars indeed but pale in the white circle of the moon. And the moon itself drew softly westward toward the pine-tops with the thin tangle of mist before its face. The dying man stirred again.

"Sammy," he whispered, "a hell of a place . . . to die in . . . you an' me . . . what?"

He drew a quick breath. Blinky knew that he was dead as well as if a voice had spoken in his ear. The eyes rolled open. It was astonishingly and terribly like a calm awakening in the morning. Instinctively Blinky reached out a hand and commenced to stroke the shining neck of the roan.

His thoughts were coming fast and confusedly now as he looked down to the leonine face of the dead man. He remembered another he had seen in a Hester Street barroom. The man had been standing at the bar reeling a little but clinging fast to the edge with one hand while he balanced his glass in the other. Then the glass had dropped, cracking and splashing noisily. And the man fell at the same moment with a breath which was half gurgle and half hiss. They made a sudden circle around him. But he writhed and kicked so vigorously that they could not put a hand on him. It was a fearful thing to watch.

Blinky had seen a mad dog shot and die in convulsions. This man in the barroom had reminded him horribly of it. It seemed as if he were fighting against death as he lay face downward, twisting and cursing. Then he stopped moving, said "God!" and then lay in a crumpled heap. When they straightened the body and turned it face up, the sight of it made Blinky weak and sick at the stomach.

He closed his eyes and thought of this. He opened his eyes and looked on the big man who lay dead before him. A flicker from the firelight touched his face and the steady smile on it and lighted the wide eyes. Blinky trembled, and then reached out with a faltering hand and closed those eyes. It was too ghostly otherwise.

It was a long while before he gathered strength and courage to drag the big man away and half bury him as he had been requested. At last he got up and slipped his arms under the limp shoulders. The weight of the body astonished him. It was obvious that he could not drag the body far.

He let it down slowly again and sat on a log to consider. The horror and the solemnity of the moment was dying out from Blinky's mind. His thoughts commenced to revert to their usual channels. A dead man was but a dead man. If he had valuables upon him, they could do him no good. And he, Blinky, was desperately broke and in a country to which he was totally strange.

He commenced the search rather reluctantly. In a trouser pocket a slight crinkling sound as he stirred the cloth roused him as the scent of game rouses the well-bred hunting dog. He brought forth a compact roll of bills.

Blinky hummed while he counted the money. One hundred and eighty-five dollars lay in his hand. He slapped the money carelessly across his knee and smiled benevolently upon the dead man. Afterward, he continued the search of the dead man's clothes.

In the breast pocket of the shirt he found another roll of paper, and again his heart thrilled. But when he brought it out, he found it merely a sort of folded poster. He would have torn it up or thrown it away, save that as he unfolded it his eyes caught what seemed to be a picture of a man.

Blinky stirred up the fire, and by that light examined the picture more closely. It was beyond a doubt the picture of the dead man dressed in his present costume, with the same wide-brimmed hat pushed back from his forehead. Then as he unrolled the paper still more, Blinky saw in great type:

REWARD!

Blinkly rubbed his chin and stared without being able to read more of the poster for a moment. Then he read on:

REWARD! FIFTEEN HUNDRED DOLLARS! REWARD!
For the Person of "Sandy" Donahue
Dead or Alive
Any person or persons whatsoever are hereby authorized to bring the body of Sandy Donahue, in any way whatsoever, into the hands of the law, and claim therefore a reward of fifteen hundred dollars. To this there is added a private subscription of five hundred dollars from individuals not named, and three hundred

**dollars more from Mr. J. J. Binkersdorf, of
El Dorado. A total reward of twenty-three
hundred dollars is therefore offered for
the apprehension of Sandy Donahue, dead
or alive.**

**For acts of murder, for robbery, plunder,
and other acts of violence, Sandy Donahue
has become a menace to the public safety.**

**In person the outlaw is between five-feet-
eleven and six feet tall, wears the clothes
customary to a cattle ranger, with a wide
sombrero with a heavy silver braid around
it. He rides a large horse of a roan color.
There are no peculiar markings on his
face. He has a long mustache of a light
color, and his whole complexion is light.**

He had read it over to himself three or four
times, and at last said it aloud before he quite understood his great fortune. It was almost too good
to be true. Blinky Meyers sighed and leaned over
to make sure. Yes, there could be no doubt of it.
He remembered several hints which the outlaw
had dropped during their conversation that afternoon. It was quite plain now. This was why he did
not wish Blinky to go back to El Dorado and men-
tion a big roan horse and a man with a mustache.

Suddenly, Blinky crumpled the poster and
threw it from him. He laughed long and loud and
with such enthusiasm that he fell into a strangling
chuckle at the end. He remembered now well
enough how he had been thrown out of a saloon
back in Monkey Hill, in good old Manhattan. He
remembered a thousand painful incidents of hu-
miliation scattered throughout his life and not
least of all the contemptuous cuffing which he had

received from the plainclothes man as he fled down the stairs that night. And now . . . ?

Blinky again burst into laughter. He reached out a foot and stirred the dead outlaw slightly. Now Blinky Meyers had done a service to the state. At least no man would ever know otherwise. Now Blinky Meyers would be a hero among heroes, a slayer of the slayers.

Blinky's mind went blank with wonder for an instant. He raised his face to the wide arch of the sky. It rolled vastly upon his struggling mind now, the possibility of this huge and naked West where nature bulks big and man-made scenery is contemptible. All was a great gamble here. At the first throw of the dice Blinky had won! He kept his face turned up for a long moment to the sky. It was the most solemn moment in Blinky's life.

V
"IN EL DORADO"

After that he started to work systematically. With some reluctance he refolded the yellowbacks and stuffed them into the pocket of the dead man's trousers. His next effort was the saddling of the roan. This was hard. He had to guess at some of the buckles, but he finally drew the cinch as hard as his strength permitted and knotted the loose strap-end to the best of his ability. Next, he led the roan to the body of Donahue.

He fixed the loop of the lariat under the arms of the dead man and passed it over the pommel of the saddle. Then came the hardest part. He had to stop sometimes and draw his breath, but in the end he managed to lift and draw Donahue to the

saddle. He fastened him lying face downward behind the saddle over the roan's broad hips. Then
he climbed to the saddle and started down the
road in the direction Donahue had pointed—toward El Dorado.

He found out later that it was eight miles he
traveled that night. It seemed thrice as long to
him. Once or twice he started to trot, but the horrible jouncing of the corpse behind the saddle re-
volted him, and he came back to the roan's long
pacing stride. The road swung through the hills
and came abruptly out onto a limitless plain.
Blinky thought he had never seen so wide a sky
nor colder stars farther away from him.

Underfoot, the road gave back a sandy crunching to the step of Sammy. So they went on for two
hours and a half until, as they topped a little rise
of the road, Blinky saw a huddling heap of houses
before him.

As he came closer he made out a little group of
buildings along what was evidently the village's
one street. They were mostly completely dark. The
largest place, however, was brightly lighted. It was
a timber building fronted with hitching racks at
which stood a row of down-headed saddle horses,
evidently victims of a long wait in the night.

They sidled hastily apart and stood with prick-
ing ears when Blinky rode in among them and dismounted to tether his mount. Then he walked
with some trepidation to the door, from behind
which issued the unmistakable clatter of bar fix-
tures and the rumble and stir of human voices.

It was a timid and faltering Blinky Meyers who
put his hand on the knob of that door. It was another man who stepped inside and looked about
the brightly lighted room with his usual pale-eyed

stare. For it suddenly occurred to him that these were doubtless the very men who stood in awe of Sandy Donahue. These were the men whom he had defied with impunity. And behold! he had ridden into this town on Donahue's roan with the body of the bandit behind his own saddle.

His entrance had been the sign for no disturbance. Only one man turned his head but, when he saw Blinky, his expression changed partly to puzzled attention and partly to amusement. He nudged his neighbor, who in turn looked, but he, lacking his fellow's restraint, burst into a hearty laugh as soon as he caught sight of Blinky.

"Hey, boys," he shouted, "look what's among us! Look at them there legs! Look at that hat!"

Every head moved to Blinky. He was the object of a burst of merriment which made him flush slightly, yet he looked back at them steadily enough.

"I'm looking for the sheriff," he said.

A big man detached himself from a group who sat around a table playing cards.

"I'm the man," he said with a grin. "What you want, a bodyguard while you're travelin' in these here parts in them clothes?"

"I want the reward," said Blinky, feeling that he could stand this mirth since his own trumps were not yet touched, "for Sandy Donahue . . . dead or alive!"

A sudden silence fell on the room.

"For what?" asked the sheriff. "What do you want with Donahue? Have you met up with him?"

"I killed him," answered Blinky, fixing his pale eyes on the sheriff.

"You did *what?*" The sheriff pushed back his hat from his forehead and glared at Blinky as if he were suddenly robbed of understanding.

"This guy's tryin' a bum four flush," said someone. "Where's his proof that he killed Sandy?"

"Outside. Look for yourself." He waved his hand toward the door.

There was no answer to this. Every man in the barroom started. There they wedged and had to fight their way out into the open. The bartender alone remained in the room, and he was staring at the door with mouth ajar. Blinky stepped to the bar and made the unmistakable sign of thirst. The bartender served him, still with his head turned toward the door. Plainly his soul was not with his business at that moment.

As Blinky drained his glass, a great shout rose from without and a chorus of shouts and curses. It was too much for the bartender. He broke for the door and disappeared. Blinky helped himself rapidly to another drink and then went to a chair, where he sat down. He was yawning deliberately when the procession appeared.

First the sheriff backed through the door, and after him the entire crowd poured into the room. They stretched the body of Donahue on the card table. Then the sheriff turned to Blinky.

"An' you did this?" he asked incredulously.

Blinky shrugged his shoulders and said nothing. He was beginning to feel that he could act up to his part.

"It ain't possible," broke in a voice. "Bah! That little runt ain't big enough to have looked twice at Sandy when he was livin'."

The heart of Blinky fell and his face paled, but his natural pallor was so great that this change of color was hardly noticeable. He saw very plainly that if he were to win reputation out of this he must play a high hand and play it at once. He rose slowly from the chair and approached the last speaker, whom he confronted with his hands resting lightly on his hips and his pallid stare turned up to the cowboy's face.

"Pardner," he said, thinking back to the dialect of Sandy and keeping his voice steady with a great effort, "it takes a lot more to prove a thing to a damn fool than it does to a wise man. Some people got to die to learn a thing."

His eyes went dizzy after this speech. He half expected that the larger man would draw a gun on him. But when his eyes cleared, he saw that his bluff had carried. The big man had changed color. The dead body of the redoubtable Sandy was probably large in his eyes.

"I was merely askin' a question," he said. "There ain't no call to fly off the handle, is there?"

Blinky shrugged his shoulders. He felt as if a lifelong weight had dropped from them.

"He's drilled clean," said the sheriff, who had conducted a hasty examination. "Right over the left breast. You must have got the drop on him . . . otherwise *you* wouldn't be here." He turned sharply on Blinky as he made the observation.

"He had his gun out before I drew," said Blinky coldly.

The sheriff drew the Colt from Sandy's holster and glanced at it. "Five shots," he said with a mighty wonder subduing his voice. "Five shots, an' you're still alive an' walkin'!" He turned to the crowd. "Boys, will somebody tell me if I dreamed this here?" He turned back to Blinky. "How many d'you fire?"

"I dunno," said Blinky carelessly, "'nough!" He

drew his gun and passed it to the sheriff, handle first.

The sheriff was greatly interested. "I seen a make like this down in a store window once," he avowed. "Look at this here toy gun, boys, that done for Sandy. Only three shots out of it."

The gun was passed cautiously from hand to hand amid exclamations.

"Three shots to five," muttered the sheriff, shaking his head. "I can't hardly believe it!"

Again Blinky yawned.

"Look here!" cried a man. "Here's a roll of cash in Sandy's pocket."

The sheriff took the money with a puzzled frown and counted it.

"One hundred and eighty-four dollars," he announced and sighed. "You didn't even go through his pockets after you done the work?"

Blinky's response was an elaborate shrug. The men were regarding him with fascinated eyes as if he were some new species hardly to be placed in the category of men.

"That man belonged to the state," he announced pompously, "and what money he has belongs to the state, too. Am I wrong?"

The sheriff merely stared at him with wide eyes. The other men exchanged glances.

"How did you do it?" asked one of them. "Ain't you a new man in these parts?"

"I needed some easy money," said Blinky with a carefully careless inflection in his voice. "I come across the poster." He stopped to draw out the poster he had taken from the body of Sandy Donahue and tossed it on the bar. "So I went out to find Donahue," he said, "and found him."

"Where?"

Blinky waved his hand toward the north. "Up by a water hole. I was down on my knees getting a drink when Donahue comes up behind and tells me to stick up my hands."

"What happened then?" inquired the sheriff.

For answer Blinky waved to the dead body on the table. "I put my hands up, but one of them carried a gun with it. It was a pretty thing while it lasted. Donahue was fast but wild."

"You must have been right on top of him when you fired," said a man who had been bent over the corpse. "Here's a powder burn."

"I was running in on him," said Blinky calmly. "Sorry I burned him, but I wasn't trying very hard to be polite just then."

A deep guffaw applauded this sally. The sheriff came up and seized Blinky's hand in a great paw.

"Son," he announced, "you're a bit different from the sort of men we see around here, all right, but I reckon you're about as regular a man as there is in these here parts. Anyone who could stand up to Sandy Donahue and account for him, man to man, I take my hat off to. About this here reward. I'll see that you're fixed up right away."

"Thanks," said Blinky briefly. "It'd come in handy. I'm a little short now."

"Old Binkersdorf offered five hundred besides what's comin' from the state," said the sheriff. "We can fix it up with the old man to pay you right away."

"I leave it to you," said Blinky, waving the subject into dismissal and turning toward the bartender. "I'm kind of fagged, been on the go after Donahue for two days. Think I'll hit the hay."

"Come this way," said the bartender and led the new hero from the room.

Once they had disappeared, the sheriff turned slowly toward the crowd. He still looked dazed as if he had just undergone some great shock.

"Boys," he said, "I've met up with a lot of queer people in my life, but never with a gunfighter who looked like this pie-faced runt. This here man appears to have went on the trail of Sandy Donahue all by himself and killed him single-handed with a toy gun. I reckon I'm getting old. I'm goin' to apply for a room in the old man's home. Well, I'm goin' to see that Sandy gets buried decent. He was sure a hard fighter, but he was always a clean one."

VI
"MARKED CARDS"

So began the sacking of El Dorado.

Ambition is like a plant in that it grows, but it grows far more rapidly than any plant, and never did ambition spring into flower in any man more suddenly than it grew into life in the heart of Blinky Meyers. At first he looked upon El Dorado as merely a place to leave as soon and as happily as possible. If his reward money had been paid to him on the first day, he would certainly have disappeared toward the nearest railroad before the night fell. But there was a delay. Old Binkersdorf could not get his five hundred all together for a couple of days. He paid an installment, and Blinky had to settle down and wait for the rest.

Before he was through waiting he had discovered that a new world lay at his feet ready to be conquered and, with the proper spirit of an Alexander, Blinky embraced the opportunity with both hands and a pack of marked cards. Moreover, there were tenderer motives which urged him to remain in El Dorado. The bulging pocketbooks of the cattlemen were hardly more attractive to Blinky than their adulation of him.

From the degradation of a hounded New York guttersnipe, starting at his own shadow and pallid for fear of the following law, he had suddenly become an awesome figure of fear to these Westerners. All his life he had found it hard to make himself current as a real man. Here he was accepted without question as a sort of a superman. It was passing sweet to Blinky.

He came once on the verge of exposure. It was the evening of the second day that Lucky Pete, black-bearded and red-eyed from liquor, swaggered into the bar of the Alsace Hotel and in pressing up to the counter shouldered Blinky.

"Get out o' my way," shouted Pete. "Why the hell can't a man get a drink in this here joint?"

He seized Blinky by the shoulder and sent him whirling halfway across the room. Blinky's hand dropped into his open coat and settled firmly on the handle of his automatic. He knew that he could never draw that gun and still less use it, but he made the motion and stood with his pale eyes steady upon Pete's face. In his heart were two conflicting emotions: one a sudden distaste for El Dorado and the men of that Western town, and the other a tremendous impulse to flee through the nearest open door.

He was kept from action by the intervention of no less person than the sheriff. He leaped from behind and grappled Blinky by both arms.

"Don't shoot!" cried the sheriff, "he's drunk! He don't know what he's doing!"

Blinky permitted himself to be overcome after

a short struggle. In the meantime, others had thrown themselves upon Lucky Pete and had wrested the gun from his hand.

"You fool!" whispered one of them to him. "Are you pinin' for an early grave? That's the man what killed Sandy Donahue face to face!"

The effect of this news was astonishing. The face of Lucky Pete changed color. "I might have known," he muttered. "He's got a bad eye . . . a damned bad eye!"

Blinky stood observing him with the pallid and changeless stare.

"Let me go, boys," said Lucky Pete, "I'm sober now. Won't some of you gentlemen introduce me to Bad Eye over there?"

The sheriff rose to the crisis. He stepped between the two would-be combatants.

"Bad Eye, my friend," he said, taking up the name with which Lucky Pete had referred to Blinky, "you got to admit that Lucky Pete here was drunk, and you got to know that a drunk man ain't reasonable. Will you shake hands with him now?"

Lucky Pete advanced cautiously, one hand stretched toward the man-killer. Blinky disregarded the question. His pale eyes were steady upon Pete. He turned and walked slowly from the room. At the door he paused.

"There's a big country around El Dorado, Lucky Pete," he said coldly, "and we ought to be able to find some place where we can meet without having the officers of the law"—here he bowed to the sheriff—"to introduce us."

With that he left the room.

That night Lucky Pete tin-canned out of El Dorado. The citizens of that city made no comment on the unannounced departure save to remark

that Lucky Pete was a sensible man. The other out-
come of the adventure was that Bad Eye became
the popular and only name by which Blinky Meyers, late of the Bowery, was known throughout the
environs of El Dorado.

But it was through cards that Blinky Meyers
was to continue and establish his fame through
the regions of El Dorado. His first exploit in this
sphere of chance occurred in the back room of the
Alsace bar. They were playing Black Jack, and
Blinky was at his best in this game. He could deal
with one hand, read the cards three deep while he
was doing so, and bury any of the three cards in
the middle or the bottom of the deck, dealing at
the same time with equal facility from the top or
the bottom, and all with the pale-eyed nonchalance which had made him notorious in New York
and which was to make him truly celebrated in El
Dorado.

To say that Blinky made a "killing" on his first
appearance in a Black Jack hand would be to put
it mildly. He stacked the cards with a skill that
would have deceived even Hoyle. He fed his op-
ponents hands which worked them gradually to
the breaking point.

He was not a large winner on this first evening,
through calculation. It was the grace with which
he lost and the nonchalance with which he accepted his successes that won admiration. Two or
three of the boys from whom he had made slight
hauls were determined to get back at him on the
succeeding nights.

They came back. So did Blinky. He was astonished at the rope which he could pay out to these
men. He was no less astonished at the size of their
rolls. Night after night the bitten ones came back,

curious to see how it was done and willing to pay
to learn. So Blinky trimmed them with increasing
rapidity. After the second day he abandoned his
double and triple set-ups and would run-up the
pack only once. They were sure to bang into the
crimp.

Then he made the discovery that they did not
insist on fresh packs of cards for even the most
important games. In fact, they were as well content to play with a greasy and thumb-marked pack
which, at one deal, became as familiar to the practiced eyes of Blinky as they were to play with the
whitest and stiffest cardboards ever flickered under a dealer's thumb. They were, in fact, so blind
and so smiling in their losses that he sometimes
felt that they were merely playing him along and
were waiting to catch him red-handed before they
rose, gun in hand, and shot him limb from limb.

The days passed. The reward had been paid. The
cattlemen were paying in still more. These were
the fat days for Blinky, and he stored enough pelf
away to keep him sustained through a long life of
lean days. He had long ago given up the New York
clothes which had excited the mirth of the cattlemen. He took now to wide-brimmed hats and
jacket-like coats of rough cloth, and bandannas
around the throat, and a great wide belt above his
hips to support the little automatic, very trim and
insignificant in its dangling holster. He got a pair
of old-fashioned riding boots whose soft leather
tops crumpled around his ankles and looked very
natty indeed.

There was just enough of the wild West about
the outfit to make it seem in place. There was just
enough Mexican dash in it to win the admiration
of the cowboys. If fashions had been possible in

The Sacking of El Dorado

El Dorado, he would have become the city's fashion plate.

As the sacking of El Dorado progressed, so grew the ambitions of Blinky Meyers. If he could plunder El Dorado, why should he not own it? It was a great moment in his life. The time came during the Saxon invasions of England when the invaders began to settle down in the country they had formerly robbed. So Blinky Meyers decided to settle down in El Dorado.

It might have seemed hazardous and an impossible undertaking to capture a modern American town. But in reality El Dorado was not particularly modern. It had one barbaric weakness which made it easy prey for Blinky Meyers. There was not one of the worthy citizens who would not gamble for everything he possessed except his six-shooter and his silver spurs.

So Blinky, proceeding with caution and forethought, made his first step toward the great conquest. He enticed Stew Young, ancient proprietor of the Alsace, into a game of stud poker. It would have seemed a brutal thing if he had sat down and deliberately won the hotel from Stew at one sitting, but Blinky staged his little game so cleverly that it seemed that the old man was the aggressor throughout. He won from him a little at a time on successive days, and each time he showed the greatest apparent disinclination to return to the play. But Stew had tasted blood and he wanted the finish. So he kept at the thing until the eventful evening arrived when Blinky stacked up two thousand dollars on the table and offered to bet it against the hotel.

It was a good deal more than the hotel was worth, but then Blinky was dealing and he could afford to be generous. Stew bit off another chunk of tobacco and took the bet. There was a crowd of witnesses to attest the point. Blinky won. It was a close deal—but he won!

The old man pulled back in his chair and stared at the money for a moment and then shrugged his shoulders. He was a game loser. The boys came around and condoled with him. Then they turned their eyes on Blinky with a question in them. Blinky wondered what that question could be.

The next morning Stew gathered his belongings into a battered trunk and hauled the trunk out to his still more battered buckboard, between the shafts of which stood a downheaded, iron-gray horse, far the most rickety of the three. Stew was on his way to become a camp cook in the open country. He had done that before he saved his pile and had bought the Alsace. He was far too old to save another pile.

There was quite a crowd gathered in front of the Alsace to watch Stew depart. They would come up one by one and examine his harness and then his horse and then shake hands with him, and then one by one they would turn to Blinky with that singular question in their eyes. Blinky was very much puzzled.

Finally the sheriff drew him to one side. "Are you sure goin' to let the old man go?" he asked Blinky gently.

"Sure, I am," Blinky said, honestly irritated. "Didn't the old fool lose his bet? Think I want to keep him around as an ornament?"

The sheriff pushed back his hat and regarded Blinky with solemn astonishment. "I got nothin' to say," he muttered, "not a word. I only thought. . . ." He never completed his thought, but turned slowly away and called a good bye after the old man. Already rattling down the road in his buckboard, he turned in his seat and waved his big hat in the cheeriest of farewells.

So the last stage of the sack of El Dorado began.

Blinky was worried by that continual question which he had seen in the eyes of the men for the past twenty-four hours. He decided that they were simply a lower and stupider order of humanity and that he could never hope to understand them. He recalled how Sandy had refused to shoot the chipmunk and also refused to be sunk in the pool, because he would poison the drinking water. Blinky made up his mind that these people possessed an element which would always be a mystery to him.

He was right. But there is the old saying about the tide in the affairs of men. Blinky's had been at the flood for a long time. It was turning now. It was turning even as old Stew drove out of town, for at the same time that he drove out another man got off at the nearest railroad station, some twenty miles away.

VII
"WHEN GREEK MEETS GREEK"

This stranger was dressed in square and comfortable lines from the blunt crown of his soft hat to the flexible, square toes of his shoes. He walked with a snappy, purposeful swing of the arms to the little store of the village.

If his appearance at first caused some amusement to the group of elders on the porch of the store and to the clerk within, he soon won their better opinion. For he was enormously alert and cheerful and he had a way of looking you suddenly and directly in the eye so that you went straight inside and had to frown to look back at him.

A peculiarity about him was that with a cigar stowed in one side of his mouth, he had a habit of whispering out of the other side, as if he were inviting you into a secret conference and imparting news of the greatest significance—and this for the most trivial matters of speech. When he had finished his long list of purchases in the town, he appeared in a costume which was more or less in tune with the clothes of the men in the community. There was the inevitable bandanna, the heavy shoes, the wide sombrero, the sagging belt from which swung the typical long and heavy Colt in its holster. Further, he collected a shaken-down buggy and an old horse and started on his journey toward El Dorado.

He reached that metropolis late in the afternoon of the day and, after he had put up his horse in the shed behind the Alsace, he took a room in the hotel. But in El Dorado the stranger at once began to attract more attention. For in spite of many physical differences the good people of El Dorado thought they noticed a great similarity between the newcomer and Bad Eye himself. For instance, there was the same habit of nodding the head backward when making a remark, and the same ability to twist words out of the side of the mouth, and to a certain extent the same vocabulary. Another point attracted their attention. He possessed the same peculiar pallor which Blinky had not yet lost.

It was a strange case. El Dorado wondered. They were eager to see these two men together.

Perhaps they were friends. They asked the new man, who called himself John Smith. He declared that he had never heard of Bad Eye.

He was not much in evidence during that day and, when evening came on, he loitered in the barroom for a while, though he drank little. They are apt to be suspicious in the West when a man will not step up for his drink when his turn comes, but Mr. Smith was so cheery about it and made so many remarks about the bad throat which forced him to lay off the booze that they passed the affair over.

Moreover, he was excellent as a listener. He had heard none of the tales which were old in El Dorado for some weeks, and particularly he knew nothing of the spectacular appearance of Bad Eye, who had slain the famous Sandy Donahue. The details of that historic combat had been circulated and added to. Blinky had contributed a little in friendly moments. His little had been magnified by gossip which he did not care to contradict. So that now the town possessed the makings of an epic whose every detail was capable of being visualized.

To all of this Mr. Smith listened attentively. In fact, he appeared to sympathize with the exploits of Mr. Bad Eye as deeply as if he had been his blood brother. By degrees the crowd was slipping from the barroom into the back room which had now been converted by Blinky Meyers into an ideal card room, with little round tables and excellent lights—lights which were peculiarly necessary to Blinky, for even the most practiced eye needs a good light when reading marked cards.

The exodus at last became so marked that the stranger said good night to the bartender and

joined the others within the card room. There was
a great deal of action there, but most of it was
centered around the table where Blinky himself
sat. He was playing his favorite Black Jack, and
the money was changing hands rapidly.

Tonight Blinky was feeling peculiarly exuberant. The possession of the hotel swelled him with
a most natural pride. He had made great the day
by partaking of a still more favorite brandy—in
ponies, to be sure, but even these count up in
quantity before the end of a long day of celebra-
tion.

So Blinky drank until he was happy, and then
until he was exuberant. There he stayed. He rarely
passed beyond that point. It was his natural limit.
Moreover, his partners had pleased him this evening. They had money. They had stomachs. The
latter were partial to whiskey. The former they
were willing to spend. Blinky showed them how
to spend it most rapidly.

Around his table watching the proverbial "luck"
of Bad Eye, the pride of El Dorado stood grouped.
Here it was that the cheerful Mr. Smith came and
took his stand. When Al Dangberg, broke, stood
up and turned his empty pockets inside out, Mr.
Smith very naturally slipped into the vacant chair,
though it seemed a rash act on the part of one who
had witnessed the amazing luck which was blessing Bad Eye on this evening.

Half a dozen deals had passed and still Bad Eye
held the deal. It seemed as if no one else at the
board could hold an ace and a face card. He never
held less than twenty. The crowd took it all good
humoredly enough. They were accustomed to see
all things fall to the will of Bad Eye.

After those half dozen deals, Mr. Smith, who

had been quietly interested in the backs of these cards all this time and particularly in the corners of these backs, though to a casual observer he had not studied them a moment, suggested to his neighbor that the cards they were playing with were rather old and that it might be well if they got a fresh pack. The neighbor received the suggestion with enthusiasm. He beat upon the table and announced his desire. Bad Eye, looking up while he shuffled the cards, smiled and consented. In so doing he glanced for the first time at the strange Mr. Smith.

At that moment, perhaps by chance, the flap of Mr. Smith's coat fell open, and Blinky, looking straight at him across the table, could not fail to note a significant little bulge under Mr. Smith's armpit. Blinky knew just what that bulge was. He had a similar one under his own arm. Nothing save a small automatic had just such an outline. Through Blinky's mind flashed a thousand suspicions. He knew now that he was playing against a man of his own training and caliber. Or perhaps a bigger caliber than his. He noted now the stranger's pallor and his tricks of speech. Beyond a doubt he was now face to face with metal worthy of his sword.

It would have seemed for that instant that Blinky had turned a little paler than usual, but as he leaned back in his chair, waiting for the fresh pack, his eyes met those of the stranger again. As Mr. Smith seemed not in the slightest degree interested, Blinky shrugged his shoulders and seemed at the same time to shake some weighty question from his mind.

When the fresh pack arrived, the game was renewed with ardor. Blinky still won, though with less rapidity than before; still his gains were remarkable during his own deals. It was also worthy of interest that Mr. Smith bet only nominal sums while Blinky dealt, but renewed his interest when the deal changed. It was further of interest to note his slender white hands which flew over the pack when he dealt with a suggestion of fondness in their light touches. And he, too, won with surprising regularity during his deals.

So the game waxed old and the night waxed old with it. A good many had left the room, and finally the last man at the table withdrew and left the possession of the board to Blinky and the stranger alone. The stranger took the deal and shuffled the cards rapidly. As Blinky's hand settled over the pack to cut, he started, as though someone had moved his chair, and he glanced up with a quick frown at the stranger. He had felt a noticeable crimp in the deck.

Blinky was fascinated. He noticed now, too, that the stranger was dealing in his own pet fashion with one hand flicking the cards over the table with the skill of long practice. A little chill began to touch Blinky's spine.

His first impulse was to call the game to an end. His second was irritation. His third was to call for a drink. He obeyed the third impulse. So it happened that the pile of coins and bills before the stranger grew and grew, and Blinky drank and drank.

He began to bet recklessly now on his own deal, forgetting that his fingers were losing a good deal of their usual skill, and the stranger began to take chances on Blinky's own deals, and won amazingly. The bystanders were breathless.

"Seems as how," said one big cattleman, "this

here fellow has come from Bad Eye's own home town and has a bit more of Bad Eye's luck!"

It was the general sentiment.

"I'm through!" cried Blinky at last. "I've been playing too long today."

There was a moment of dead silence around the table. It seemed the height of bad sportsmanship. It was the second black eye for their gunfighter that day. The first had been the departure of old Stew.

"A few more hands," said the strange Mr. Smith. "I got a story that'll interest and maybe make you want to play some more."

"One more hand," said Blinky, noting that the sentiment of the crowd was turning against him and anxious to make a graceful exit from this losing game.

"The story," said Mr. Smith, "isn't much to tell a gunfighter like yourself. But it happened to a friend of mine. He was a detective in New York."

Blinky looked up with a very real interest. "Are you from New York?" he asked.

"Sure."

It became necessary for Blinky to loosen his collar. "Go on!" he said.

"This here detective friend of mine," said Mr. Smith amiably, "was working with a bunch of the force who were raiding a gambling joint. One of the gamblers got away and ran down the stairs my friend was guarding. He jumped the gambler and started searching him when the gambler jumped away down the stairs and shot my friend when he started to follow. It wasn't a severe wound, just a graze, but it was enough to stop him from following. Then the chief of detectives got wind of it, and how his detective, this friend of mine, had let the crook get away, and he docked the detective. So my friend, he lay in the hospital sick for a while. You see, he was a married guy. He needed his job pretty bad. And he hated to lose it because of a damned crook. And when he got out of the hospital, he got a clue as to where the crook had run, which was a long way from New York. Then he started out after him with just enough money to buy his grub on the way. Had to beat it on freight cars . . . but, say, I guess you aren't very interested in my story."

Blinky had an unmistakably sick color. "Not very much," he murmured.

"Well," said Mr. Smith, "anyways, let's play a few more hands."

"Anything you say," submitted Blinky, almost humbly.

Thereafter a prodigy occurred, for Blinky lost with amazing regularity. It was almost as if he had lost interest in the game and in life itself. He played his cards mechanically. Mr. Smith accumulated a vast pile of money. At last Blinky rose, somewhat shaky on his feet and his eyes depressed.

"I'm broke," he said. "I haven't another cent."

Mr. Smith eyed him critically. Evidently Blinky was broke in more than a money way.

"Lay you the whole pile for the hotel here," he suggested.

The crowd closed around them silently in their fascination. Blinky waved a hand in submission and slumped into his chair again. When the deal was past, he sat staring at a nineteen-hand, while the stranger showed an even twenty. Suddenly Blinky started up fiercely.

"Damn you!" he said. "You're a crook. You can't

get away with this . . . not in El Dorado!"

A flash of steel showed in his hand. There was a sudden motion through the room. Every man who could reach the bar dived behind it like a fish into water. Those who were too far away sprawled flat on the floor. There was a moment of silence and then a laugh sounded, a calm and clear laugh instead of a pistol shot. It was the strange Mr. Smith who laughed.

He rose where he was and said, still laughing: "What a rotten little cur you are, Blinky; what a yellow deuce!"

The crowd shrank closer to the floor. The shot would surely come now. Instead, they heard the voice of the stranger again saying opprobrious things to their hero.

"Why, you hound," said Mr. Smith evenly, "did you think I'd be broke and stand for it? Did you think the earth was wide enough to hide you from me? Not a hope. Not a hope, my boy. Here I am. Now, take water. Don't point that gun at me. You had the guts to shoot on a back stairs. You haven't the heart to fire before a man. Have you?"

Here some of those on the floor slowly raised their heads far enough to look and wonder, for the strange Mr. Smith was standing, leaning across the table, and not an inch from his nose was the gun of Bad Eye. But the gun was wobbling, and Mr. Smith smiled. Then his hand went up very slowly, so that a child could have seen it, and took the gun from Bad Eye's hand.

"Get out!" said Mr. Smith.

The crowd rose as one man to their feet, still too paralyzed with horrified astonishment to move further.

"Get out!" repeated Mr. Smith. "Beat it back to

where you belong. If I had a warrant, I'd be company for you. Get!"

The terrible Bad Eye turned and moved toward the door. He had almost reached the entrance. He had opened the door upon the night. Then Mr. Smith took a light step forward, poising himself upon his left foot, and swung his right so that the stout, square toe landed with an audible precision. As the result of this action, Bad Eye sagged in the middle and pitched forward through the door.

A clamor began and rose suddenly through the room.

"Get him!"

"Let's see what sort of a guy Bad Eye is!"

"We've all been bluffed!"

"He never plugged Sandy!"

They were starting toward the door with danger in their eyes when Mr. Smith interposed with raised hand.

"Fellers," said Mr. Smith, "don't chase after him. He ain't worth your attention. I wouldn't have hurt my toes kicking him just now except that he had me a little peeved. Boys, I happen to own this hotel just now. Suppose we all line up and have a drink . . . on the house!"

Some applause greeted this popular suggestion and, when they stood with glasses lifted, Mr. Smith spoke:

"Fellers," he said, "I got to say that I come a long way to get back at that dirty guttersnipe I just kicked through the door. He plugged me in New York while I was makin' an arrest. I was in a hospital a while. Then I come after him. Well, I got more than his skin. I got his whole goat . . . am I wrong? . . . and several thousand dollars and this hotel! For this hotel, I don't want it. I wouldn't

The Sacking of El Dorado

keep it as a gift, which it was. It goes back to the old chap who owned it before. As for Bad Eye, let me tip you off, his name in Monkey Hill is Meyers . . . Blinky Meyers . . . because he never had the guts to look a real man square. He's bluffed you boys. He never did in Sandy Donahue. If Sandy was killed, he killed himself. Get me?"

"By Gawd!" shouted a voice, "I always *did* have a hunch that that was what happened! Remember that powder burn? I'll bet he was foolin' with Bad Eye's gun and got plugged himself!"

"Hey!" called another. "I always wanted to punch that pasty face of Bad Eye's when he was winning from me. Now, why the devil didn't I?"

Mr. Smith smiled behind his hand. "Well, boys," he said, "here's a toast to a real man, whatever else he may have been. We're drinking to Sandy Donahue!"

About this time, mounted on a fast-running horse, Blinky plunged from the outskirts of El Dorado into the wide night of the plains to be seen no more—at least in this story.

Max Brand is the best-known pen name of Frederick Faust, creator of Dr. Kildare, Destry, and many other fictional characters popular with readers and viewers worldwide. Faust wrote for a variety of audiences in many genres. His enormous output, totaling approximately thirty million words or the equivalent of 530 ordinary books, covered nearly every field: crime, fantasy, historical romance, espionage, Westerns, science fiction, adventure, animal stories, love, war, and fashionable society, big business and big medicine. Eighty motion pictures have been based on his work along with many radio and television programs. For good measure he also published four volumes of poetry. Perhaps no other author has reached more people in more different ways.

Born in Seattle in 1892, orphaned early, Faust grew up in the rural San Joaquin Valley of California. At Berkeley he became a student rebel and one-man literary movement, contributing prodigiously to all campus publications. Denied a degree because of unconventional conduct, he embarked on a series of adventures culminating in New York City where, after a period of near starvation, he received simultaneous recognition as a serious poet and successful popular-prose writer. Later, he traveled widely, making his home in New York, then in Florence, and finally in Los Angeles.

Once the United States entered the Second World War, Faust abandoned his lucrative writing career and his work as a screenwriter to serve as a war correspondent with the infantry in Italy, despite his fifty-one years and a bad heart. He was killed during a night attack on a hilltop village held by the German army. New books based on magazine serials or unpublished manuscripts or restored versions continue to appear so that, alive or dead, he has averaged a new book every four months for seventy-five years. In the United States alone nine publishers now issue his work. Beyond this, some work by him is newly reprinted every week of every year in one or another format somewhere in the world. Yet, only recently have the full dimensions of this extraordinarily versatile and prolific writer come to be recognized and his stature as a protean literary figure in the 20th Century acknowledged. His popularity continues to grow throughout the world.

THE WORLD'S MOST CELEBRATED WESTERN WRITER!

Donnegan. He comes from out of the sunset—a stranger with a sizzling six-gun. Legend says that he is Donnegan. And every boomtown rat knows he has a bullet ready for any fool who crosses him. But even though the Old West has fools enough to keep Donnegan's pistols blazing, the sure shot has his sights set on a certain sidewinder, and blasting the deadly gunman to hell will be the sweetest revenge any hombre ever tasted.

_4086-7 $4.50 US/$5.50 CAN

The White Wolf. Tucker Crosden breeds his dogs to be champions. Yet even by the frontiersman's brutal standards, the bull terrier called White Wolf is special. And Crosden has great plans for the dog until it gives in to the blood-hungry laws of nature. But he never reckons that his prize animal will run at the head of a wolf pack, or that a trick of fate will throw them together in a desperate battle to the death.

_3870-6 $4.50 US/$5.50 CAN

Dorchester Publishing Co., Inc.
P.O. Box 6640
Wayne, PA 19087-8640

Please add $1.75 for shipping and handling for the first book and $.50 for each book thereafter. NY, NYC, and PA residents, please add appropriate sales tax. No cash, stamps, or C.O.D.s. All orders shipped within 6 weeks via postal service book rate. Canadian orders require $2.00 extra postage and must be paid in U.S. dollars through a U.S. banking facility.

Name_____
Address_____
City_____State_____Zip_____
I have enclosed $_____ in payment for the checked book(s).
Payment <u>must</u> accompany all orders. ☐ Please send a free catalog.

RIP-ROARIN' ACTION AND ADVENTURE BY THE WORLD'S MOST CELEBRATED WESTERN WRITER!

GUN GENTLEMEN

MAX BRAND

Renowned throughout the Old West, Lucky Bill has the reputation of a natural battler. Yet he is no remorseless killer. He only outdraws any gunslinger crazy enough to pull a six-shooter first. Then Bill finds himself on the wrong side of the law, and plenty of greenhorns and gringos set their sights on collecting the price on his head. But Bill refuses to turn tail and run. He swears he'll clear his name and live a free man before he'll be hunted down and trapped like an animal.

_3937-0 $4.50 US/$5.50 CAN

MAX BRAND

TROUBLE IN TIMBERLINE

"Brand is a topnotcher!"
—*New York Times*

Barney Dwyer is too big and too awkward to be much good around a ranch. But foreman Dan Peary has the perfect job for him. It seems Peary's son has joined up with a ruthless gang in the mountain town of Timberline, and Peary wants Barney to bring the no-account back, alive. Before long, Barney finds himself up to his powerful neck in trouble—both from gunslingers who defy the law and tin stars who are sworn to uphold it!

_3848-X $4.50 US/$5.50 CAN

THE WHITE WOLF

MAX BRAND

"Brand is a topnotcher!"
—*New York Times*

Tucker Crosden breeds his dogs to be champions. Yet even by the frontiersman's brutal standards, the bull terrier called White Wolf is special. With teeth bared and hackles raised, White Wolf can brave any challenge the wilderness throws in his path. And Crosden has great plans for the dog until it gives in to the blood-hungry laws of nature. But Crosden never reckons that his prize animal will run at the head of a wolf pack one day—or that a trick of fate will throw them together in a desperate battle to the death.

__3870-6 $4.50 US/$5.50 CAN